APRONS & VEILS
BOOK THREE

The Enchanting of
Miss Elliot

GRACE HITCHCOCK

VALMONT
HOUSE PUBLISHERS

The Enchanting of Miss Elliot © 2024 by Grace Hitchcock

Published by Valmont House Publishers

GraceHitchcock.com

Names: Hitchcock, Grace, author.

Title: The Enchanting of Miss Elliot / Grace Hitchcock

Other Titles: the enchanting of miss elliot

Series: Aprons and Veils; book 3

Identifiers: 979-8-9858217-8-9 Hardback | 979-8-9858217-9-6 Paperback | 979-8-9858217-7-2 Ebook | 979-8-9912707-5-5 Large Print Paperback

Subjects: Christian Romantic suspense fiction

All scripture quotations, unless otherwise noted, are taken from the King James Version of the Bible.

Cover design by *Carpe Librum Book Design*

Author is represented by The Steve Laube Agency

For My Little Darlings

"Trust in the Lord, and do good;
Dwell in the land, and enjoy safe pasture.
Take delight in the Lord,
And He will give you the desires of
your heart."

Psalms 37:3-4 KJV

CHAPTER 1

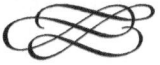

*T*opeka, Kansas
October 1898

OF ALL THE dares Lorna Elliot had accepted from her older brother, this one was by far the dumbest—and she had pulled some pretty foolhardy antics in the name of pride. Ride a dangerous mustang? Yes. Canoe down a raging river? Certainly. But becoming a Harvey Girl waitress? She swallowed back a groan as she paused in her work to mop her forehead with her pristine white apron. Her back was sore. Her feet were swollen, and she was pretty sure she stank from sweating through the high collared black uniform that allowed for precious little air to kiss her skin. She sucked in a bracing breath and continued scrubbing down the lunch countertop after a dust storm of cowboys descended upon the training Harvey House on their way through Kansas with a herd of cattle. And there would be more guests arriving on the Atchison, Topeka, and Santa Fé Railroad in half an hour.

Out of all her adventures, this might be the one that did her in. She had done it to herself in a fit of pique over a Texas Ranger who was mooning over a woman he considered a catch—another man's mail-order bride who became a Harvey Girl instead of marrying her intended. Lorna didn't need this job, being the daughter of one of New Mexico's wealthiest ranchers, but she had longed for distraction at the time of Gaston Reid's pursuit of Belle Parish. However, after twenty-five gruesome days of training in Topeka, she was going to keel over and die in the middle of the dining room floor with a plate of pie in one hand and a pitcher of coffee in the other.

But she was an Elliot. And Elliots never quit. The only thing she ever quit was trying to win the hand of Gaston Reid. She scrubbed the counter all the harder, as if she could scrub away the secret affection she had stored in her heart for him since childhood. It had about near killed her when Gaston up and joined the rangers, leaving her to wonder where he was, but those letters he sent her over the years with little treasures from his travels—a glass bead here, an eagle's feather, and, heaven preserve her frantically beating heart, a stunning length of expensive lace for her gown —they planted hope in her heart that he cared for her more than as his best friend's little sister. Truly, her hope for a future with him had not faltered until that Belle Parish rolled into town with her ebony hair, and perfect skin, and perfect story that apparently made every man's heart *bleed* for her.

"Lorna?" The petite blonde waved a hand in front of her. "What on earth are you brooding over? You've nearly worn a hole in the countertop with all your scrubbing."

"Sorry, Freya." Her cheeks sparked with shame. The other thing that Elliots did not do was wallow over something that could not be changed. Her pa would be ashamed if he knew she was wallowing and complaining in her jealous heart. She shook off the resentful thoughts, determination filling her once more. She would prove to everyone that she was not spoiled.

And even though Belle broke Reid's heart when she chose to wed a former outlaw, Lorna would not begrudge Belle her happily ever after since she really had been through such a trial to get there. No. Lorna would work until her fingers fell off if that's what it took to forget *him* and set her heart to rights.

"I got lost in thought. I won't let it happen again." She glanced about the dining room as Harvey Girls flurried about the tables with linens, cups, and place settings, their black skirts swishing, and their large white aprons crisp and bright with every hair brushed into place with a large white bow atop their chignons. "Did you need help setting the stations?"

Freya shook her head. "The girls from this week's batch of new recruits need to learn to be faster. I was only concerned that someone might have said something to upset you. You are usually so diligent in your work." Freya rested a hand on her arm. "You need only tell me, if—"

"No one upset me." *No one here, at least.* She offered Freya a bright smile and tossed her rag into the bin under the counter. She wanted to stretch her back, but that would look weak—another Elliot trait was to be a hard worker and *not* complain.

"Good. But I do believe it is time for your ten-minute break."

Thank God. Lorna nodded, secretly relieved that she could catch a moment alone before the next train arrived. She enjoyed being busy, but she missed the out of doors. On the ranch, she could help with the cattle and chase down coyotes on her stallion under the open sky. Here, she barely had a chance to see the sun before the long day of serving was over, and she fell atop her bed exhausted, only to repeat the process the next day. "Would you mind if I took a short walk outside? I'm afraid that it's a little stifling in here."

"Of course." Freya moved behind the counter and checked the large coffee urn that Lorna had already refilled. She nodded toward the door. "Be mindful of the time. There will be another train in twenty-five minutes that we will need to prepare to serve based on their telegraphed order, and then we need to discuss the details of your transfer to the Montezuma Harvey resort in four days."

"The Montezuma?" Her breath caught. She had hardly dared to hope they would deem her ready to leave the training program, but to be granted her absolute last choice of placement that would see her returning to New Mexico? *Oh, dear, this will make the plan to forget a certain devastatingly handsome ranger a lot more difficult.* She had chosen two little towns in Texas as her first choices, knowing that *no one* would make those her first pick. She had only added the

Montezuma because she had done some promising to Pa before she departed that she would at least try to get one of the Harvey Houses in or near Las Vegas. She had chosen the Montezuma, which was only five miles from the town of Las Vegas but would give her a sense of being independent from home, unlike the Castañeda Harvey House which was in the middle of town. "I-I had thought one of the other girls would have been placed there, or someone who was already working on the railroad line somewhere and was far more experienced."

"Experience isn't the only factor the Harvey House looks in to when awarding positions. Given your work ethic and attention to detail, the management thought you would be perfect for the resort. You have been marked as one of our most dedicated girls." Freya gave her a beaming smile, even as worry flickered in her eyes. "I tried to suggest you might like the other position, given what you've told me about your, um, gentleman friend, but they were most insistent. You and your roommate, Corinna Victoria, are our best waitresses from this group of recruits."

Blast. Sure, she worked hard, but it was the Elliot way, and now it was coming back to bite her in the derriere. *I should have tried less, but trying less would mean thinking, which would lead to Gaston Reid creeping into my thoughts.* "Wonderful. I am honored you all think so highly of me," she said instead with a forced smile.

"I thought that would encourage you, despite the complication returning home might bring." Freya pushed her toward the front door. "Best hurry and take your break before you lose it."

Lorna lifted her hand in a wave and nearly frowned at the redness of her hands. She was a hard worker at home. But holding massive coffee pots and heavy plates were a different type of hard work. She ducked outside. She stepped off the front porch and leaned against the side of the building. She closed her eyes, basking in the sun on her skin and the brisk wind on her cheeks.

Laughter brought her eyes open once more, and her heart skipped at the sight of a giant of a man sporting a Stetson that looked just like—he lifted his gaze to hers and sent her a crooked grin. Nope, not Gaston Reid. She sighed and caught herself *again.* She straightened. *Stop it! This is ridiculous. You came out here to take charge of your life, for better or for worse, and not get buried in the past.*

The cowboy lopped her way, encouraged by her momentary confusion. She spun on her heel and sped down the boardwalk. Maybe a brisk walk would take her mind off of *him.* She would have to speak with Freya later about her new location and see if there was any way she could be posted to a house in Texas instead. She certainly could not stop working as hard to get herself moved to a smaller house. As much as she loved her beautiful Gallinas Mountains, visiting her family on Sundays for their traditional dinner with the former Texas Ranger attending would be more troublesome to avoid than a pie left on the windowsill to cool with a herd of raccoons on the hunt.

And after years of pining for the man,

she was done being that girl, silently begging for scraps of his love when he had no clue of how much he affected her. Gaston was a good man—the best of men—but he would never be hers.

SHERIFF GASTON REID finally worked through the last of the mountain of paperwork on his desk. Having a job that allowed him to think of settling down had been exciting after a decade in the saddle and camping under the moon and stars, living wherever his job as a ranger led him. But now that he was in the actual work of being the new sheriff of Las Vegas, he was beginning to think that this job would lead him to an early grave from atrophy brought on by this infernal wood chair. Considering his adjustment as difficult was an understatement. He *missed* range life. The excitement of capturing a criminal would charge through his veins, spurring him on to the next mission and the next. Here, the same men ended up in his two-prison cell every Friday night after drinking away their wages. At least he had Sunday lunches to look forward to at the Elliot's, even if the visits were a little less lively these days without Lorna.

He had been beyond shocked when he had visited a few weeks ago to find that Lorna had left the ranch—and not for a visit, but to Topeka for a job as a Harvey Girl. He kind of always thought she would be in sleepy little Las Vegas. But he supposed that was a foolish assumption as she was a woman now and probably would be thinking of marriage sometime soon, and then babies would follow, and their friendship would fade. He gritted his teeth at the thought. *Another adjustment that I did not account for in my spur of the moment decision to leave the rangers.*

He shook off the strange, mixed feelings regarding Lorna's departure. He was proud of her for striking out on her own, but maybe a little surprised that she didn't confide in him, or even say goodbye before she left. But she must have departed quickly as she left her new stallion to her parents care instead of bringing her favorite horse with her. Since his horse was nearing retirement age, Pa Elliot asked Reid to switch mounts to see that the young horse had plenty of exercise while his old mount was put into pasture until Lorna returned. He had been happy to take over Bunny's care for the time being.

Reid exhaled his aggravation with Lorna leaving without a word—he had done it often enough to her in the past. He shouldn't take it personally. He had simply gone through too many major life changes to focus straight. Sure, he missed Lorna, but it was nothing like the ache when he had discovered Belle Parish had married that Lawson fellow. Anger still clawed in his craw every time he thought of her married to that former outlaw, but every time the anger came, he paused to give it to the Lord. He knew from a long life on the trail that bitterness and rage only blinded the person holding on to the offense. He had too many enemies to allow himself to develop a blind spot.

The door banged open, launching Reid from his seat. The town's mailman flapped something in his right hand. "Wanted. Poster." He panted, lifting his visor and swiping at the sweat coating his shining widow's peak. "Thought this one couldn't wait until you came for your mail."

Reid snatched it up, his heart pounding at the face that greeted him. Hardened jaw. Cruel eyes. A smug, leering smile. His stomach clenched. "Grant Lawson is on the run?"

The man groaned. "Seems so. Jumpin' Jehoshaphat, this is going to mean trouble for us all."

"Not if I get the jump on him first." He reached for his gun belt that hung on the clotheshorse behind him, buckled it, and tied the leather strap to his thigh, securing the holster.

"You going to ride out after him? But you ain't no ranger now."

"Still have the training and the know-how. Thanks, Mike!" He grabbed his Stetson and rifle on the way out the door to where he kept Bunny saddled and at the ready. He threw the rifle in the gun harness, flung himself up, and wheeled Lorna's stallion, nudging it into a gentle trot out of town until he passed the last home. Reid pressed his mount into a gallop for *Belle Ranch,* crossing under the threshold with its freshly painted sign—another shining beacon of his failure to woo the former Harvey Girl. He crested the small hill and spied the ranchero set in a field with a cedar at the corner that offered the house shade in the harsh summers.

The door flung wide, and Colt Lawson appeared in the threshold with a hand poised above his gun belt until he recognized Reid and relaxed his stance. "What's wrong?"

Reid halted the horse in a cloud of dust. "Your brother."

"Grant escaped?" A melodic voice greeted his heart, the panic in Belle's voice making his gut clench with the desire to protect her.

She is no longer mine to protect . . . except as a citizen of Las Vegas. He nodded to the petite beauty in a blue gown as she joined her husband on the porch. "Yes, Mrs. Lawson. I wanted to ask you where you think Grant would go, Colt."

Colt wrapped his arm about his wife's waist, concern etching his brow. "We had a base in the canyon, which I told you about, but I doubt he would go there again since his arrest . . . and there was our hideout near Topeka, Kansas."

"Topeka . . ." He clamped his jaw. What were the odds that Topeka was exactly where Lorna Elliot resided, Las Vegas' wealthiest rancher's daughter, and was connected to a family Grant despised? *It's too coincidental to dismiss.* "Can you draw me up a map of the location in Kansas? I don't have time to waste if I am to get there ahead of him."

"You are heading to Topeka now?" Belle rested her hand on the porch beam. "Why are you convinced he is there?"

"Because he is a thief with a vendetta and no fool. He knows Colt is protecting you and that it is only a short ride to Elliot Ranch, where even more guns await. In Topeka, there is a woman unprotected that he could snatch up and still achieve his end." He frowned. "We all know how he tends toward ransom."

Belle paled and Colt took her hand in his, no doubt remembering all that she had endured at Grant's hand.

"What do you want me to do besides drawing up a map?" He frowned at Reid. "I can't leave Las Vegas to chase after him."

"I'll need someone to act as sheriff while I'm gone, and I need someone I can trust who knows his way around a firearm." He sighed. "That narrows the field exponentially—you and Gilbert Elliot. Between the two of you, it could work."

Colt gritted his teeth. "I can't leave Belle out here alone—not after Grant failed in killing her the first time."

"You have ranch hands. Have them watch her." Reid challenged. "And, if you are afraid of her being too isolated, bring her to the Castañeda Hotel in town. Do you still have friends there, Mrs. Lawson? Surely your former Harvey House will welcome you with open arms."

She nodded. "I will be fine there, Colt. Draw the map as quickly as you can, love. If Ranger—I mean Sheriff Reid—is correct, he has no time to spare if he is going to save the life of Lorna Elliot." She squeezed his hand. "Harriet Lane Elliot is one of my dearest friends. Do you really expect me to protest your leaving me at the hotel when this could help save her sister-in-law?"

Colt sighed. "I'll find some paper."

"And a Bible for the swearing in," Reid added, swinging down from his mount. "We can't leave anything undone in case Grant doubles back to attack Las Vegas. I'll need you to tell the Elliots of my plan and assure them that I am doing everything in my power to see to their daughter's safety. Gil will not protest helping at the sheriff's office, but if he says he wants to join in the fight for his sister, remind him of how much trouble I put the Lawson brothers and their Death Riders through on my own."

Colt kissed his wife's hand and led her

inside as if already afraid for her safety. If Reid had a wife, he too would do anything to protect her. But he didn't, and, right now, all that mattered to him was reaching Topeka before Grant and saving Lorna.

CHAPTER 2

"No, sir. We do not offer alcohol at the Harvey House. I can offer you any beverage from our list. We have an assortment of tea, iced tea, coffee, or milk." Lorna repeated the following day as she stood before the white linen covered table of three dusty cowboys. All had a severe ring of matted hat hair and had donned a jacket from the row of jackets that Mr. Harvey required each Harvey House to keep at the ready should any man arrive without a dress coat. Mr. Harvey said it was to aid the fine dining experience and remind guests to be on their best behavior. In a restricting jacket, manners of a sort would follow and usually, it worked. However, these three were not minding their manners with their raucous laughter, leering at her every time she turned, and downright appalling muttered comments. *Perhaps I should offer them a second coat to make them so uncomfortable they remember they are in a restaurant and not some saloon.*

"I'm so fancily dressed right now, I reckon I'll take tea." The man nearest her proclaimed, his gold tooth winking in the sunlight pouring through the windows.

"Any particular leaf? Green, white, black, or herbal?"

The man grinned at her proximity, the liquor on his breath making her fight a gag. "I reckon I'll take herbal, as it will remind me of how good you smell while I drink— like a flower."

She reached across him and flipped the cup over in its saucer to follow the cup code of the Harvey House, turning the handle to the correct position for the type of tea desired to alert the server. Her cheeks burned at their chuckles, but she ignored their crude gazes, thankful for the high collar and long sleeves—a nun habit could hardly be more modest than her uniform. The remaining two men each parroted their desire for tea, guffawing as she bent to flip the cups over in their saucers. Given the girl who usually followed with the tea pot was absent, Lorna would be doing the pouring herself. But, if she did not follow the code, she would be reprimanded. *Maybe it wouldn't be such a bad idea. Maybe I'll lose the vote for the position at the Montezuma.*

"And for your meal, *sir?*" She gave him a pointed look as she tapped her pencil against the page of her narrow notebook. Acting impatient could get her reprimanded as well, but there were exceptions when it came to ogling guests.

"We will take the special." The man with the gold tooth winked at her. "Are you the special? Because I might need another meal to take home with me to eat later."

His friends threw back their heads in laughter, stomping their feet under the table and rattling the dishes.

She darted away to place an order for three specials in the kitchen. She grabbed the filled teapot and moved about the room with a tight smile, flipping and filling any cups that were upside down in the saucer, saving the bawdy group for last as she swapped her pot of black tea for the herbal. She had been raised on a ranch filled with cowboys, and she had heard rough talk a time or two, but when she had been sixteen and a new hand made a flirtatious comment to her, Gaston had knocked him on his backside. She would have to fight her own battles today.

Bringing the men's plates of steak, mashed potatoes, and peas, she set down two, and when she turned around for the last one, she felt a hand graze the back of her skirt. She gasped, and, at the man's leering smile, she narrowed her eyes. "Keep your hands to yourself."

"I thought service with a smile was a requirement." The man chortled at her discomfort.

"Get out of my restaurant," she said through clenched teeth.

"Not until we get our meal and . . . dessert." His eyes flicked over her.

"If you act like a pig, you are going to start looking like one." She flipped the plate on his head, mashing the contents into his hair.

The guests in the house gaped, women gasped, and a cowboy shot to his feet in the corner. Beau Carson had come in three times since last night and had always been a perfect gentleman, even bringing his own coat to dine, though it was a little dusty.

She curled her fists, resisting the urge to glide into a fighting stance. She may be on the small side, but her brother and Pa had taught her how to defend herself, and, growing up as the town pariah, she had thrown a punch, or two, in self-defense before. "Pay for your food and leave. I won't ask nicely again."

Beau crossed the room and stood behind her, arms loose as if ready for a fight too. "The lady asked you and your friends to leave, Stan."

"Always the knight in shining Stetson, eh, Beau? Mind your own business. We are on our break and enjoying our meal." Stan lifted his spoon to his head and scooped up the mashed potatoes dribbling down his hair, stuffing them into his mouth, his cheeks billowing.

If she wasn't so angry, she'd laugh.

"When it comes to you bothering ladies, I make it my business." Beau Carson narrowed his gaze and nodded to the door. "Now, leave your money and get."

"Not until we finish our vittles."

Beau bent and whispered into Stan's ear. The filthy man straightened, a few peas rolling off his head to join the mess on the floor. Stan dug into his pocket and dumped a few coins on the table and skedaddled, his friends following, all grumbling under their breath.

Lorna sagged against the chair back. "Thank you, Mr. Carson."

Four Harvey Girls surged forward with a broom, mop, bucket, and rags at the ready. Freya stood in the corner, arms crossed as she inclined her head to Lorna, as if asking if she were well. Lorna smiled and nodded.

Mr. Carson scowled after the men. "Those three have always been trouble. I haven't rightly liked working with them over the years, but on a cattle drive, there's hardly anyone better than them." He smiled. "And it's Beau, Miss Lorna."

"I'll get you some fresh coffee, *Beau*. Please, return to your table and relax." She snatched the coffee pot and a plate of pie from the kitchen and refilled his cup of coffee, setting the plate before him. "And it's on the house."

"It's not necessary, but you won't never see me turn down pie." The cowboy grinned up at her and dug in, his zest thanks enough.

The waitresses weren't really encouraged to chat up the guests, much less the men that frequented the house, but Mr. Carson—Beau—had saved her from having to throw those men out herself. The least she could do was be kind and offer him another piece of pie on the house. She returned with a second piece.

He patted his stomach and exhaled. "You know, a few seconds ago, I didn't think I could eat another bite. But now you bring me a chocolate pie? It would be criminal to let this go to waste." He picked up his fork and went to work.

"Where are you driving your cattle?"

"Outside of Montezuma Hot Springs, ma'am."

Is everyone heading for Montezuma? "That is where I'll be going in three days. I'm to be positioned at the Montezuma Resort." *Unless I can get out of it, but judging from the way my conversation with Freya went last night, I am stuck going there, or risk getting in trouble for not following the contract.*

"Yup. Got me a little ranch on the other side of the mountain. I like to visit the Montezuma Harvey House Resort a few times a month for some good cooking."

"That's a lot of effort to cross the Gallinas for some good cooking."

He raised a brow. "You know the Gallinas?"

"I was born and raised in Las Vegas, New Mexico."

His eyes brightened. "We are neighbors then." He chuckled. "Yes, it is a little more effort, but it's worth it. There is a certain

Harvey Girl there that I have set my cap for since I met her nearly eight years ago."

"Eight years?" This fellow was almost as bad as she with hankering after someone for that long without any hope of affection in return. "She must be a catch."

He sighed and polished off his pie. "She's a beauty inside and out, but she is married to her work. I've been asking to court her for years, but she has always teased she won't even think of marrying until the new century. I've tried to set aside my dream of marrying her, but no one compares to her."

"Why, that's only fourteen months away! There's a chance at least for your love to bloom." *And as a man, you at least can ask the woman to court you, while I'm stuck waiting without any hope.*

He shrugged. "Maybe. I would be willing to wait forever for her, but if January first arrives and it is indeed hopeless, it will be time for me to marry someone who can love me. My ranch is beautiful, but I get lonely."

She topped off his coffee. "Well, you wait

until January first of the new century, and ask her again. Maybe she is in earnest."

"Maybe. I've learned the hard way not to hope too much." He sipped his coffee. "Do you mind if I sit at this table for a couple of hours and read the paper? I'll order my weight in coffee. I have a few hours left to relax before heading back out to watch the herd."

She smiled. "After rescuing me, I'll make sure no one says a word against your staying put. When you need a refill, lift your cup, and you'll be helped right away."

The gong sounded, and she quietly excused herself to go stand in a straight line with her Harvey sisters to greet the approaching train. On the way to the platform, she whispered Beau Carson's request to Freya who nodded as they joined the ranks. Lorna folded her hands demurely before her apron. Working to appear meek had been a task in itself when she was used to running wild on the ranch with her hair down and in a loose blouse, split skirt, and thick boots. But, if her time hankering after Gaston had taught her anything, it was time for her to move on, and, to do that, she needed to become a lady and prepare her heart to marry another.

She smiled at the passengers disembarking from the train. At the sight of a massive cowboy with dark brown hair and piercing blue eyes, she blinked. *Gaston?* But the cowboy turned and headed in the opposite direction. She shook her head. She needed to drink some water to rid herself of these mirages and forget him. She had three days left of training before she was put to the test of how well she could handle the sight of the man without her knees going all wobbly like a newborn calf.

A LINE of Harvey Girls clad in black gowns and white aprons with large white hairbows stood smiling at the station platform as a man in a black suit and tie banged a gong, welcoming all the weary travelers to the Harvey House. Reid spun on his boot and headed the opposite direction. Before he announced his arrival in town, he needed to discover if Grant was already here. It was nearly eight hundred miles from Las Vegas. By horse, it would take time, unless he took the baggage car and made his way here undetected. Grant had outwitted him too many times in the past for Reid to ignore any possibility.

Reid waited outside the cattle car for Bunny. Now that his old, trusty mount lived like a king on the Elliot Ranch, the ache of riding another horse was soothed by this magnificent stallion. He rubbed the mount's nose and hoped that Lorna would not mind sharing Bunny with him when she found out he had taken her horse from the ranch. He hoped her family accepted his word through Colt, who should have told them by now of Reid's suspicions and not to worry yet as his theory could be unfounded. Reid had chosen to leave out the fact that he doubted he was wrong, but he did not want to worry them unnecessarily.

He saddled the stallion and mounted, guiding Bunny down the main street, taking in the town. It looked much like every other Western town he had travelled through while chasing gangs and thieves as a Texas Ranger, with its row of businesses, including a saloon, lining the main street and the storefront facades built high to give the appearance of being larger within. At the end of the road stood a weather-worn chapel with paint peeling and a few shingles missing. But even though he may have seen a town like this many times, he was thrilled to be out of that horrible wooden chair.

He chuckled to himself. It had taken all of a month before he had grown bored with life as a small-town Sheriff. However, he had given the townspeople his word to stay in office for the year, and he never went back on his word unless life and death was in the balance. Grant posed a threat to his town—the man had too much history in Las Vegas, and with its citizens, to be left for others to find. As sheriff, it was his duty to protect his town, even if it meant leaving to find Grant.

Reid was well aware that he had been one of the best of the rangers, and if anyone was going to find this murderer, it would be him. The only other man he knew who could do the job better was his good friend, Tanner Sterling, a famous bounty hunter, because the man always delivered and kept every outlaw alive with minimal wounds. He was known for mercy, but not weakness. First, Reid needed to send the telegram he had drawn up on the train to Tanner and then, follow the map that Colt had provided.

Reid patted his vest for the sketched map to the hideout near Topeka. On the train, Reid remembered that Grant's wife Jill had been arrested as well. He needed to send a message to the prisons in New Mexico and see where she had been taken. With crimes across the West, there were a number of places they could have sent her. It was a long shot that Grant would go after his wife, given that he never really loved her from what Colt said, but again, no stone would remain unturned when it came to this coyote.

He located the telegraph office and, tying Bunny to the hitching post, strode inside. He withdrew the paper from his pocket and slapped it on the desk, setting a coin atop it. He pulled aside his jacket to reveal his sheriff's badge.

The telegraph operator pocketed the coin and lifted the note, reading it. "You looking for a man who is over six foot five? Dark blond hair, beard?"

"You confirming my writing, or asking?"

The telegraph operator scratched his beard. "I'm pretty sure I saw a fellow matching that description go into the saloon across the street yesterday."

"Thanks." Reid tipped his hat and tossed him another coin. "See anything else, or receive a response, you can find me at the hotel, and there will be a good tip awaiting you."

The man's eyes shone with interest. "Yes, sir."

Reid left his horse at the hitching post in front of the telegraph office and crossed the street to the saloon, keeping his hat pulled low over his eyes. He pushed open the short shutter doors that swung closed behind him, *thump thumping* into place. His spurs jingled as he crossed the filthy hardwood floors to the man at the counter who stood polishing a glass with a disgusting mottled rag. A man in a worn suit pounded out a ragtime tune for the few customers playing cards on the circular tables with a few saloon women roving about in too short costumes. He avoided the women's hopeful stares and leaned against the bar with one arm. He unfolded the wanted poster and slid it over to the barkeep.

The barkeep's brows raised. He leaned over the counter and studied the picture. "A murderer, eh?"

"Yup." Reid kept an eye on his surroundings in case Grant was lurking in the shadows.

"Can't say I've seen him."

"I don't like being lied to." Reid growled, pulling back his jacket to reveal his gun belt and star. "He's wronged my town and needs to be put away before he kills again."

The barkeep lifted his hands and laughed in short, puffy gasps. "I don't want no trouble. People come in here all the time from out of town looking for a good time and a drink. I don't study their faces, or ask questions. I give them what they want and make sure they leave with empty pockets."

"You see him, and you tell me. I'm at the hotel." Reid kicked off the metal foot bar and headed for the doors. Time to follow the map before Grant caught wind that Reid was looking for him. He trotted across the street to his horse, untied him, and gripping the saddle horn, swung himself up, riding as quickly as he could out of town without raising suspicion.

If Colt hadn't traced the trail on the map and noted the trail marker, a unique oak tree that was split down the middle from a lightning strike and somehow managed to stay alive, Reid might have missed it. Riding just beyond the split oak, there was a trail hardly visible from the road. He bent low in the saddle and ducked through brush to reach it. He scanned the undergrowth and found a broken twig. He grinned. Grant was here. He continued down the trail, following a brook until he reined in Bunny at the sight of the dilapidated cabin nestled under a giant white oak with an outhouse at the edge of the overgrown clearing.

No smoke rose from the chimney, but that didn't mean it was vacant. He tied the reins to a branch and, keeping low to the ground, crawled to the cabin and peered through the grimy window. Boot marks scuffed the hardwood floors in an erratic manner that made it impossible to gauge the boot size from the window. Not much else hinted at the cabin being occupied, except the placement of a crowbar thrust into the ashes of the fireplace. Had Grant used it to melt off his cuffs? He scanned for the cuffs but could not see it from this angle. He'd have to get inside, but he didn't dare yet, not while Lorna was in town and unprotected from this beast that roamed free, bent on revenge. Reid crawled back to his horse and leapt into the saddle, pushing the stallion to his limits to reach Lorna before it was too late.

CHAPTER 3

Time slowed as the fried chicken thigh hurtled through the air, followed by the glorious roasted brussels sprouts, and the world-famous apple pie as the Normandy hand-painted plates tumbled from her hands, and she plummeted to the floor. Her hip caught the corner of the table, and she braced herself as she slammed to the hardwood in a heap of black hose and white petticoats. She swallowed a few choice words that she had picked up from a ranch hand.

"Miss Lorna!" The staff about her exclaimed, questioning if she was injured.

A pair of strong hands gripped under

her arms and gently dragged her to her feet, she stumbled back, and the arms wrapped around her chest, hoisting her upwards when the front door slammed open. *Oh, dear Lord in heaven.*

Gaston stood in the door, raw fury nearly splitting his face. "Let her go." He boomed.

Lorna found herself smashing onto her derriere as Beau scrambled back, hands raised at Gaston's lightning reflexes that brought his pair of revolvers out from their leather holsters.

Lorna gasped from her place on the floor. "Leave the poor man alone."

"Keep out of the way, Lorna." He pulled the hammers back.

She scrambled to her feet and rubbed her hip, swallowing a groan. "Nope. You've misunderstood the situation."

"I come in here to see you in a man's arms like you were some saloon dove—"

"Watch your mouth. You put those in their holster, or so help me, I'll tell everyone in this room your first name." Lorna plopped her hands on her hips and stood between the two men.

Beau rested his hand on her shoulder, gently pulling her behind him as if intent on putting himself between her and danger.

"Get your filthy hands off of her!" Gaston shouted.

Lorna crossed her arms and rolled her eyes. "You keep behind *me*, Mr. Carson. He won't shoot with me in the way. Will you, *Gaston?*"

Something flickered in Gaston's eyes, and he seemed to take in the situation for the first time, including the broken China on the floor and food bits strewn across the table and floor and clusters of guests, all gaping at him. "No, I won't shoot you." He released the hammers, twirled his guns once, which was meek for him, and tucked them back in his gun belt.

"Now that we have that settled," Miss Freya muttered and waved the girls in the room with their rags to clean *again*. "You go weeks without a single incident and now you have two accidents back-to-back after I tell you about the Montezuma?" She lowered her voice and grasped Lorna's arm, "Miss Lorna, go change into a fresh apron, and then we *will* discuss what happened away from our guests."

Lorna escaped the Harvey House dining room, cheeks flaming. Of course, Gaston would arrive the moment she had made a mistake after being a nearly flawless worker. She glanced down to the culprit. Her half boot snagged on the edge of a guest's chair when they unexpectedly decided to adjust their seat by shooting backward four inches. Her sole had ripped from the toe to her arch. It slapped against her foot as she raced out the front door and shut it behind her only for Gaston to shove it open.

His eyes widened at her uniform that was fairly clean given the flying food, save for a corner that had a long gravy stain. "Well, this is a surprise, Gaston." She kicked herself. She needed to address him as *Reid* like everyone else, not her name for him that she used whenever they were alone. *Distance must be had.*

"I suppose it would be." He gripped his Stetson, trouble in his eyes.

"Why are you in Topeka?" Her heart pounded as she realized for the first time why on earth he would be here and seeking her out and not Gil or Pa. "I-is it my family? Is it Ma? She had a cold when I left and—"

"Everyone is well." He grasped her hands and stroked his thumbs over her palms.

Did he notice the fresh callouses? She pulled away from his grip, reminding herself a second time that she needed to distance herself from him and not give into the pleasure of him holding her hands like he missed her.

"I'm sorry I frightened you and for-for that display." He jerked his head back to the restaurant. "I can explain why I acted so odd, but what on earth was going on in there? Why was he holding you around your, um—"

"My chest?" She supplied and lifted up her boot, displaying the broken sole. "Accident."

He snorted. "I'll say."

"Why are you here, Gaston? I thought

you retired from being a ranger? Who is watching the town?"

"Colt Lawson and your brother are the acting sheriffs while I'm away." He cleared his throat. "I came for you."

Her gasp caught in her throat, accidentally inhaling some spittle, and bringing on a coughing fit. *For me? He's here for me? He missed me?* "What?"

He patted her on the back. "You okay there?"

"No." She blinked back tears from holding in her cough. "Why?"

"I have some bad news." He reached into his vest pocket and withdrew a folded piece of paper and handed it to her, his gaze never leaving her face.

She unfolded it, confusion blooming. "Grant Lawson? Isn't he in jail? Why are you showing me an old poster?"

"The wanted poster is new, Lorna. He escaped, and it is believed that he is in Topeka."

"Topeka?" She paled. "Why would he be here?"

"He has a hideout here, but I thought it

was too coincidental as you were here too and would be the perfect means of exacting his revenge on me."

"Pardon? I've never spoken to this man in my life. How on earth did you leap to the conclusion that I was in danger?" She shoved the paper back in his hand and crossed her arms. *Do I mean so much to you?*

"You are an Elliot. He knows that I practically grew up on your ranch. He has a bone to pick with your brother after he confronted the gang this summer. And Grant is not stupid. He probably kept abreast of your family's whereabouts, and when he learned you were unprotected, he could not only get his revenge, but fund his new Death Rider posse. Since your pa owns so much of New Mexico, your abduction and ransom would replenish his coffers and help him evade the law again." He folded his arms over his chest. "Therefore, I've come to take you home."

"What?" She snapped up. "No. I just got here, and I've already signed a three-month contract with Fred Harvey."

"Where are you stationed?"

"They want me in Texas." She lifted her chin at the half-truth that was more like a full falsehood. They wanted her, but *she* wanted to be in Texas more than anything. Or did she? She could already feel herself cracking when it came to Gaston—*Reid!*

"Nope. Too far. I have to keep an eye on you. See if they can transfer you to the Castañeda. If you are as dedicated a waitress as you are a cattle hand, they won't want to lose you."

"It's full." She scowled up at him as if that would help her fend off his charms. "And for your information, I am a great waitress."

"If you do not get a position there, what about Montezuma?" He tugged his hat back into place, his contrite expression long gone as he rose to the challenge. "It could work, but it is awful close to Grant's canyon."

"Where I work has nothing to do with you."

He leaned down to her, mirroring her frown, and coming entirely too close, his musk of leather and outdoors enveloping her. "It has *everything* to do with me."

Was he *trying* to torture her? How could

he smell so heavenly after traveling? "I think not."

"I am not about to allow you and your family's famous pride get you killed. I owe Mr. and Mrs. Elliot a great deal."

"So, it is not because of a great love you have been harboring for me?" She laughed, proud of herself for the jest given that only a few weeks ago such a comment would have cost her dearly. *Huh, maybe I am getting over Gaston Reid and his many charms.*

"Of course, I care for you." He pulled her hand free and began stroking it with his thumb again.

Nope. Not impervious. Good thing her sleeve went to her wrist as he had sent chills up to her shoulder.

"Listen to me. I would not be here unless I considered this threat real. Now, will you pack your bags, or do I need to go up in your dormitory and pack them for you?"

At this, she jerked her hand back once again. "You can't. It's against the rules. And you can't tell me what to do, Gaston Reid."

"Watch me." He fairly growled, taking a step closer to her.

She smirked and poked his solid chest with a single finger. "Don't think that intimidation tactic works on me. I've seen you laugh so hard that milk squirted out your nostrils."

He smirked, that dimple at the corner of his mouth taunting her. "You know I'll do it, Lorna."

She knew he had logic on his side, and it was a lost cause in convincing the board to allow her to change positions from the resort. "Look, I have three days left of my training before I can go to the Montezuma. I doubt Grant will throw me over the back of his horse and make off with me by that time."

He ran his hand over the back of his neck, groaning. "You can't expect me to think that job is important enough to risk your life."

"It's important to me and my future. If you cannot respect my decision, I'll make you respect it." She growled.

"How?" He frowned down at her.

"Easy. I'll tell my brother you tried to kiss me, and he will send you packing."

"What! Lorna." His jaw slacked. "I did no such thing."

She smirked. It was playing dirty, but how else was she supposed to get Gaston Reid to bend to her will? *And what's wrong with a little threat?* She shrugged. "You might have."

"You are incorrigible." He flicked the brim of his hat upward. "Fine, but I will see to your safety myself, and you won't go anywhere without my knowing about it. Agreed?"

"What are you going to do to achieve that? You can't rightly sleep in my room, nor outside my door." She snorted.

"No, but I will not leave your side until I set you in the Montezuma, and, even then, I will get a room to stay close until a fellow Texas Ranger, or a friend, can be reached to come help me."

"So much for avoiding you to forget you." She mumbled under her breath. It seemed her trial of temptation would begin at once.

"What's that, Lorna?"

"Nothing," she mumbled. Even if he

didn't love her in the way she wished, he did care for her, or he wouldn't have come. But, unlike the old Lorna of almost a month ago, she would not misconstrue the truth to suit her unrequited love. No. She, Lorna Elliot, was determined to be disenchanted by his charms and focus on the true meaning behind his actions—friendship and loyalty to her family. And that only. She sighed and offered him a smile half as bright as usual. "Thank you for your concern, Reid. You are a true friend to give up so much to keep me safe."

He blinked, a weariness settling over his expression. "You are acquiescing mighty fast. What are you planning, Lorna?"

"I'm not planning a thing. I'm mature enough to see your point. Now, if you'll excuse me, I need to change my apron and shoes and get back to work. If you wish to stay near, you can wait at the bottom of the steps to the dormitory while I make myself presentable."

HE FLICKED BACK the brim of his hat and leaned against a storefront near the Harvey House, keeping an eye on Lorna as the sun set. Why was she calling him Reid all of a sudden? She always called him Gaston when they were alone because she knew how much he hated that name. And then, it became the way only *she* addressed him, and it became rather nice. However, she would not dare to call him that in public—except for the Harvey House incident when she had been trying to snap him out of his stupor.

But he had been in a trance. Seeing Lorna dressed as one of the elegant Harvey Girls that displayed her curves to perfection and *in* a strange man's arms had done something to his heart. She didn't look like the wildling in split skirts with a braid flying over her shoulder as she rode hard over the foothills in chase of a coyote pack threatening her herd. The Harvey uniform, modest though it was, made her seem . . . older and far more mature. He massaged a hand over his chest. *This is ridiculous. I've seen her in her Sunday best before. Why is this any different?* He shook his head at this absurd feeling. It was *Lorna.* He had known her forever and never had he ever felt *this* in his chest in regard to her.

He must be hungry. Good thing he was near the best place to eat for a hundred miles. He needed something to clear this nonsense out of his mind. At the quick clicking heeled footsteps behind him, he turned to find Lorna approaching him, and the nonsense flooded his vision all over again. Somehow, in the span of a month since he'd seen her, Lorna Elliot had turned into the most beautiful Harvey Girl he had ever seen—even more so than Belle Parish. Her flaming red hair against the black uniform took his breath away.

"Reid? You okay? You are looking a mite peaked." She rested her hand on his forearm, her brown eyes not dancing with their usual mischief but, instead, flickering with concern.

"Why would I not be?" He managed to grit out.

"You're breathing heavy and," she lifted her little hand to his forehead, "you are sweating, but not in the way of fever. You are probably hungry and exhausted. Come along. I best see to you before you pass out." She tugged him along. He had been tugged along plenty by this fiery little redhead, but never had her touch sent charges up his arm. He must be sick. *Probably picked it up on the train.*

At the door, Lorna dropped his hand, and he at once felt the absence of her warmth as she led him into the dining room that was emptying of the passengers as a gong sounded for the final warning for them to board the train again. She showed him to a small linen covered table in the corner with a window to the main street where he could keep watch until the sunset. That man who had helped her was still in his corner, staring at Reid over his newspaper.

"I'll fetch you some coffee and your usual order."

"How do you know what my usual is?"

"You told my brother often enough of your times at the Harvey House and what you ate as you visited your old beau. I'm sure

Gil would remember what your order is too." She chuckled and patted him on the shoulder as she moved to the kitchen to place his order as another Harvey Girl approached his table with a smile and a pot of steaming coffee.

"Good afternoon, sir. Are you new to town or passing through?" She poured his cup slowly, as if she actually wanted to hear his answer.

"Passing through. Came to pick up something." His gaze flicked to Lorna as she wiped down a newly vacant table.

The Harvey Girl's pleasantness faded, and she pressed her lips into a thin line. "You know she signed a three-month contract. If she marries during that time frame, she will forfeit a month of wages."

Jealously surged through him. He gripped the edge of the table. "Married? Who is talking about marrying her?"

Lorna appeared with his plate of steak, baked potato, and green beans. "What's this talk of marriage?" She set the plate before him, her expression stiff as if she were fighting back her emotions.

"You tell me. A-are you planning on getting married?" He was dying to look toward that cowboy in the corner but kept his gaze on her. Could one really fall in love in a matter of weeks? His stomach tumbled. He thought he had with Belle, but his Lorna couldn't possibly be getting married. Could she?

The Harvey Girl nodded to him, plopping one hand on her hip with the other gripping the pot handle. "This man said he was picking up something and looked straight at you." She shook her head and laughed, bitterness making it sharp. "Here, you've gotten yourself the best Harvey House to serve at, and you will be breaking contract before you even step foot off that train. What a waste."

Lorna frowned. "You misunderstood him, Miss Vara. He is a family friend. I am to serve the Harvey House for at least three months. Who knows? If I like it, I may sign on for another year."

A year? His gut clenched at the thought of not seeing Lorna at Sunday dinners that long. The food lost its allure. *Oh, boy. I'm in trouble.*

"Is there something amiss with your food, Reid?" Lorna snapped her fingers. "I'm so sorry. I forgot your gravy." She darted back into the kitchen, and by the time she returned with the dish, Miss Vara had moved on to another table. Lorna poured it over his potato and greens and glanced over her shoulder. "While it is nice to see you, Reid. I really must get back to work. Good luck with that hotel. I heard bed bugs run the place."

"You can't keep me from staying to watch over you, Lorna. I sleep as well under a tree as I do in a feather bed sans bed bugs." He scratched at his scalp as if already imagining the bugs eating him alive as he attempted to sleep. "Come to think of it, I may sleep under the stars tonight, which window upstairs belongs to you?"

She worried her bottom lip. He knew she was warring against the idea of him protecting her. He dug into his plate, pretending to enjoy the steak, letting her think. This was supposed to be her grand adventure, and here he was inserting himself into her life without an invitation.

"Do you really think I am his next target?" Lorna whispered.

"I wouldn't be here if I didn't think it a credible threat." Reid set down his fork and gripped his coffee cup, holding her gaze.

She sighed. "I'm the corner window on the rear left of the second floor."

CHAPTER 4

*L*orna perched on the edge of one of the four single beds in the tiny room and jerked off her boots, wrinkling her nose at the sour odor. Her pa would be proud of her for working so diligently as unto the Lord, no matter how pungent her shoes had become. She would need to borrow some baking soda from the kitchen. She drew back the lace curtains to the single window to let some air inside and spied Reid's bedroll beneath a small redbud tree with its few remaining leaves. She smiled to herself. He did care. *As a friend, Lorna. He cares as a friend.* She flopped on her bed and flung her arm over her eyes for a few moments of rest before dressing for bed when she heard a thumping on the dormitory roof.

She whipped about. Her three roommates were still on their shift. She snatched up her silver hairbrush that had been a gift for her twenty-third birthday last year. It was supposed to be for her wedding trunk. Everyone wondered why she hadn't married yet, but she had her heart set on one man. *Where is that man? I know he doesn't sleep that hard.* The only way he would have not heard an intruder was if he had been knocked unconscious. Worry churned her belly. She lifted the brush and leapt to the window, ready to smash whoever was approaching her open window. She shoved back the lace and swung, smacking Gaston in the jaw and sending him rolling to the ledge.

"Lorna!" He gasped, gripping the edge of the roof. "*Why* on earth would you do that?" He scrambled for a better hold, his round boot tips not finding purchase.

"Reid?" She climbed through the window and crawled out onto the roof, skirts pooling about her ankles. "Why wouldn't I? I didn't know it was you."

He grunted, adjusting his hold. "I was testing how easy it would be to get to you."

She tossed her hairbrush back inside, aiming for her bed. "I'm sorry I accidentally walloped you. But, ever consider that you would be a peeping Tom by climbing up here?"

"No." He grunted, his knuckles white in the moonlight. "I'm going to fall now."

"Don't do that. There are rose bushes lining the path!" She extended her hand to him. "Take hold."

"You can't pull me up. I weigh twice as much as you."

"I can rope a bull calf for branding. I can pull you up." She grasped his wrist with both hands, tugging.

"Let go!" He commanded a breath before his fingers slipped from the ledge and he fell, lugging her down with him. She gasped as the ground hurtled toward her, but instead of being cut by bushes, she found herself wrapped in Gaston's arms. He shifted at the last moment to land on his feet and rolled with her caged in his arms.

They tumbled to a halt with her atop him and Gaston groaning. Her body already ached from the fall, but knowing he took the brunt, she gently pushed off his chest and ran her hands over his shoulders and arms, looking for anything broken. "Gaston. What on earth were you thinking? You could've killed yourself! I would have been fine if you had focused on catching yourself."

"You were plunging headlong. You would have been seriously hurt." He grunted, slowly sitting up and wincing.

"I know how to fall." She murmured, still unconvinced of his health as she examined his head, tilting it one way and the next. "Are you certain you didn't break any-thing?" She ran her hands over his collar bone and methodically moved her fingers down his torso. She had seen the doctor perform such examinations at the ranch often enough to know what to look for after a hand took a hard fall from his horse, or

while making repairs to the stables or out-
buildings.

"I know how to fall too," he echoed her
words with a grin and a wink. "I appreciate
your concern, though." His gaze rested on
her hands that were currently examining
his abdomen of steel.

She jerked them back as if they were on
fire. "And I appreciate *your* concern, but
Grant Lawson is nowhere in this building.
It's just us Harvey Girls, and there is only
one person who has the key." She rubbed
her neck, closing her eyes against the sting
that was roaring to life now that she was
certain Gaston was well.

His eyes flashed with concern, he jerked
upright, his hand resting on her shoulder.
"You are hurt. Where?"

"It's not that bad." She sighed, adding,
"You took the worst of it. I may be proud,
but even I can admit that you spared me a
broken bone, so thank you."

"You can thank me by letting me check
out your injury." He flicked his fingers, motioning for her to come closer so he could
have a better look.

She turned around in the dirt and lifted her thick braid.

He sucked in a breath through his teeth and ran his finger over the mark, sending a chill down her spine. "You've got a nasty brush burn. How? I blocked you with my body."

"Your whiskers grow back quickly." She scooted away from his touch. "My collar will hide it."

"I'll pick up some salve at the general store." His eyes bored into hers. "You sure you aren't hurt elsewhere? Are your ankles fine?" He nodded to her exposed feet.

She tucked her stockinged feet under her gown. "Gaston Reid. I am a lady, and I won't be showing you my ankles."

His cheeks flushed. "I know that. I was asking if you need to be carried to the doctor. And I've seen your ankles before, so they are hardly a great mystery."

"Not for some time." She narrowed her eyes at him, making his blush deepen.

He glanced away and rolled to his feet, extending his hand to her. "We best get you back up the trellis before anyone sees you covered in dirt, sprawled on the ground beside me."

She ignored his hand and shot to her feet, dusting off her skirts with a few good whacks. Her gown would have to be laundered. "What a thing to say. I can take care of myself, thank you very much."

"I know you can, Lorna. You can do anything."

She pursed her lips, tilting her head. "What's the catch, Reid? You never compliment me outright without trying to butter me up like a piece of toast."

He chuckled. "Do I really? Well, that is something I will remedy in the future, but," he cleared his throat, "you aren't wrong about me needing to tell you something. There never seemed to be a spare moment during your day, but your parents lent me Bunny while you were away."

She blinked. "My stallion?" A surge of longing filled her being. "Bunny is here in Topeka?"

He nodded. "I brought him as I wasn't sure what I'd find here and might need to ride out after you."

"Where is he now? The Main Street stable?" What she would give for a moment on her horse.

"Yup, but I don't think that nightfall would be a good time to take him for a ride in a terrain that you aren't familiar with and given the fact that I don't know where Grant Lawson is at the moment."

She sighed. "You are right. I'll bring him a treat before I start my shift in the morning."

"You don't mind my borrowing him?"

"Bunny deserves to be ridden and often." She shook her head. "That was the hardest part of joining the Harvey Girls. I knew I'd have to give him up for a month during training before I knew where I was stationed, and, even then, it seemed cruel to keep him in a stall when he could roam free on my parents' ranch, but I'm selfish and requested that they care for him while I was gone and send him to me once I knew my post. Thank you for exercising him for me."

He nodded. "He's a beautiful animal as well as swift, but don't worry, I won't steal him from you for long."

She tossed her braid over her shoulder. "He is loyal to me. Even if you tried, he wouldn't let you." She looked up to the window. "I best be on my way before any of the girls return and the rumors start circulating. Now, turn around." She waited until he did so to hike up her skirts and climb the trellis. She scrambled through her window. "Goodnight, Reid." She called down and shoved the window shut behind her and locked it, flinging the curtains closed. She crossed her arms and turned her back to his upturned face. She would not look out the window at him again. She would not think about his arms about her, or how solid his chest felt. She wanted to flop into her bed, but now that she was filthy, she'd need to bathe in order to be ready for work at dawn.

She shuffled into the hallway to the shared bathroom and checked the bath schedule even though she knew it was likely free during this hour, but rules were rules. Schedule confirmed, she gathered a clean nightgown, her bar of honey and vanilla soap, and drew a bath and settled herself in, allowing the heat to sooth her sore muscles as her thoughts once again returned to the handsome former Texas Ranger. The question was, how was she going to convince Gaston that she was safe as a Harvey Girl under the fatherly arm of Fred Harvey and his laundry list of rules? Because if she was unsuccessful . . . *How am I supposed to forget Gaston when he plans to be by my side every moment for the foreseeable future?*

REID HAD a quarter of an hour before the next train arrived, which meant the Harvey House would soon be swarming with new guests, potentially with an outlaw among them. He was loath to leave Lorna's side for even a moment, but he had a word with the Harvey House manager about the situation, and the manager agreed to sound the gong rapidly at the sight of anything amiss while he was gone for five minutes. Reid trotted over to the telegraph office, flinging the door open. "Any reply?"

The telegraph operator nodded, drawing

papers from his half apron pocket. "Two actually. Both came in this morning. Was about to head over to the hotel."

"Camping outside the Harvey House now." He tossed a coin to the man as he handed him the sealed envelopes. He opened the top one.

Meet in Las Vegas. T.S.

The panic plaguing in his chest eased a bit. If Tanner Sterling was after Grant, the outlaw would be in chains and behind bars before long. He lifted his Stetson, swiped his brow with his forearm, and tucked away the telegram into his pocket. The second slip was from the Texas Rangers headquarters, saying that they already had men out looking for Grant. Not exactly the support he was hoping for, but he supposed the rangers couldn't spare any men for guarding Lorna. It wasn't their job, which mean Reid would do everything in his power to see her safe, with or without her permission.

"Thank you. Shouldn't be any more news, but you can find me at the Harvey House if you see or hear anything."

The man nodded and waited with expectant eyes.

Reid tossed him another coin to ensure his helpfulness and shoved open the door, the bell dinging overhead. He crossed the street to the saloon, informed the barkeep where he could be found in the event of any news, and checked on Bunny in the nearby stable, barely taking a moment to rub the stallion's nose before Reid's gut pulled him back to the Harvey House porch. He paced along the outside, keeping an eye out for trouble, while watching Lorna through the windows.

She moved with grace, and there was an elegant gentleness he had not seen formerly in her. She smiled brightly to the little girl who couldn't be much older than three and allowed the little girl to touch the big white bow in Lorna's brilliant coiffure. Lorna laughed and disappeared into the kitchen to place an order. Over the next few hours, he could tell that she was by far one of the best waitresses in the training house. Many made little mistakes, but he noticed how the head waitress never corrected Lorna.

"Why are you watching Miss Elliot?" The man Lorna had called Beau Carson joined him on the platform facing the train as another burst of guests streamed out of the train cars.

"There's been trouble." Reid crossed his arms and studied each face, man and woman. He wouldn't put it past Grant to disguise himself. "And that trouble is likely to come for Miss Elliot."

"Las Vegas is no stranger to trouble . . . what with it being the former headquarters of the Death Rider gang."

His brow lifted. "You must be from the area if you know that."

"It's the closest town to my ranch. It used to be a wild township before Fred Harvey arrived. Don't doubt that there is some legacy of that trouble remaining, despite the two Harvey Houses in the area. I'm heading back over the Gallinas Mountains now. I would have left yesterday, but one of my hands was sick, and I don't leave anyone behind. What should I be on the lookout for?"

Reid withdrew the wanted poster he kept folded in his vest, handing it to him. "Grant Lawson. As you well know, he is the leader of the Death Riders. I put him away only weeks ago. He escaped and has a vendetta against me."

"And that would effect Miss Elliot in what way, and why do you care so much?" His eyes narrowed. "Do you two have an understanding?"

"She's a dear friend that I would die to protect. And why are *you* asking about her?"

"Harvey Girls hold a special place in my heart. And I don't like to see men take advantage of women." He pushed off the Harvey House wall. "I best get my last good meal until the Montezuma. God speed on your capture of the outlaw, Sheriff Reid."

CHAPTER 5

*L*orna stood on the train platform with Corinna and Freya, blinking to keep her tears at bay as passengers bustled about their way. No amount of hinting would see Freya changing Lorna's assignment. The only consolation was that her roommate, Corinna Victoria, would be joining her at the Montezuma Resort in Hot Springs, Las Vegas. The golden-haired beauty had been difficult to get to know, but she was an exceptionally hard worker with a gentle spirit that was a balm to any busy Harvey House. Corinna was already proving herself to be a friend in her thoughtful actions and kindness, even if she was reluctant to open up about her life before becoming a Harvey Girl, but they would have plenty of time for bonding at their new post.

Gaston rapped on the inside of the train's window with the gold signet ring that he always wore on his little finger. Lorna made a show of rolling her eyes at his impatience. She had insisted Gaston board the train before them so she could say her goodbyes to Freya on the platform alone, and she would draw this out as long as possible. She embraced Freya. She hadn't thought thirty days would be long enough to form such a deep friendship, given she had lived a lifetime in Las Vegas and only had Harriet for a true friend . . . and that was because she was married to Lorna's brother Gil. She had never had a true friend that was a woman before Harriet. She pulled back, still clutching Freya's hands. "I'm going to miss you."

A burst of steam from the engine enveloped them. It was time to go.

"We are going to miss you, Lorna. Remember to be strong." Freya squeezed her hands. "You have come so far in a short amount of time. Remember your goal, and when you waver, count all the blessings the Lord has given you, and pray that He changes the desire of your heart."

She dipped her head. "I know. I want to be content. I am content. I don't need *him* to have a full life when I have the Lord in my heart and at my side in life."

Freya nodded. "It's so hard when the desires of our hearts do not come to fruition. But I know the Lord has a plan for you, dear Lorna. There is a reason you are a Harvey Girl now and not a certain someone's wife."

Lorna cast a glance to the train, but Gaston was seated with a newspaper cracked open. There was no way he could hear them above the shouted goodbyes from family to passengers, porters calling out directions to new arrivals, and the Harvey House gong that was directing guests into the restaurant. "I-I know, and I'm learning to trust my unknown future to my God who knows all, no matter how hard it is for me to surrender control."

"Amen." Corinna whispered behind them, surprising Freya and Lorna.

Lorna smiled through the pain of parting with Freya. "Are you certain you want to stay in Topeka to train Harvey Girls? You could come with me? Now that I finally have a bosom friend, I am not eager to leave you behind."

Freya slowly shook her head. "I'm tempted, but for now, my place is here, ministering to and serving the new recruits and readying them for their futures. Most are not as prepared as you and Corinna Victoria." She smiled at the Harvey Girl who stood a few feet away, staring anywhere but at the two Harvey Girls. "Corinna," she waved her over, "I know you are shy, but you two look out for one another and lean on each other. It can be lonely at a new post, but you have each other. I will write and will visit you on my next holiday. It would be wonderful to meet your family, Lorna, after all that you have told me about them. It's really too bad that you do not have another unmarried brother."

"Like you need any more proposals."

Lorna giggled, but she appreciated the sentiment. "I'll see you soon?"

Freya nodded as the train whistle sounded the final warning, and with one last hug, Corinna and Lorna joined Gaston for the journey to the Montezuma. She wasn't surprised to see that Corinna had chosen to sit in the bench seat across from them in the opposite row. She removed her ball of yarn, needles, and her folded project. Lorna offered the woman a smile who returned it and set up her knitting. It appeared she had been working on it for a while, given the length, but the stitches were uneven, and the pattern was undecipherable, but she turned all her focus on it, knitting away. Lorna had never had the patience to learn, but she admired Corinna's determination.

"You going to stand in the aisle for the whole of the journey, or take a seat with me?" Gaston folded his paper and scooted closer to the window.

The bench seat was a mite narrow, but she figured it would prove even more awkward if she did not join him. *And the test be-*

gins. Lorna sank down beside Gaston. "Anything interesting in the news?"

He pressed his lips in a firm line. "It's an old paper that a passenger wedged between the wood bench and the wall . . . dated from the morning of my arrival in Topeka, which was how I missed seeing it." He grunted and passed the paper to her. "I should have done a better job, but I allowed my worry over Grant to make me careless and forgot to read it." He flicked the top of an article on the third page.

Lorna gasped at the headline over the small article. "*Jill* Lawson escaped?"

He rubbed his forehead, resting his elbows atop his thighs. "No doubt it was Grant's work. I cannot believe I didn't at least check and see if Jill was still secure, but I honestly had no idea where she was imprisoned."

"So, he was never in Topeka?"

He shrugged. "I wouldn't say that. I checked out his hideout cabin right outside of town, and there was proof that someone had been there recently, but it is my belief that he passed on through here before he freed his wife. She was a working member of the Death Rider outlaws as well. They had hideouts in Colorado, New Mexico, Texas, and Kansas. She committed the bulk of her crimes in Kansas along the Atchison, Topeka, and Santa Fé railroads and was most likely in a prison near Topeka."

"I didn't know they covered so much ground." She shivered.

"Which was why it took me so long to capture them all the first time." He draped his arm over her shoulders, brows raising as she tensed. "I'm not telling you this to frighten you, merely inform."

She never used to be so stiff around him. She tried to force herself to relax.

"You are safe. I am not going to let anything happen to you, and without the rest of his riders supporting him, Grant is significantly less threatening."

"I know. I still think it is odd that he would mark me as his target." She shifted out from his arm in the guise of checking her carpetbag at her feet, pulling out a romance novel. If she could read, she wouldn't have to look into his beautiful eyes that touched her soul.

"I can understand your hesitation, but I chased Grant and his gang for years before I put him away only weeks ago. I know how he thinks and operates. I agree, it seems far-fetched, but I *know* Grant, and this would be his move. He needs funds to breathe new life into his outlaw group. Getting his hands on you would provide revenge against me and Gil while still filling his pockets."

Revenge against you? She dared to look up at him. Did he care so much for her? Or was it merely because of her last name that he sought to protect her? Her thoughts threatened to swirl and take over her resolutions not to read into things. She flipped open her book.

Desmond embraced Lady Giselle, his lips seeking hers once, twice, until the last kiss sent her into a faint—

She slammed the book shut. A romance novel was the worst idea with her own dashing Desmond beside her. As she packed her Bible in her trunk to keep it from getting damaged, she only had one more book in her bag, a dictionary. She picked it up and flipped it open, dredging up enough willpower not to think about a certain man.

Gaston chuckled. "Is my company so inferior that you would prefer a dictionary?"

She blinked up at him in what she hoped was an innocent manner. *Perhaps some form of the truth will keep him from pressing.* "There is a lot going on right now. I need to distract my thoughts from spinning out of control."

"I'm so sorry." He gently grasped her elbow. "I didn't mean to frighten you. You've never been one faint of heart." He gritted his teeth, shaking his head. "I shouldn't have told you everything."

"I'm glad you did. If you didn't, I wouldn't be so compliant." She grinned at him, her gut twisting with guilt over the half-truth. She *was* distracting herself, but from him—not Grant. She had total trust in the man beside her to protect her from everyone but himself. She lifted her book. "I better get back to reading." She turned to the *E's,* but not before she noticed the question in his eyes.

The train ride was torturous. He checked on her state of emotions every twenty minutes it seemed. She even changed seats to be beside Corinna, saying she wanted to get to know her better, but that did not stop his asking about her heart. It would have been better if Gaston talked nonstop about some other woman, but he was attentive and thoughtful—everything she had ever wanted him to be toward her. But now her eyes were opened to the fact that Gaston Reid would never love her more than a friend. And so, she did what she promised Freya. She took her thoughts captive and did not make more of his actions than what they were. He was a sheriff, and she was a citizen in danger. He was doing his job, and she would do the job before her, even if it killed her. She was an Elliot after all, and Elliots never shied away from a challenge.

HE SCRATCHED his jaw as they stood in the aisle to disembark in Las Vegas, scowling after the hours he and Lorna had traveled with Corinna Victoria. Lorna had been friendly, with her changing seats back and forth between her two companions, but their conversations lacked the vibrancy he usually enjoyed. Reid had even gone out of his way to make sure she was taken care of, along with the quiet Harvey Girl, Miss Victoria.

But Lorna's distant conversation remained the same, no matter what he did to draw her out from behind that dictionary. What happened in Topeka that brought such a change? He knew he had been distracted before she left. Or, more accurately, *obsessed* with Belle Parish, but that was before Belle had run off and married Colt Lawson. And Reid wasn't distracted anymore.

He hadn't sent Gil a telegram telling him of Lorna's post at the Montezuma in case Grant had a telegraph operator delivering him tips. Instead, Reid planned to escort her to the Montezuma, see her settled, and then return to the sheriff's office to speak with Colt and Gilbert there, and perhaps Tanner, if he had already arrived. Tanner hadn't said where he had been though, so it could be a few days yet.

Reid held his hand out to Lorna to help her down the steps, but she gave a slight shake of her head and nodded to the attendant on the platform in a black suit. Behind him, the Montezuma Harvey Resort surrey with a gold fringe along the roof stood beside the rails and was drawn by two white horses.

The attendant greeted them with a smile and a nod. "Miss Lorna Elliot and Miss Corinna Victoria. Welcome to Las Vegas. I am to escort you." He looked to Reid. "Are you staying at the Montezuma as well, sir?"

Reid nodded, not bothering to explain his intentions with Lorna's safety. Instead, Reid motioned for the ladies to proceed him and asked Lorna to wait in the surrey while he fetched his horse. He trotted to the stable car and shifted from boot to boot as the hand guided Bunny down the ramp. The stallion tossed his head eagerly. By the time he returned to the surrey, the trunks had already been stacked in the back of the surrey and the two Harvey Girls sat together behind the driver.

Reid climbed into the back seat, glancing about for any signs of danger. Instead, he was met with smiles and waves from the townsfolk as they rode down the main street. He knew the people would have some questions once he was back in the office. It was strange to have to answer to a town full of folk after being the one questioning whomever he needed to and ignoring those he didn't want to answer.

Lorna whispered something to Corinna who giggled while Lorna pointed out places in the town. "You are going to love it here. I've been to the new resort many times. This is the third time it's been rebuilt."

"What? Was this the resort with the fire?" Corinna gasped. "I heard one burned down."

"There were not one, but two fires, that destroyed the resort. The last fire was in 1885. The resort was rebuilt again using the same design as the second building because it was, in truth, a beautiful building with lovely architectural elements. It was dubbed

The Phoenix for a short while, but then Mr. Harvey decided that he would rather not remind the public of the Montezuma's past and risk people thinking it is cursed."

"*C-cursed?*" Corinna replied, eyes wide.

She patted her arm. "There was a perfect excuse for each time. The last one, a horrible criminal on the run, named Wellington, burned it down. He died in prison."

"How shocking." Corinna pressed a hand to her chest. "How do you know so much about this? If it was so long ago. You weren't *there* were you?"

"Oh no!" Lorna threw Reid a glance over her shoulder, grinning. "I had a friend once who believed in the curse of the Montezuma Resort and would never stay there on holiday with us, even with the mule trail and hot springs that he could have enjoyed. And the view—oh, the view of the Gallinas Canyon and its mountains is simply breathtaking from the rooms. Pa liked to bring us all after he returned from the cattle drives to give Ma a break from cooking and cleaning as a thank you for holding down the ranch in his absence."

"Sounds like a storybook childhood," she whispered.

"It was." She clasped Corinna's hand. "You are going to love it there, and as we were trained together, you know we are going to be roommates, and I foresee a beautiful friendship ahead."

Who was this confident girl? He grinned, loving this side of Lorna. For years, he had seen her try to buy her friendships with gifts to the town girls. They never had accepted her, and the result had seen her turn more and more to the ranch and to her animals, her only friends being him and her now sister-in-law.

The surrey pulled past the last house on Main Street and crossing the wooden bridge, the horses pulled them up the steep mountainside to the Montezuma Resort. At the first bend, Lorna pointed out the pointed roof of the Montezuma's tower that was visible from the tree line if you craned your neck. The surrey wound with the road until they pulled up before the impressive resort with lovely grounds set in the picturesque mountains.

Corinna gasped and Reid couldn't help but be impressed by the resort that he had avoided for all these years—a castle-like building with its reddish-brown sandstone exterior on the first two stories, but it was done in such a manner that it complimented the mountainside with its gray slate roof. The architect had made it feel homey, though, with its verandas, dormers, and bay windows, and elegant with three towers. He could see why it was a popular destination and why Fred Harvey was so determined to see the resort rebuilt again and again.

The driver halted the horses, and a young boy secured the reins of the horses as the driver dismounted and lifted his hand to the women, giving Lorna a wink.

Reid scowled at him, but the man merely grinned up at him. "Enjoy your stay at the resort, sir. If you head to the lobby, which is right through the front door, you will be taken to your room directly." He bowed to the ladies. "And as for our new members of the Montezuma staff, please follow me."

Reid wanted to protest that he would stay with Lorna for the remainder of the day, but knowing she was safe enough in the daylight surrounded by guests, he swallowed his protest and sent her a wave and an encouraging grin. She returned a ghost of a smile and linked her arm with Corinna, fairly skipping away from him. *Ouch.* So much for hoping that Lorna saw him as her knight in shining Stetson.

CHAPTER 6

*A*fter resting all afternoon, Lorna didn't have much of a chance to enjoy the beauty of the resort before her shift in the massive dining room that would last until the wee hours. As the newest addition to the Montezuma staff, only the worst shifts should be expected for the first two weeks until she could prove herself. Below each stained-glass window that added a touch of elegance to the room, there were even larger windows. She knew from her time here as a guest that each window boasted of a stunning view of the reservoir. And as dusk approached, one might catch a bit of wildlife coming to the edge of the forest.

Because of this, every table at her station along the wall of windows was filled with guests. Thankfully, she was paired with Corinna who worked diligently to ensure each guest was given the best of service. While Corinna hadn't spoken much with her Harvey sisters over the staff dinner, she blossomed while working, speaking so clearly with each guest that no one would think that she was impossibly shy with strangers.

Lorna removed the dishes after a family of four vacated their table and hustled back to the kitchen, placing the stack of plates in the surprisingly empty dirty dish bin for the dish boy, who eyed the fresh pile with exhaustion and reached for the top saucer with a sigh. She offered him an apologetic grin and darted out with a pile of fresh linens in her arms as Corinna slid past with the dirty linens. While they may have been the newest of recruits, she could see why Freya had sent them here. The Montezuma was bursting with guests and needed fresh girls with energy.

The house mother, Ella Ashby, stood in the corner with a notepad, watching them, along with the head waitress, Maura Carr. Lorna spread the linen and with Corinna's arrival with the clean dishes, set the place efficiently and to perfection before checking on her tables with a coffee pot in hand, refilling cups without interrupting any of the guests as they enjoyed their meals.

Despite the long hours and aching back ahead of her, Lorna was finding that she loved working in the resort. She would write Freya tonight and tell her so. She took an order for dessert at one of her tables, one her favorites from her childhood holidays spent at the resort, triple chocolate cake. Her mouth watered at the thought of tasting it once more. The resort held so many happy memories for her. A sense of purpose filled her, and she determined to give these families good service to make their stay as enjoyable as possible and make those same memories she treasured. Why, she had been so busy she had not even thought of—

Gaston Reid strode into the dining room, his freshly washed hair gleaming in the gas lights of the metal Art Nouveau chandeliers with their curling, vinelike fixtures and shades that resembled blooming flowers. *Focus on the chandeliers. Your guests. Anything but his beautiful blue eyes.* But that did not help when one needed to navigate a sea of tables with heavy plates of food and therefore, avoid tripping. She lowered her gaze only to be captured in his. Her heart did a little flip. *No. Stop that. Gaston is not yours.* She gave him a stiff nod and set the plates before the family.

Gaston spoke with the head waitress, and Lorna swallowed as he was escorted to the freshly set table in her section.

Wonderful. Join the Harvey Girls! Get over Gaston. Travel! Have an adventure. She straightened her shoulders and smiled like he was any other guest. "Good evening, Sheriff Reid. Can I get you started with tea, coffee, or milk?" She withdrew her notepad for his order.

"Coffee, as always, *Miss* Lorna."

She took away the glass, leaving the cup upright. "And to eat?"

He rested his elbows on the table and intertwined his fingers. "Are you mad at me?"

"What?" She blinked.

"It's a simple question." He cracked his knuckles and picked up his overlarge napkin and gave it a snap, draping it over his lap. "You've been stiff toward me for days, and I cannot figure out what has you all in a knot."

She bit her bottom lip as Corinna paused to fill up his coffee. "I am not mad at you. Why would I be? You are only trying to help me." *I only meant to keep myself from treating you like you were the most special person on earth.* But she supposed that when one was used to such treatment . . . they might notice when the treatment ended.

"Then what is it?" He reached out, but stopped as if he realized that his touch might not be appropriate in the setting.

She glanced about. "I really can't talk right now, *Sheriff Reid*."

"So, there is something." He leaned back in his chair, frowning. "What did I do? Tell me so I can fix it, and we can go back to being friends."

"No! There's nothing. Not really. Do you just want something you'll like?" She nodded, tucking the notepad in her apron pocket. "I'll order something for you." She darted away, avoiding any response.

Miss Ashby met her at the kitchen doors. "Sheriff Reid spoke with me this morning about your unique situation. While I gave him my approval for watching you, I must ask that you keep your conversations with him to a minimum while on duty, unless of course there is some sort of threat that you need to discuss." She frowned. "You look flushed. Is there something amiss?"

"Yes, ma'am. I mean, no ma'am. It won't happen again." She pushed the swinging door to the kitchen and ordered the pork chop, collard greens, and mashed potatoes for Gaston. She grabbed Corinna's arm as she passed by. "Can you see to Sheriff Reid's table? Miss Ashby doesn't like me talking to him while working. He always tries to chat, and I thought that between the two of us—"

"I'm the one who talks the least," Corinna guessed with a wink. "Go ahead. Table seven is ready to be cleared."

The rest of the evening passed in a blur of activity until around midnight when the guests trickled back to their rooms and the tower parlor. While the resort kept the dining room open for any late-night meals, the staff was reduced to Lorna, Corinna, and two other girls that Lorna met upon her arrival, Pernilla Margot and Jean May. Gaston remained in the corner table with a book and a cup of coffee. As Corinna was busy mopping one section, Lorna grabbed the coffee pot and approached his table.

"Sheriff Reid, you really should be getting to bed," she whispered. "I'll be fine. I won't be able to retire until five in the morning, and I don't think all this coffee can be good for one man—even an invincible one such as you."

"That long?" He released a low whistle,

set down his book, and lifted his cup. "You said we'd talk. I didn't know your first day here would be a ten-hour shift."

"All my shifts are ten hours." She poured him another cup. "A new girl is arriving tonight and therefore, Miss Ella Ashby will be coming down to greet her, and I don't want her to catch me talking to you."

He tapped the rim of his coffee. "Keep them coming. I'm not going anywhere until I know you are safe in bed. I can rest when Tanner Sterling arrives in the morning."

Her lips parted in surprise. "You received word from him?"

He sipped his coffee. "Tanner was closer than I thought. I'll sleep after he arrives, while he watches you for me."

"That's good news, but I fear you are going to make yourself ill drinking so much, and by the time my shift is over, you won't be able to sleep a wink."

"If you would just talk with me for ten minutes, I promise I will retire for the evening."

"Reid, this is my first evening here. I really don't want to get into trouble. Do you want me to get you some herbal tea? Chamomile, perhaps, to help you sleep when you finally do go to bed?"

"Fine. Please bring me some pastries too. It will be the only way I can choke down my flower water while I watch you work."

"You are ridiculous." She muttered, but couldn't subdue a giggle, which died the moment she saw Miss Ashby in the doorway, scowling at her, arms crossed, a weary looking new arrival in a rumpled Harvey Girl uniform behind her.

Lorna stifled her grimace and grabbed the tea pot and a fresh cup. She removed his coffee and poured the tea, motioning with her eyes that they were no longer safe to chat.

Miss Ashby lifted her hand, motioning the Harvey Girls to her. "Ladies, gather around," she said, keeping her voice low. "This is Miss Sylvia Williams. She has just arrived on the last train into town tonight from Texas. I want you to make her feel at home here. We are lucky to have a Harvey Girl with so many years of experience. She will retire tonight and will be given the day tomorrow to find her way about the Montezuma before she assumes the position of second head waitress. If you are on duty with her, she is in charge."

Sylvia's chin lifted at this, a spark in her eyes that Lorna didn't quite like, but Lorna smiled anyway. She would give Sylvia a chance before judging her . . . even as it seemed that Sylvia was not extending her the same courtesy. *She is likely only tired and doesn't know she is coming across as anything other than friendly.* She bobbed her head in greeting as Miss Ashby introduced her and moved down the line.

"Now, let's see to her needs with a meal served to her as a guest." Miss Ashby patted Sylvia's arm and motioned for her to take a seat by the massive stone fireplace.

She was in Pernilla's and Jean May's section, but Lorna's feet pushed her forward to make small talk and lifted her tea pot. "Good evening, Miss Sylvia, I—"

Sylvia lifted a staying hand. "Miss Lorna, I haven't given the direction for tea yet." She nodded to Pernilla. "Miss Pernilla was about to ask what I would be having."

Pernilla coughed, likely to cover her own shock. "Would you like milk, coffee, or tea?"

"Coffee, and I'm too tired to have anything else but a piece of apple pie." She pinched the corner of her napkin and lifted it, her lips curling upward. "This has a spot in the corner." She tossed it to Lorna. "Fetch me a new one. Standards will be kept while I am in charge of this dining room."

Pernilla turned pursed lips and wide eyes to Lorna before scooting away.

Lorna retrieved the coffee pot and filled the cup, Sylvia's narrowed eyes never leaving her face. Lorna made the mistake of meeting her gaze and overfilled the cup, the scalding coffee drenching the tablecloth.

AFTER THE GREAT DEBACLE, Lorna hadn't dared return to his table. He figured it was to avoid the ire of the new second waitress. He grimaced at the dressing down that Sylvia delivered upon Lorna's spilling the coffee. Lorna disappeared into the kitchen for a while, and when she returned, her hands were red and her face sweaty. What had the woman sent Lorna to do?

"Sir?" A young man in a fitted suit approached with a silver tray. "A telegram just arrived for you."

He shot to his feet and snatched it up, tearing into it. Tanner Sterling was arriving this morning. His shoulders sagged, and the knot in his belly eased. Relief was coming. As much as his chest burned over the thought of another guarding Lorna in his stead, he needed to sleep, and Tanner was more than capable.

Finally, at five of the clock, Reid stood and stretched. *And I thought I was free from the confines of a wooden chair for a few weeks.* Lorna reappeared from the kitchen, her apron removed. She signaled him to follow her with a slight jerk of her head. She led the way through the parlor and out onto the tower veranda. She leaned against the rail, her head in her arms, groaning.

"Well, that was rather a rough start with your new second waitress. I never knew Harvey Girls could use that tone before."

"Me either." She lifted her gaze. "It was

mortifying. But Miss Ashby had retired, and the head waitress was no longer there, so I had to bear it as she is my superior." She shrugged. "I've dealt with mean girls before. I only hoped I wouldn't have to deal with them at my place of work."

He hated to bring up the topic that had she clearly wished to evade earlier, but he had never been very good at letting matters lie when he could fix an issue. "So, why are you mad at me?"

"I knew you weren't going to let that go." She turned to him, her back against the rail. "I told you. I am not really mad at you. I needed a change and didn't expect almost *nothing* to really change after all my efforts to strike out on my own."

He blinked. "Nothing has changed? You live about eight miles from your parents' house now in Hot Springs, you haven't seen them in weeks, are working constantly, earning a good wage, and making friends. So that means your 'almost nothing' change is in regard to one thing. Me. You weren't expecting to see me so much. Do you resent my being here, Lorna?"

"Not at all. I appreciate it. I was merely hoping to gain some independence and have an opportunity to grow in character without the help of the people who have known me my whole life." She twisted her hands behind her back. "I wanted to stand on my own feet and make my own way. I cannot wait around on the ranch forever for . . . things to change."

There was obviously something else that was bothering her, but if she didn't feel comfortable sharing, he reckoned he needed to respect her privacy after all that he had asked of her. "I understand that."

"Thank you." She attempted to suppress a yawn to no avail.

He chuckled, laying his hand on her shoulder, and guiding her to the door. "Let's get you to bed before you fall over."

Her cheeks reddened. "Gaston, I may be more tired than I have ever been, but I can see myself to my room. There are rules in place to protect us ladies, and if I allow you to go traipsing in the women's section, I'll be fired without a second glance."

"I know, which is why I've gotten permission to bend the rules under the circumstances. Promise that you'll stay on your floor until it's time for your breakfast? I have to see to a few things in town. I don't like the idea of leaving you unguarded for even a short amount of time, but it can't be avoided until Tanner arrives this morning."

"No worries on that account." She released a splitting yawn again. "I'll likely sleep through breakfast and lunch."

Reid escorted her to the ladies hall, pausing outside of her bedroom door. Corinna was likely already asleep, and he had no wish to frighten the mouse of a Harvey Girl, so he merely waved in farewell. He trotted down the service stairwell, exited the Montezuma, and located the stables. He didn't bother waking the groom and saddled Bunny. He hated leaving Lorna alone in the resort, but he had to return to the sheriff's office eventually and speak with Colt. While she slept seemed like the only option, and he was used to sleeping less while on a job. Hopefully Tanner had arrived on the first train and could give him a break. By the time Bunny trotted into town, dawn streaked across the sky. He halted Bunny outside his office and knocked on the door before pushing it open.

Colt jerked awake from the cot in the back room, his hand instinctively going for his gun, eyes bloodshot. "Finally. What took you so long? And don't you ever think you are leaving me with this deputy job again. I've got a ranch to run, Reid, and I don't have time for you to be riding all over the countryside looking for my older brother while my bride is at the Castañeda with only Harvey Girls and my ranch hands to guard her."

"Hello to you as well." Reid crossed to the back room and withdrew a fresh, red shirt from his dresser. He unbuttoned his plaid shirt and filled Colt in on his findings. "And then I read about Jill's escape en route to Las Vegas."

"I'm aware of Jill's escape." Colt combed his fingers through his hair and settled on his Stetson. "I've been a nervous wreck. Belle is putting on a brave face, but I know she is worried. She is having nightmares about the cave again. She needs me."

Reid gritted his teeth at the thought of the winding, never-ending cave with the underwater lake where she and Colt were forced to cross to find another exit or die from Grant's hand. "Why do you think I'm trying so hard to put him away?" He lifted his hand at Colt's coming protest. "And no, it's not because I still harbor love for your wife, Colt. I don't think of her like that anymore. I am trying to protect the citizens of this town and the people that will most likely be in Grant's riflescope. I sent telegrams to the ranger's headquarters and Tanner Sterling."

Colt released a low whistle. "The bounty hunter they call the Angel of Justice?"

"There is a massive bounty out on Grant and a fair one out on Jill Lawson." He poured water from the pitcher into the basin, splashing his face before drawing on his fresh shirt. "I received a telegram at the Montezuma that Tanner will be arriving this morning to relieve you and to give me a reprieve in watching Lorna. While Tanner doesn't know much about Jill, he understands Grant's ways. I don't know about you, but Grant is the one I'm most worried about."

Colt shoved his hands into his pockets. "Don't underestimate her. Everyone does because she is a woman, and, therefore, cannot possibly be as evil as a man. Last I saw of her, Jill was unhinged, making her loyalty to Grant more dangerous than any of his other riders." He shuddered. "I wouldn't want to stand against her. She is a crack shot and would do anything for her husband."

"Not going to argue with you there . . . what woman in her right mind would be in love with Grant Lawson?" Reid packed a small carpet bag with fresh clothes. Even though he had been able to bathe at the Montezuma, his clothes were beginning to stink. Lorna had ridden many an hour beside him on the ranch when he was a boy becoming a man, and he had not put much stock in cleanliness, but the thought of stinking in front of her now, dressed in that pretty Harvey Girl uniform, was humiliating. "I was hoping that Tanner would have arrived on the first train, but it seems he may be on the late morning train, so I need to get back to the Montezuma to watch after Lorna, but I wanted to let you in on the updated plan. Tell Tanner that I'll be back at five o'clock when her shift begins." He hefted the bag up. "You heard anything that I should know about before I head back up the mountain?"

"No. I've been stuck in here," Colt answered flatly. "But I'll tell you this. If Grant was in the cabin in Topeka, or Jill, it means they got their hands on the reserved gold and arsenal there and will be set for a few weeks of hiding at least before they make their next move."

"Reserved arms *and* gold? Why on earth didn't you go and take it once he was locked up?" Reid dropped his carpet bag on the floorboards and crossed his arms.

"Because *he* buried it, and only those two knew the location." Colt fired back. "I've been more than helpful when I didn't have to be, so don't you go on acting like I'm not doing my part or impeding the law. I have been on the right side of the law for years now and do not intend on ever going back to that life again, especially when I have a family now."

Reid raised his hands, backing off. "Sorry. I forget you're tender about that topic."

"You bet I'm tender. I was nearly put in jail by you! I'm an honest citizen now." Colt crossed his arms, scowling.

"So, being a former Death Rider, do you think he is after Lorna, or am I barking up the wrong tree?"

"Seeing as how all the Death Riders are either in prison or in the ground, he wouldn't have enough manpower for a train robbery unless he rounded up new recruits. However, it takes too much time to train them to jump a train or a coach right away." Colt scratched his chin. "Nah, I think your first instinct about Lorna was correct. He has it out for the Elliot family after they helped put him in jail with Gil and his wife testifying against them—not that their witnessing should have made much difference in the eyes of the law after you caught him red-handed robbing a train. He knows the Elliot family is special to you too. Getting Lorna would be almost as good as getting a bullet between your eyes because it would shatter your heart. Stay alert and protect Lorna."

"I intend to."

CHAPTER 7

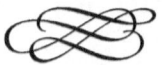

*L*orna scrubbed under the seat of her twenty-second dining room chair. It was official. After two days of working under the new second waitress, Sylvia Williams did not like her. Lorna was used to the townsfolk treating her differently given her pa's unfortunate history with the town's beloved Lane family, which one would think would be resolved with Harriet Lane *marrying* Lorna's brother, Gilbert, but no. The town held onto its grudge that Pa had inadvertently killed his best friend, Mayor Lane, who had his eye on moving back to Texas and becoming governor. When in truth, Mayor Lane visited the

Elliots before they were aware they had been exposed to the scarlet fever that had nearly taken Gilbert's life. Harriet's father did not last the week.

Lorna and her family had become pariahs that day. She had lost all her friends and had wondered why no one wanted to come to her birthday that year. If she closed her eyes, she could see Gaston riding over the hill, balancing a giant wood box with a red bow atop. Inside, was a perfect, cream and orange bunny. She marked that day as when she had fallen a little bit in love with Gaston.

Lorna wiped her brow and tucked the chair under the table, reaching for another. She had hoped that animosity would stay in Las Vegas and not follow her up to the mountain resort. But how would Sylvia be aware of the town's ire, and why would it matter as Sylvia was not from Las Vegas? It didn't make much sense why she would be so dead set against Lorna.

She hadn't done anything to the second waitress. Sure, she nearly burnt the waitress with scalding coffee that first night, but she checked the schedule and Lorna had been slotted *all* the night shifts for the next month and was being assigned extra cleaning duties that the other girls weren't subjected to. The bottom of the chairs had been neglected for years it seemed, for who thought about cleaning them . . . except Sylvia.

And what a treat awaited under each chair. Lorna wrinkled her nose and kept scrubbing. She'd cleaned many a horse stall. She could scrub unmentionables without grumbling. She would prove herself to Sylvia. She only needed time to demonstrate that she was worthy of her respect.

"Come with me."

Lorna nearly collapsed from fright at Sylvia appearing at her elbow. She glanced about the dining room. No guests had been down in over an hour, and she had already sent Reid to bed. His eyes were more bloodshot than she had ever seen, and she was certain it was only because of his extreme exhaustion that she was able to convince him to leave her side. She ran her fingers over a fresh rag, weighing the risks of disobeying Gaston's wishes . . . and objecting to Sylvia's order. "But you already sent Corinna to bed. Who will watch the counter?"

Sylvia shrugged. "The guests will have to wait. We need to talk and put some matters to rest between us. We shall call it your ten-minute break."

She frowned at this but did not argue. She didn't dare, lest Sylvia send her to scrub something worse. She followed her down the hall, to the stairs, and out to the moonlit lawn. "Um, may I ask why we are talking outside?"

Sylvia smiled with a sweetness Lorna hadn't seen directed her way yet. "It's a lovely night, and it will help clear away any animosity between us. Who can be angry with a full moon shining down upon grounds such as this?" She linked her arm in Lorna's, strolling about the groomed gravel pathway. "We Harvey Girls need to be in harmony, and I can think of nothing more calming, nor bonding, than taking in the fresh air under the stars together."

She really should tell Reid where she

was headed, but in this pivotal moment, she had a chance to become friends. And she had determined to make as many friends as possible after a lifetime of loneliness out on the ranch with only thoughts of Gaston to warm her heart and her journals that she burned before she left for Topeka, due to all the embarrassing recordings of unrequited love.

"Unless you want to keep scrubbing chairs?" Her lips quirked. "Surely, my company cannot be so inferior that you prefer cleaning?"

"No! I was only thinking of letting Gaston know where I am going. He was so adamant about me not leaving, and even though I am not going off the Harvey House grounds, I am pretty sure he meant for me not to depart the dining room," Lorna rushed to explain.

"Of course. You should tell your devoted shadow." She released a yawn, the first time Lorna ever saw a crack in the woman's infallible armor. "I'm only so tired that I might not be up for a walk and talk by the time you get back from reporting to him and then your break will be over." She giggled softly. "I only wanted to walk to the end of the old mule path and back. I wanted to show someone what I found the other day at the copse of trees there."

"Other day? Didn't you just arrive? You've hardly had time to rest."

She giggled. "I know, but I've always been full of verve and love to find things in nature to use in an artistic way. If you see my bedroom, you will see pressed flowers, pinned butterflies, and smooth stones that caught my eye over the years. What I found the other day, I didn't have time to retrieve. It is a glorious, abandoned beehive. It's not high at all and I want to fetch it before it is destroyed. Come with me? I understand if you don't want to."

"I'm not sure that is a good idea, Sylvia. It is quite the walk and would take far longer than the time we have, and Reid would be beyond upset with me."

She pursed her lips, silent. Was she thinking of all the ways she could torture Lorna for not accepting this odd olive branch? "Very well. Let us walk to the end of this path and turn around. That should be long enough for us to sort out our differences."

"If it's a short stroll, I'm certain it will be fine." Lorna followed Sylvia down the path, basking in the silence after evenings filled with guests yammering for food. At the ranch, it was always quiet, save for the low of cattle and the call of the cicadas in summer. She missed this.

"What has you so quiet? Out of all the girls, I've noticed you are the chattiest, even when you don't have anything to say."

She chose to ignore that obvious barb. "I was thinking that I have never been away from the ranch this long, but if I take off a day so soon to go visit, I would be proving my brother right in that I can't do this job."

Sylvia quirked a brow. "What do you mean by proving your brother right?"

"My brother dared me. He said that I could never become a Harvey Girl—that it was too hard, and I was too spoiled to do the job well."

She chuckled. "A good dare. I'm curious, how did it come about?"

"It's a long story." *Well, it stemmed from my bratty comments about Belle stealing Gaston Reid with her uniform, smile, and a plate of pie.* And Lorna had been a self-centered brat for those weeks Belle had caught Gaston's attention. There was so much more to this job than she had given Belle credit for. While she had kept most of her feelings on the matter to herself, she couldn't help but feel that she owed Belle an apology for judging her so harshly. *But wouldn't an apology like that hurt her and the confession would be more for me than her?* Yes. Yes, it would.

She bowed her head. *Lord, I know I've been running around like a headless chicken, but I want to thank You for this opportunity to grow —to become the woman you want me to be. Help me to bless Belle in some way. To welcome her into this community, even though we both know I'm not an appreciated part of it. But help me to do it, nonetheless. Let me become more like You.*

She glanced up from her prayer and found they were far from the well-kept grounds and were nearing the head of the old mule trail and an old cabin. Since the last fire, the resort had moved the trail to entice more guests with new spectacular views from atop the mules and demoted this one to a hiking path with dangerous drops for the more adventurous guests. She halted by the old mule cabin and stock yard that the Montezuma kept for their own type of folly, a destination to draw guests toward in their ambles. "Should we turn around now, Sylvia?"

She lifted a single brow. "Not much for adventure, are you? Just a little further? Being indoors all the time is difficult on my soul. Besides, we still need to discuss how to move forward in our working relationship."

She well understood the feeling. Lorna glanced at the hole in the woods that created the mouth of the trail. There was adventurous, and then there was foolishness. She was no fool. She shook her head and took a step back. "We don't have a lantern, or a gun. Any kind of wild animal could jump us."

A man leapt from the shrubs, his thick, meaty hand clamping over her mouth as she released a guttural scream. She bit his hand. He cursed and dropped it from her mouth long enough for her to cry out to the stunned Harvey Girl, "Run! Sylvia, run!"

She did not. She merely stood there as the man seized Lorna's jaw, squeezing until her cheeks ached. Why wasn't Sylvia running?

Sylvia lifted her skirt and removed . . . a revolver from a calf holster? "Where are the horses? Grant is expecting me by tomorrow. I do not like to disappoint him."

Sylvia is working for the Death Riders? She kicked at the man, screaming around his hand, desperate to free herself.

"Horses are up the path and around the bend, Miss Williams."

"Good." She gripped the gun in one hand and gathered up her skirts with the other, hiking up the path. "Gag the girl."

What is going on? Is Sylvia even a Harvey Girl, or did this woman do something to the real Sylvia Williams?

The man stuffed a handkerchief that smelled like the inside of a ranch hand's boot in her mouth and tied a bandana about her head to keep it in place as she fought from retching. He wound a rope about her hands and tossing her over his shoulder, joined the other Harvey Girl. "Where's my money, Sylvia? I don't do charity work."

Sylvia tossed him a small leather pouch, coins jingling. "I added funds for your silence. Put her on the horse and get out of here before that former ranger sees us."

Lorna kicked against the man as he plopped her in the saddle. She swung around, her heel meeting his jaw, and for one glorious moment, Lorna's heart burst with hope.

Sylvia aimed the revolver at her belly. "Please, stop thrashing. I'd hate to shoot you, Lorna, and it would make the journey so much harder on the both of us, even if Jill would be happier if I delivered you to Grant a little more bloodied than intended."

With a whimper, she sank into the saddle, gripping the horn with her tied hands. She didn't need the reins. She could try to direct the horse with her thighs. She squeezed, but the animal did not respond. Not all horses were as intelligent as her stallion.

"I suggest you hold on tight unless you

have a wish to meet your maker earlier than you intend. This is the trickiest piece of the puzzle." Sylvia laughed and wheeled her horse. She charged down the path, pulling Lorna's horse by a short lead rope. Sylvia dropped the lead at the ledge as her horse leapt down an impossibly steep slope, Lorna's horse following suit.

Lorna gripped the horn, eyes wide as her gag muted her scream. She leaned back in her saddle, her legs propped forward as she had been taught. If she wasn't a proficient rider, she would indeed meet her maker. Tree limbs loomed dangerously close, their thin branches snagging her skirt and slapping her arms. But, with her bun almost pressed against the horse's rump, her face remained unscathed. The horse leveled out and, at the bottom of the cliff, Lorna finally jerked upright and nearly lost the contents of her stomach as Sylvia cackled with laughter and secured the lead of Lorna's mount, guiding them up the road around to the north side of Las Vegas. No one would spot her unless they were in the no man's land between the two towns. *I'll have to get out of this on my own.*

"At the train station up a ways, you and I will use our passes for the train that I swiped when Corinna went to bed. No one will question two Harvey Girls heading to Colorado. But if you so much as whisper that you are in distress, I'll put a bullet in your back and then send an order to have the same done to your precious family that you are always yammering on about. You hear?"

An order? Who is this Sylvia Williams? And why does she wield so much power? She swallowed and nodded. *Is she part of the Death Riders, or Grant's second in command?*

Sylvia pushed the horses at a trot for the twenty miles between them and the next town, Watrous. With only a station and a general store, Lorna didn't have much hope for rescue in the almost ghost town. As they neared the depot, the four o'clock train was just arriving from Las Vegas. Sylvia paused behind a bolder alongside the road, whipped off Lorna's gag, and sliced off the ropes at her wrist, tossing the bindings in the brush.

She patted her pocket and motioned her forward. "I'm a fast draw, thanks to my fiancé's training. You make one wrong move and you will pay with more than your health," she reminded her and nodded to the train. "Dismount and keep your mouth shut while you fix your hair. No one would think you are a Harvey Girl with bits of leaves in your hair."

They took a few moments to make themselves presentable, and each led their horses to the station. Lorna cast a glance up and down the red dirt road. *Not even a freight wagon.* She swallowed her disappointment, but she knew that Gaston would never stop searching for her. The man was dogged when he set his mind, much like her, and it was up to her to mark the path. She rubbed the horse's neck and slipped her hand into her pocket, withdrawing the handkerchief with her initials embroidered in the corner, dropping it. *Please, Lord, let Gaston find it!*

Sylvia smiled to the conductor and

handed him their two Harvey House train passes. "Good morning, sir."

"What an unexpected pleasure to see two Harvey Girls in uniform, but why are you boarding the train here and not in Las Vegas?"

She smiled prettily up at him. "Me and my cousin were visiting my grandparents. It was easier for us to board the train here as they wanted us to take our horses on up with us to Colorado so we could get about town at our new Harvey House post."

"Congratulations on your new posting." He motioned a porter to take the horses to the cattle car. "Have a good trip and remember, if you need any food, head to the dining car. Food is all paid for by Fred Harvey. Just keep your ticket on you to claim the vittles."

"Isn't he the most generous employer?" She smiled at Lorna, linking arms as they boarded their train car, which was vacant. Out of earshot, Sylvia whispered, "Good work. I see what it takes for you to listen, but I would think taking a gun to work would be frowned upon." She giggled at her poor jest. She pointed to a bench seat in the rear of the train in the corner. "Get some rest. We change trains in Trinidad."

Lorna didn't budge out of the aisle. "Why are you doing this, Sylvia?"

"Out of a motivation that you would agree with, given your confession."

"My confession? We've *never* talked." *Which was how you tricked me.*

"No, but I share the wall with you and Corinna, and you've talked and talked about a certain gentleman who 'fills your thoughts and heart.'"

Her stomach lurched at the quote, and she sank into the corner bench seat. *Sylvia had been listening?* "And what would that motivation be?"

"To possess the love of the man who holds my heart."

Okay. That tells me nothing, given Grant is married . . . unless she is his lover, but she mentioned a fiancé? "Would you care to tell me about the man who holds your affection?"

She eyed her. "Why would I?"

"If I am helping you win a man's love, mayhap I would be more agreeable to your abducting me if I knew more about him."

Lorna laughed without mirth. "You said you wanted to bond with me."

"I never wanted to bond with you, much less confess my whole plan. I've been a Harvey Girl long enough to know that you all think you are above such things as being desperate for love. You are nothing but a bunch of goodie girls playing in nun habits —so afraid of being alone that you snap up any proposal that sounds like you won't have to work another day in your life."

She wanted to deny her claim and to point out the obvious, that Sylvia herself was in the same uniform, but she would do the impossible. She would do what Gaston would do. She bit her tongue and instead of arguing, would ask leading questions. Maybe Sylvia would make a mistake in her ranting—a mistake that Lorna could use.

SOMETHING WAS WRONG. An ache pressed against his ribs, crying out to him. *Lorna.* Reid jerked awake, morning light splaying from the crack in the heavy curtains. He tugged on his boots and buckled on his gun harness and gun belt and ducked into the hallway of the Montezuma. He tromped up the stairs to her room in the women's hall, not caring for their rigid Harvey Girl code of conduct. He may have been allowed to bend the rules, but this was completely breaking them to venture into the hall without Lorna escorting him. He kept his eyes on the baseboards, in case any women were about. He prayed that she was safe, and it was merely a dream that sent a charge of panic through his veins.

He pounded on the door and within a moment, Corinna threw it open, eyes widening at the sight of him as she moved to slam it. He set his boot in the crack, wincing as the door bounced off it. "Is Lorna in bed? I need to know."

Her head appeared in the doorway, her golden braid spilling over the front of her nightgown. "Her bed is still made, but her shift was over hours ago. I just awoke. Maybe she's at breakfast?"

He gritted his teeth. "Something's wrong. Would you please dress and look for her, and if you cannot locate her, tell Miss Ashby, and get a search party together. I'm going to check the grounds. I feel it in my gut that something has happened to her."

"You can count on me, Sheriff Reid."

He kneaded at the spot atop his chest and bolted for the side stairs, taking an exit door that spilled him out into the vast garden. If Grant had gotten to her this easily, he must have had help, or someone would have heard her screaming in the building. *Father God, direct my steps.* He whipped about, scanning for anything out of place on the ground. Nothing. He closed his eyes and listened. Nothing but the chirping of birds. His eyes flashed open and spotted the mountainside path. If she had been led outside by someone she trusted, wouldn't she seek the solace of the mountainside, as he would?

He pumped his arms as he shot up the worn path, almost relieved to find the path churned in one place, quickly followed with a pang of terror. A heavy imprint of boots came from the bushes, aiming toward her small footprints while another stood off to the side as if watching the whole affair. The tiny footprints disappeared, and the boots marched after the other woman's heeled prints. His gut twisted. Lorna had been here, and she had been taken.

He followed the trail as best he could, noting the broken branches from Lorna's tussle until he found the horse hooves. Grant had been prepared, and he had help. Knowing these first moments were precious, he raced back down the mountain path to the stables, saddling Bunny as he shouted for the stable hand.

A young man approached him with a pitchfork full of hay as he dumped it in the next stall over. "Sir? Can I help you?"

"Go into town to the sheriff's office. Tell whoever is on duty that Miss Lorna Elliot has been kidnapped by Grant Lawson. He is extremely dangerous."

The man's eyes widened. "One of our new girls?"

"Yes. Go!" He shouted and flung himself on the stallion's back and wheeling him around, he trotted him through the grounds and up the path and followed the loop to the other side of the Montezuma. He didn't dare run the horse while in an unknown territory along a mountain cliff. However, the stallion, though freshly broken, was surefooted. He halted the horse at the cliff top that was the old turn around point for the mules. The hoof prints disappeared off the ledge. He bent over in his saddle. Not many trees, but the sheer angle made his belly lurch. Grant had ridden down the side of the mountain with Lorna.

He drummed his fingers on his thigh. If he went the long way, Reid might miss where the trail led. He rubbed the horse's neck. Bunny was a mountain stallion. He could do this. Reid swiped at his brow, uttered a prayer, and wheeled his mount, retracing his steps before turning once more. They surged forward and the horse leapt off the ledge, down the steep slope of the mountain. Reid angled his body backward and his boots forward in the stirrups, leaving a long lead and giving the horse full rein and trusting him to run as he would have with his wild herd.

The ground at last leveled. He turned

Bunny about, seeing the hoofprints disappear toward Watrous. He swallowed. If he knew Grant like he thought he did, Grant would have a fresh set of horses at every twenty miles to switch and keep going toward Raton, heading to another of his favored hideouts on the other side of the pass —Colorado.

Reid yelled in a burst of frustration. He should have prepared more. He should have stayed with her instead of allowing himself to be lulled into the false sense of protection that the Montezuma had offered Lorna. He dropped his red bandana in the path, hoping someone would see it and kicked Bunny into a gallop, riding hard for a mile until he slowed him to a canter and then a trot, keeping his eyes on the pair of tracks.

He had chased criminals more times than he could count, but this time . . . it felt different. It felt as if he did not reach Lorna in time, he might not be able to draw another breath.

Nearing the next town, he caught a flash of white, caught on the root of a juniper tree. He leapt off the horse and scooped it up. The scrap was a handkerchief. He traced his thumb over the embroidery. *L.E.*

Tucking the cotton in his pocket, he hauled himself back into the saddle, following the trail that ended at Watrous depot. Grant had taken her on the train. He slapped his Stetson against his thigh, dismounted, and trotted up to the depot window. If they went North, like he supposed they would, as the train South went through Las Vegas, they were likely heading to his hideout in Colorado. "When is the next train to Colorado Springs?"

"Coming through in a quarter of an hour. You want a ticket?"

"One for the animal car and one passenger. And I need to send a telegram," he said, sliding a coin forward and picking up the pencil and pad of paper nestled in the outside corner of the window. "Did you happen to see a Harvey Girl on the train heading north?" He pulled back his coat to reveal his sheriff's badge.

The man's eyes widened. "Sure did. Don't see too many board here. Saw two. Why? They in some sort of trouble?"

Two? His heart hammered. Who else did Grant take? Who was she on duty with? Corinna was obviously safe. Sylvia and one other girl had been working that night. His heart hammered with dread. What did he want with *two* Harvey Girls? Was the second from a wealthy family as well? "Yes, they are in grave danger. Where did they purchase their tickets?"

"Oh, no. Them poor dears." The elderly man's brow furrowed. "But they didn't need to purchase tickets. They used their passes."

Smart. "And was a man with them?"

He scratched his white scruff. "Can't say there was. No one else boarded the train here but those two ladies."

Well, that doesn't mean Grant didn't have someone in the woods with a rifle should they disobey. He could have been waiting on the train for them. He jotted out a telegram addressed to the ranger headquarters.

Lorna Elliot and another unidentified Harvey Girl abducted by Grant Lawson. Lorna is five foot one, red hair. Likely in Harvey uniform. Last known location, North of Las Vegas on train. Reply to Raton Pass Station. G. Reid.

He brought Bunny to the attendant of the cattle car and boarded the train at the last car. Grant would head to Colorado Springs. Reid would bet his life on it, which was good because he was certainly betting Lorna's. He ran his hands through his hair. This was too similar with what happened to Belle, but this time, there was desperation in Grant's moves that was making him sloppy. The Grant of this summer would have never left a trail behind him as obvious as today's.

"You've got it bad."

He turned at the familiar voice. "Tanner!"

Tanner pulled off his dusty hat and shook the blond curls from his green eyes and settled his gambler's wide brim hat back into place, the single crimson bead holding the leather strings of his hat swayed beneath his chin. "The Montezuma staff member arrived at the sheriff's station as I did. Put my horse in the cattle car, or were you too consumed to see my golden palomino stallion?"

"Silver was in there?" He plopped onto the bench seat across from Tanner. "Good thing you are here. I need to sleep before we get off the train. I'm losing my touch."

"Being in love with the victim will do that." Tanner crossed his arms.

"I'm not in lov—"

Tanner chuckled. "You called for the rangers to guard a single citizen and sent for me to catch the man terrorizing her. You never share the glory of an arrest, or thought you needed help, especially when it came to Grant. And now that his bounty is massive, I *know* you wouldn't be sharing his capture unless your heart was involved. And before you protest, I'll ask you one question. Where's your hubris motto now?" He chuckled. "'One riot, one ranger' indeed."

"You were the one who turned down a job as a ranger. Don't sound bitter."

"I'm not. I never wanted to be at the beck and call of anyone but myself and my brothers."

Reid was desperate to pull his hat over his eyes and fall asleep, but if they were going to be a team, he needed information. "What do you know?"

"Grant escaped with another man from the prison in Texas. The man's name is Frank Hill, and he is some religious warrior."

"A what?" He sat up straight, never expecting that.

"Judging from what the warden was telling me, it's no religion I've ever heard of —or anyone for that matter." He chuckled. "But apparently, he and Grant became friends. I tracked them to the prison where Jill was being held. They busted her out. All signs point to Colorado Springs."

"Just as I thought. Think we can track them?"

He snorted. "I didn't become the best tracker in the West by not being able to find a man leaving a train. Don't worry. We will find your woman, Reid."

"She's not my woman," he ground out.

"Then we better find her so you can ask her to be." Tanner grinned, elbowing his side. "You should have heard the chatter over your telegrams. All were wondering about this woman who had captured your heart at last." His eyes twinkled despite the heaviness of the matter.

Reid wasn't that affronted by his teasing. When one was in their line of work for so long, one had to seize any bit of humor and joy to avoid their mind being taken over by the oppressive darkness of their duty.

"That is neither here nor there." Reid adjusted to focus on the window as it pulled out of the station. "I'll tell you what I know about the case so far. Then you stop hooting and hollering in my ear and let me sleep."

CHAPTER 8

At one of the through stations, Sylvia had Lorna shed her apron and white hair bow with her, making them merely appear as two women in mourning colors, which had any passengers graciously giving them room. Lorna feared her window for sending a warning telegram to her family was narrowing. Her plan didn't hold much hope anyway as there was the small matter of securing a pencil and paper and then the monumental task of handing over a note to a stranger and trusting them to *pay* to send it to Las Vegas.

Prayer was all she had and pray she did, for her family, for Gaston's following the feeble trail, and for safety over her and her loved ones. Grant's was a clever plan, even Lorna had to admit it. The passes kept anyone from being able to recall them purchasing tickets and knowing the direction they were heading . . . except for the changing of the horses from car to car, which would be a unique fact for two Harvey Girls. And Lorna clung to that one fact, knowing that if anyone could track them down, it would be Gaston. The former Texas Ranger would save her.

The hours on the train had proven how dark a heart this Sylvia possessed, and she was fairly convinced Sylvia was not only working for the man, but desperately in love with Grant. Though, she had mentioned a fiancé. Things simply did not add up. Perhaps Grant was her lover and not a fiancé? If he was anything as handsome as his brother Colt, he'd likely have a woman in every town he had a hideout, no doubt. And this Harvey Girl was obsessed with him.

"Colorado Springs! Arriving in Colorado Springs." The conductor moved through the car, sending the passengers into a flurry of gathering their belongings.

Sylvia gripped Lorna's forearm, her fingernails digging through the sleeve. "This is us. Remember, you try anything, and your precious family will pay for your attempts of escape. The minute we get off this train, do not speak. Not. A. Word. Understand?"

"Yes."

"Good. Now, follow my lead."

Lorna suppressed her urge to fight Sylvia. She may be smaller than the other girl, but she was raised on a ranch and had roped many a calf in her day. But how could she fight to save herself when it meant that her family would pay the price? Lorna folded her hands and followed Sylvia to the station's powder room. Sylvia opened the satchel and tossed a calico dress at Lorna that would be far too big for her while Sylvia donned a blue blouse and a split skirt, slinging a leather gun belt across her hips and moving her revolver from her pocket to the belt. Out in this wild West, Lorna knew no one would question Sylvia, nor her skills with a gun. If a woman openly sported a gun, she was better than good.

They claimed their two horses and headed out of town. Sylvia pressed her mount harder than she should have down the red earth road and over a hill, as if anxious to be away from the train and anyone who might recognize them as Harvey Girls.

Lorna's lips parted at the shocking beauty of a canyon of red rock that reached to the sky in various peaks, mounds, boulders, and cliffsides in brilliant hues of red, burnt orange, pink, gold, and brown of the exposed rock. Tourists wove about the rock formations on foot, in pony carts, and on horseback. *Why would Sylvia bring me to such a populated area?*

Lorna openly gaped at the men attempting to scale one massive red rock. One misplaced foot and they could plunge to their deaths, save for the single rope connecting them to a metal hoop a guide must have hammered into the rock. Sylvia paid the tourists little mind as she wove about the red rock formations. How she knew where to go was baffling.

The sun beat down upon them as they reached the far side of the red rocks to the patchy dirt foothills with its sheer drops, jagged rocks protruding from the earth, spiky bushes, and fallen tree limbs from the scraggly piñon pines and the occasional lush juniper evergreen that was a welcome spot of color after the vibrancy of the red rocks. But there was no way she would seek solace from the sun in the shade of the pines and junipers. Hidden in the foliage, there was no doubt scorpions, rattlesnakes, and all manner of deadly creatures.

While it was nearing winter, the intensity of a ride in the sun atop the foothills was making her head swim and spots appear in her vision. She closed her eyes, trusting her horse to guide her. She pressed the back of her hand to her forehead. If she didn't drink water soon, she would faint. She did not want to be unconscious when she reached Grant. "D-do you have any water?"

Sylvia twisted in her saddle and narrowed her gaze, hand resting on her gun belt. "I thought I told you not to say a word? You want me to gag you again?"

She shook her head, pressing her lips together and holding in her whimper for a drop of water to stave off the nausea.

"Won't be much use to me if you die." Sylvia sighed, her hand sliding from her gun belt, and loosened the canteen on her saddle horn and tossed it back to Lorna.

She caught it easily and drank deeply, her throat raw from the ride in the sun. Was this part of Sylvia's plan to have her so hungry and weak that she wouldn't be able to put up much of a fight?

After an hour more of riding, Lorna could at last make out a path that led down to a cliff face to a valley where the mountain rock arched as if it were a theatre straight out of the New York papers. It formed a shelter over a small dwelling that looked like it had been chiseled from the rock itself, but on further inspection, it appeared to have been made of mortar and wood as well. From the tools lying about, it seemed that someone lived here, and that someone was no doubt Grant Lawson, had plans to add more rooms. Her lips parted. With a building so camouflaged and isolated . . . how on earth did she ever hope to be found? Even by one so determined as Gaston Reid.

Her heart pounded. She could ride for safety, but the only thought that stayed her was the wellbeing of her family. She lifted her chin. She would do anything to protect them. Ma, Pa, Gil, her sister-in-law Harriet, and their baby on the way. If she had to die, so be it. She knew where she was going . . . *but* she really did not want to go there yet if she didn't have to. She had so much life left to live. She wanted to marry, to have babies, and grandbabies, and watch their family grow. She blinked away at the sudden onslaught of tears. *Oh, I should have listened to Gaston. And what did I do? The opposite. Why am I so stinking stubborn?* She swiped at her eyes. If she could listen to anyone over her own hubris that she could take care of herself, maybe she wouldn't be facing Grant Lawson.

At the base of the trail, Sylvia called out,

"Sugar, I'm back! And I brought you what you wanted."

Sugar? Her blood ran cold when the roughhewn plank door on leather straps swung open. A massive man with scraggly dark golden hair appeared. The woman with muted blonde hair at his side sent Sylvia a scowl that could brand the hide of a calf. *That has to be Grant and Jill.* She braced herself for Grant's wrath.

Grant bowed in the doorway. "Peace be with you, and with you, Lorna Elliot."

Chills enveloped her body. Peace-spouting Grant was somehow even more terrifying than gun-wielding Grant. *What on earth is going on here?*

Grant loped out to them and lifted Sylvia from the horse, kissing her soundly. "There's my woman."

Did he just . . . kiss her? In front of his wife? She snapped her gaping mouth shut as an open show of judgement would only get her killed that much sooner.

The second front door to the right of the dwelling cracked open and another three women appeared. Their hair was pulled up in neat buns. Each wore split skirts and calico tops that matched Sylvia's.

Is this the new Death Rider uniform? Lorna gritted her teeth and glanced down at her calico dress that was made from the same material. *Lord . . . what is happening? Please protect me.*

Sylvia nestled into Grant's side. "Oh, how I've missed you, my love."

The blonde woman pushed off the porch and moved to Grant's side, glaring at the girl. "Well, you did the impossible, Sylvia. Now get the Elliot girl off the horse."

Lorna swallowed back her surprise. From all the stories that Gaston had told her, Jill was violently jealous and yet, Sylvia seemed *accepted* by her? *What is going on with this group and between Grant and Sylvia?*

Sylvia motioned Lorna down with her revolver. "Yes, ma'am, I found her, and she is all in one piece just liked you required, Jill," she replied, pride in her voice.

Lorna's gaze darted to Jill. *Grant* did not require her? Her mouth went dry. What did Jill want with her? She kept her shoulders back and confidence in her stance. She would not show a hint of fear that could be seen as weakness and therefore, make her prey.

Grant crossed his arms and smiled. "My, my, isn't she a pretty one. Maybe I should change my plans and add her to my collection."

Collection? Her gaze darted to the matching women. That did not sound good. A collector pinned butterflies . . . put rare items on display in a glass cabinet . . . or had a secret graveyard in their basement.

"One at a time, Grant. You know who is next in line. Besides, everyone must *earn* their position in this family." Jill patted his arm. "Sylvia, you did well."

"Did I do good, honey?" Sylvia tucked her hands behind her back and looked up at Grant with a coy expression. "Do you have a reward for me? I've waited so long."

Grant grinned, snatching her up at the waist and kissing her so thoroughly that Lorna didn't know where to look.

Who is Sylvia to them, and why did they send her to get me, and why on earth is kissing him a reward? He was handsome, but there was a darkness that clung to him that sent her skin into gooseflesh. Something was quite wrong with this picture.

Sylvia slowly pulled away from him. "And as our agreement, the wedding shall take place?"

"I have no objections," Grant fairly growled in her ear. "As you well know."

Sylvia crossed her arms and narrowed her gaze at Jill, as if daring her to object.

Wedding? "What is going on?" Lorna finally managed, her voice breaking from lack of water. "Why did you bring me here?"

"That's enough from you." Jill snapped. "You are lucky to be alive."

"Peace, Jill." Grant scowled at his wife, ignoring Lorna. "We know your requirements." He nodded to Sylvia. "Good work getting the girl, Sylvia." He eyed Lorna in a way that made her cross her arms over her chest. He turned on his heel to face Jill. "I think we need to change the plan and move up the timeline. Won't it inflict more pain on his family that way?"

"I will not budge on the matter. It is not

fair to Sylvia. She earned her way. The girl will have to do the same."

He sighed. "Very well. Ready her while I talk with Sylvia. I need to know what kind of attack to expect before we proceed with the ceremony."

"Ceremony? Why do you need to ready me for a ceremony?" She blinked, looking to the five women who ignored her stares.

"You'll see." Grant grinned down at her.

If I could get my hand on a gun, this would be over real fast. She could out-ride and out-shoot any man, including Gaston Reid most times. Unfortunately, she was on the petite side and would never be able to overtake Jill physically, much less Grant, and Sylvia, *and* those other women, but thanks to Jill's jealousy, maybe she could talk her way out of this, using Sylvia as a shield.

"Come, girl." Jill drew her inside to "ready" her for who knew what.

She blinked in the sudden darkness. There was a single window cut out from the mortar that was narrow enough for air and a rifle barrel to poke through, but not much in the way of allowing in light. The flickering flame of the lantern standing atop a long narrow table was the only source of light. There was a lumpy looking bed in the corner with a quilt atop it. A faded blue trunk stood at the foot of the bed. "You don't have to do this, Jill," she whispered.

Jill snickered and shoved her into one of the six chairs surrounding the table. "Yes, I do. I need to keep my husband happy. He got me out of jail. He told me for the first time since our marriage that he loves me. I will do anything to keep his love, including allowing him to take another wife."

CHAPTER 9

She swallowed against the bile rising in her throat. Did a fate worse than death await her? "Another . . . wife? But that was made illegal years ago."

Jill released Lorna's hair from the braid, running a brush through her tangled locks. "You do realize that you are speaking about an outlaw. Do you think he and I care much for society's rules on what *is* and *isn't* acceptable?"

"But I-I thought he had a code of honor regarding marriage." She blinked, recalling Colt and Belle describing how Colt had saved Belle's honor from Grant by marrying her.

"He does honor marriage." Jill plaited Lorna's hair. "So much so that he wishes to take more wives to honor them."

She fought against the urge to scrunch her nose in confusion. "And you are okay with this?" A sharp tug of her hair brought tears to Lorna's eyes.

"I will always be his first wife and therefore, as you like to point out, his only *legal* wife. I control the others. It will be nice not to worry about the domestic chores that come with being a wife and besides, it allows me to focus on what I really care about —the job."

"So . . . was Sylvia really a Harvey Girl? That doesn't exactly make her a formidable Death Rider member."

"That's how my husband met her before he got arrested. She worked along the line in Colorado. While in jail, he heard about polygamy and wanted to make a change." She snorted. "He thinks he is following religion to do so, but it's more like a religion according to Grant Lawson. He spouts phrases about peace that make no sense, but he will allow me to run the group, so how can I complain when he asked the woman he was obsessing over to marry him? I had a few requirements, including having you brought here as her induction as a Death Rider. She is a member now and therefore, eligible to marry him."

"Well, that's one way to form a new outlaw gang," Lorna murmured. "And the other women? Are they awaiting induction to the gang as well?"

"They already are one of us. They are the wives of the former Death Rider men. Their husbands were all shot or are serving their time in prison because of that Ranger Reid. But I saw to their needs, which is why they are loyal to me now." She pulled a plait into place, making Lorna wince. "We all have a bone to pick with Reid, so it stood to reason that he would be our first target."

Her gaze flickered to the mirror as she waited for Jill to pin up her hair. "Why are you readying me exactly?"

"I have my reasons. My husband wants you to be a part of the collection. However, you will need to wait for your turn to be-come his wife, but if that is what he wants, I will see to it that he will have it, one way or another."

Her stomach threatened to revolt again. "Jill, if he loves you, letting me go won't change that." She sincerely doubted that what the depraved man felt for his wife was love, but that would not help Lorna's case to say so. "Please. Let me go."

"Do you have any idea what I went through in prison before my Grant saved me?" The awe in her voice doused any hope Lorna harbored that she could awaken this woman from her stupor. "No. He is my knight, and I will never risk losing his favor —and definitely not to save some spoiled Harvey Girl."

"I know you must love him. Colt told me how you met Grant all those years ago. You had a sister and well understood the bond of—"

"Do *not* speak to me of sisterhood." She snapped. "I lost all love of *sisters* when Alice stole the heart of my husband. He withheld his love from me until he broke me out of prison, telling me that I was worth twice what my sister ever was to him. He said that if I loved him, I would allow him to take another wife—that I owed him my life."

Okay. So, no talk of sisterhood. "My pa will pay you twice what you ask for in the ransom note if you let me walk away now."

"Shut it." Jill pressed something hard to Lorna's side.

She gasped at the knife pressed to her corset, the whalebones protecting her from being nicked. "Jill, Grant's revenge is not worth giving up your life. If you kill me for him—"

"I believe you are misinformed about the situation. Allow me to enlighten you. It's not Grant who seeks revenge, but me and all the other women riders." She twisted the blade.

"What?" She whimpered as the blade pricked her skin.

"Because when Grant was sent to prison, he found religion, and felt he should give polygamy a try. He spoke of turning over a new leaf, one of peace. I outwardly agreed to his terms because I knew the only way to snap him out of it was to remember his true love—the Death Riders. Once he sees the money you will fetch, along with Ranger Reid who will undoubtably bring the ransom, he will forget all about Sylvia and adding you to his collection of wives and give in to the violence that he was so fond of only months ago. Sylvia!" Jill shouted, making Lorna nearly jump out of her skin. "Your turn."

Sylvia shut the door behind her, cheeks drained of color, a far cry from her earlier enthusiasm of a bride about to marry. What had Grant told her to cause such a change?

Jill pulled up a chair and flipped the knife from hand to hand as Sylvia lifted the lid of the trunk and pulled out a faded gown of pink silk that looked like it required a bustle.

Perhaps a show of kindness would give her an advantage? "May I help you?" At the woman's nod, Lorna moved to Sylvia's side. "Sylvia. What's going on? Why would you want to wed an already married man? As a Harvey Girl, you have your pick of bachelors," she hissed under her breath as she shook out the dress. *Is he brainwashing these women? What kind of power does he possess to make them lose all reason? Is this some sort of cult?*

"He saved me."

She looked to Jill who stared at her blade. She flipped it, caught the handle, and strode out of the door.

With her departure, Lorna's shoulders sagged in relief, and she worked at the buttons of the pink silk gown that was stained with age. "That's what your sister-wife-to-be said. But you weren't in prison. You were in a position that most girls long for. What did he offer you?"

"A life of adventure." Sylvia stared at the narrow slit of window. "He offered me riches."

Lorna looked about the rough room. She had seen cliff dwellings firsthand before. This, like everything about the situation, was a poor imitation. She grasped Sylvia's trembling arm. "Sylvia, what did he say to you out there that frightened you so much?"

She sank onto the bed, resting her head in her hands as she rocked back and forth. "He's never been cruel to me. Not once. Many men in my life have been horrible.

Grant is different . . . I thought he was different."

"Sylvia, the man has been lying to you since the beginning. He is a liar, a thief, and a murderer."

Her hands dropped at that. "A murderer?"

Lorna refrained from rolling her eyes at the woman's naivete. "Why do you think Gaston Reid has been watching me so closely? Grant is extremely dangerous. He may spout being peaceable, but would such a man be *agreeable* to abducting me? To breaking the law by taking a second wife? He has no qualms with breaking the law because, in his mind, it doesn't apply to him, and there are no consequences that can hold him—proven all the more by his prison break. He is a man without a ruler."

Sylvia twisted her hands. "I-I didn't believe anyone when they called him a murderer . . . until now."

"What did he say, Sylvia?"

Her eyes filled with unshed tears. "That if I ever crossed him, he would kill me. I-I don't know what happened. After you went inside, I told him about Reid watching you at the Montezuma and at that name, something in him switched. He called the rest of the ladies over and made plans to guard the cliff." She whispered, "He is going to use you as bait, to bring in ransom, kill Reid, and then wed you."

Her knees weakened. She grasped the back of the chair. *Just like Jill wanted.* After all of this, he was still going to kill Gaston. And if he planned to kill Gaston, he wouldn't stop to hurt her family. She had been a fool to think otherwise. *There is still time.* She pushed back her shoulders and repeated out loud, "There's still time. Help me, and I can get you out of here. You are worth more than being his second choice, or another member of his Death Rider gang that is expendable in his mind."

Tears trickled down her cheeks. "It's too late now. I'd go to prison for abduction."

"Better a prison, or an asylum, than to be powerless under a cruel man."

The door banged open. Grant stood in the doorway. His gaze rolled over Lorna and settled on Sylvia. "Time for you to become a full Death Rider, Sylvia." He motioned her to follow him.

Outside, the women stood in two short lines under a scraggly pine, bandanas affixed to their necks, and all armed with revolvers, and one with a rifle. *She must be a sharpshooter.* She swallowed, thinking of all the danger that awaited Gaston when he came for her. She had been as misled as Sylvia to think she was protecting him by being compliant. She could have saved him by fighting.

Grant stood in the center, under the branches, his gaze on Sylvia. "Before our wedding, it is time to swear you into the gang."

Lorna nearly sagged with relief. She was beginning to think it was too late for Sylvia. "Thank God," she muttered. *But, why the pink gown?*

Jill flipped her blade over in her hand. "What? You thought we were readying you for a wedding to Grant? He's not good enough for you? You'd be lucky to bear his name."

Sylvia's eyes flashed in alarm. Even

though she was the reason she was in this predicament, the Harvey sisterhood pulled Lorna into action. She could not turn on Sylvia. If Lorna betrayed any of Sylvia's doubt regarding this marriage, she knew what would happen to the poor girl. Grant would marry her anyway and treat her horribly, or Jill, crazed as she was, would kill Sylvia for the insult on Grant's behalf.

"It's not that—I'm already married to Gaston Reid!" Lorna blurted, her stomach churning with the lie. Here, she had left her hometown to get over the man and now she was claiming him as her husband. God help her if Gaston Reid ever found out . . . or her brother and father. There would be a reckoning, and she would die of embarrassment. *If I do not die now that is.* Surely this was a Rahab and the spies moment? She worried her bottom lip. *How many people have used that as an excuse to get away with a lie? But truly, it does apply here.*

"What?" Jill swiveled to Sylvia, her eyes flashing. "Is this true? Is the Elliot girl married to our greatest enemy?"

"I was about to state my suspicions."

Sylvia crossed her arms, head up. "She didn't tell me as much, but it isn't hard to believe it. It's little wonder why now that Reid has been hanging around so much."

Jill growled and seized Lorna's arm, pulling her back into the mortar cabin, slamming the door behind her as she flung Lorna to the dirt floor. "Do you swear it?" Jill tossed her blade from hand to hand.

Lorna pushed the lie out even as it burned her insides to do so. "We were married when he came for me in Topeka," she babbled, terrified of the blade and even more so of Jill's unhinged mind. "I love him." The truth was a balm on her tongue after the lies, and she saw the first flicker of belief in Jill's eyes. She sighed, releasing her secret. "The truth is, I have loved him since I was a girl. It's why I never accepted any other suitors. No one has ever caught my attention but him, and no other will do. I'm sure you know how that feels with you being in love with Grant."

Jill grunted, slipping her blade into the sheath at her waist. "Being tied in a marriage doesn't keep eyes from wandering. I should know with Grant being as he is," she mumbled.

"True, but I won't let my eyes wander from anyone but my husband." She bowed her head, even now picturing Gaston's broad smile and dimples—that smile had stolen her heart all those years ago. "Many men have tried courting over the years, but it was too late. My heart was no longer my own." *And no matter how hard I try, it will not be taken back.* Tears spilled over her cheeks at the hopelessness of it all. *God, help me surrender my love for him.*

"What are you blubbering for?" Jill snapped. "You'll see him again soon enough once your ransom is paid."

"Will I?" She sniffed, swiping at her cheeks with the rough calico sleeve.

"I've never been more certain of it. A man in love will always come for his bride, guns a'blazing." Jill cackled and lowered her voice to a whisper, "Look at me forgetting my manners in my glee. I should thank you. When Grant sees Reid with weapons drawn, it will wake him from this stupor of finding a so-called religion that suits his desires."

Lorna's heart sank. What had she done? "Y-you can't mean that Grant would gun down my h-husband?"

"If Grant doesn't, I will." She patted her on the arm. "The only gamble I would be taking with this action is if Grant does not in fact give up the idea of plural marriage and takes you, the new widow, as his third bride." She grinned. "That man has asked a lot of me, and I love him, but this had better be a phase."

"And if Grant decides it isn't a phase?"

"Come now, Lorna, you are not addled." She wove her arm through Lorna's as if they were the dearest of friends and kicked open the door. "Meaning, if he doesn't turn you two out after he grows bored of you, I will make it a phase by ending your life, as well as Sylvia's."

REID FINISHED INTERVIEWING the last porter on the job and paced at the Colorado

Springs depot, exhausted and hungry, but all he could think of was getting to Lorna before Grant did anything to her.

"Reid!" Tanner Sterling trotted up the platform as his long great coat flapped in the gentle breeze, his Stetson shadowing his face, along with his reddish beard that was already growing after a day of not shaving. "I checked with a few townsfolk. There were witnesses that said two women, one fitting Lorna's description, left here early this morning on two horses." He looped his thumb in his gun belt and flicked up the brim of his hat to look Reid dead in the eye. "But, according to talk in town, the two women rode into the Garden of the Gods. No one has seen them since. My guess is that Grant has a hideout in the foothills or used the trail through the foothills to go beyond Manitou Springs to keep us guessing. I figured we could split up and cover more ground. This train heads into Manitou in five minutes. Thought I'd take it while you follow the lead into the Garden of the Gods, so we don't miss anything."

"It's a plan." Reid extended his hand. "I appreciate your help."

Tanner grasped it, giving it a firm shake. "You would do the same for me. You've talked about Lorna Elliot and her family as long as I've known you. I know she is important to you."

A lump formed in his throat. He cleared it. "Yes. I would hate for my past with the Lawson family to hurt her."

Tanner rested his hand on Reid's shoulder in a rare show of comfort. "Brother, remember your old creed of 'one riot, one ranger.' And I'm better than any ranger." He grinned. "There are two of us, and the Lord is on our side. We will find your woman."

A man in a telegraph operator's black visor darted toward them, a wrinkled paper in hand. "Sheriff Reid! You asked if I had any odd wires. Well, one just came through, and it is addressed to you."

"Do you know from where?"

"Origin is Manitou Springs." He handed it to Reid and waited with an expectant gleam in his eyes.

Reid handed him a bill and gave a nod of thanks. He unfolded the letter and turned for Tanner to read it as well.

Lone Balanced Rock. 5,000. L.

The paper trembled in Reid's hands at the thought of his sweet Lorna Elliot at the mercy of Grant Lawson. "How are we going to come up with such a sum? I won't have time for her family to send the funds or get them myself."

"We won't have to. We can fill a sack with all the coins we carry between us and make it heavy with rocks of a like size *after* we get in position. He obviously will wait until nightfall to show himself and he thinks you'll be alone, judging how you've worked in the past. He won't know what hit him."

"And we know he definitely will not be alone." Reid huffed. "The man has more connections to outlaws than should be possible."

Tanner grinned. "One riot—one ranger . . . and a bounty hunter. We got this."

CHAPTER 10

"You promised I could marry Sylvia as soon as she brought the captive, and then you say I have to wait until tomorrow, which I agreed to, and now I find out you had one of the women send a telegram for a meet-up with Reid?" Grant screeched to Jill. "When will your schemes and demands end? Who is the leader of the Death Riders?"

"You, of course." Jill finished saddling her horse.

The rest of the women mounted, rifles cradled in their arms, gun belts weighed down with extra bullets and two revolvers each. They had even packed spare clothing, some food, and filled their canteens. They were leaving no room for error.

"But the job ain't done. You want your money, don't you, my husband? Stop arguing, and get on your horse, or I might change my mind about the wedding all together."

Lorna had no doubt now that Jill was merely buying time with the exchange to keep Sylvia from marrying Grant. *Does she intend on killing Sylvia after the trade?* She cast a glance behind her at the former Harvey Girl. As much as she disliked the girl's actions that led to this moment, she would be horrified if a bullet ended her young life. *Lord, save us.*

"She did her part." Grant crossed his arms, leaning against her horse and glaring at his wife.

Again, she wondered why Jill loved Grant Lawson. She glanced over at him. Certainly, he was a mountain of a man, and, as he was Colt's brother, possessed ruggedly handsome features, but there was an evil to him that permeated the very air. Being near him made her breath hitch with anxiety and yet, up until this afternoon, Sylvia had been under his spell and had been bent on the marriage taking place before the trade . . . *if* anyone had come for Lorna in time.

Jill was convinced Gaston would be there by nightfall and seemed to be waiting for her husband's ire to appear, but the man was focused on his bride-to-be. Although, he wasn't quite as saintly as he acted. Lorna had caught him staring at her a few times that made her want to clutch the high collar of her gown. She was convinced the only thing keeping her from becoming his intended was her lie that Jill had confirmed to the group as soon as they were outside.

And as terrible as it was that they wanted to make her a "widow," she knew Gaston better than anyone else. He would protect her and keep himself safe in the process. No man was as good with a gun than Gaston Reid, and as soon as she got her hands on a weapon, she would join him in the fight.

"Look, if you want a second wife, you are going to need my permission, judging from your loose interpretation of your buddy's religion." She jabbed a finger at Grant. "We've been together for *years* in marriage, as well as Death Riders members, so don't think she can flutter her pretty lashes at you and make it out alive without my permission."

Lorna tried to make herself smaller by hunching her shoulders in her saddle. Jill was downright scary. Her stomach rumbled, drawing their gazes.

Sylvia gave her a sympathetic glance while Jill narrowed her eyes as if Lorna's stomach should be shot for talking.

"Sorry," Lorna whispered.

"Time to go." Jill jerked the rifle from the saddle harness and waved the barrel to Lorna. "If you try anything, I'll shoot you first and your precious husband second."

"Peace, wife, there will be no talk of shooting the girl this night." Grant mounted his horse and drew it beside Sylvia's. "We only need the money, and then we can begin our new life."

Jill rolled her eyes at her husband's statement. "Sure, honey. I saw how you reacted when I mentioned Reid was coming to fetch his *wife*. You forgot about being all peaceable for a good ten minutes. I'm sure when you see Reid, you'll be feeling a lot less forgiving." She turned to the ladies, shouting, "Remember, Reid was the one that saw all your Death Rider men put in jail. We want him taken care of once and for all. This is for the future of your children!"

Lorna swallowed back a cry as the women released guttural shouts, lifting their weapons in the air, calling for revenge.

Jill lifted her hand, the group silencing at once. "There will be gold aplenty for all you ladies and your families. No woman here will ever be in want again under my watch, no child hungry." She lifted her chin. "You are all Death Riders now. We are family. And we see to our own—no matter the cost." She lifted her rifle above her head and released a shrill yell that the ladies joined, their shouts echoing off the cliff face. Jill took the lead and the ladies followed behind in a single row with Grant ahead of Lorna and Sylvia behind her.

Lorna kept her head down as her mount

followed the pack. There had been no chance to secure a weapon, but she knew Jill was serious. If Lorna tried anything at all on her own, her life would not be a long one. At the top of the hill, Lorna turned in her saddle as the sun set, casting the Rocky Mountains in a beautiful glow as the chill of the evening descended upon them. Sylvia shivered, but Lorna could sense it was more from terror than from the cold. She returned her attention to the trail and gripped the saddle horn. The ground turned treacherous with the fading light, but Jill led them through the canyon as if she knew it by heart.

Jill lifted her fist, voice low. "Ladies, take your positions about the garden. Hide, but have your weapons at the ready. As soon as we have the money, take him out."

Lorna gasped. "No! You said I would see him again."

"Don't worry. I'm not so heartless as not to let you kiss your husband goodbye first." Jill grinned. "After all, you said it yourself that we women have to stick together."

THE RIPPLING ROCK slab dug into his stomach as Reid gripped the top of the red rock formation, keeping his body hidden as he scoped out the area. He peered down the barrel of his gun through his riflescope that was trained on the path that was most likely the way to Grant's new residence. He was about to try a closer spot when movement topped the path and a line of women, all in blouses and split skirts with crimson bandanas over their faces, dribbled into the clearing with Grant behind them and Lorna in tow with another woman behind her. His chest ached at the sight of Lorna. Her red hair had pulled free from its braid and spilled over her shoulders and her nose was ruddy. Lorna Elliot was crying.

He gritted his teeth. Never in his years knowing this brave woman did he ever see her cry, much less sob like this. "What have they done with you, love?" If Grant had laid a single finger on her . . . his grip tightened on the barrel, and he drew in a bracing breath. He had to see where they were hiding before nightfall when the trade would happen at the massive balancing rock.

Grant gesticulated to a woman that looked vaguely familiar. He trained his scope on her—dark hair, slender, and his jaw dropped. *The new Harvey Girl was behind her capture?* Sylvia Williams must have lured Lorna away.

Jill commanded something and the group split, leaving Grant, Jill, and Lorna. Reid stared at Jill. She was giving the orders. Grant only had a single revolver in his gun belt. This man was always armed with knives, at least four firearms, and a long rifle. He was clean shaven, and his shirt was fresh looking, buttoned to his neck. *What is going on?* The Grant he knew took orders from no one, especially not Jill, and was always covered in a layer of grime. And what was with all these women? Where did they come from, and who were they? Surely, they were not hostages given he was allowing them free rein of the red rocks.

More likely he brought them into the Death Riders . . . but what woman in her right mind would become an outlaw? He chewed the inside of his mouth. *Unless it was a woman with nothing to lose and everything to gain.* He hadn't thought much about what would happen to the families of the outlaws that died or were locked away for life. His job was to protect the innocent citizens Grant and his crew were terrorizing. But if he had paid more attention, would he have found the women left behind to be desperate for a way to live without their men? *Would they be so desperate as to become outlaws themselves?*

Jill shoved Lorna to her knees, and she blocked her fall with her tied hands. She did not cry out, but he could spy her face twisted in pain as she was jerked to her feet again. They were heading for balancing rock.

Reid released his hold on the top of the slab and slid down the slanted rock. His feet struck dirt, and he raced toward Tanner's hiding position. Sweat coated his body as he pumped his arms, running and ducking behind brushes and pines to keep himself in the clear. He dove for the brush beside Tanner with the balancing rock within rifle range. He panted out his findings, Tanner nodding, chewing on a dried twig.

"Sounds like we have a situation on our hands." Tanner mumbled around the wood. "It's a shame we don't have more men, but lucky for you, I am the best sharpshooter this side of the Mississippi and probably the other side too. We proceed as planned."

"I'll be a sitting duck with all these extra guns."

Tanner moved to his overlarge saddle bags, withdrawing rounds of bullets from one side and from the other, a vest of sorts. He lifted it to Reid. "Put this on under your shirt and keep on your long coat to disguise the added bulk."

Reid hefted it. It was heavy—really heavy and solid. "Is this a bullet proof vest?"

He grinned. "It's got thick aluminum plates in them. Bullets won't go through. Tested it myself, but with a cactus as a body first. It's saved my life many a times, but it will leave a nasty bruise. It's my secret weapon when I face off criminals at close range."

His jaw dropped. "That's why they call

you the Angel of Justice? Because they can't shoot you down and bullets bounce off you." He whacked his Stetson against his thigh, chuckling. "I'll be. This is the best kept secret in the West."

"See to it that you don't let word slip, Reid. It could cost me my life."

"And lose my own secret weapon? Never."

"Remove your shoulder harness, pull off your shirt and let me help you put it on. It's tricky the first time." Tanner motioned for Reid to hand it back. "Lucky for you, I'm only an inch taller than you. Otherwise, you'd have some dangerous gaps that Grant could fill with lead." Tanner fitted the vest, tugging and tying it into place, and once Reid shrugged back into his shirt, vest, and coat, Tanner nodded. "Perfect. You look like you've had a few more pies than usual, but that plays wonderfully into your being around a Harvey House all the time. Sylvia might be the only enemy to notice, but I doubt it as she is likely a new convert to Grant's crew and doesn't know what to look for during a job."

With the weighted vest and shoulder harness hidden by the overlarge coat, Reid felt a mite better striding out into the open for the exchange. But even without the vest, he would do anything for Lorna . . . and he was beginning to think that it was not just because she was an Elliot. He loved her family like his own, but she was more than a friend now. His heart recognized her as everything that was beautiful in life.

"I've got your back." Tanner laid on his belly, fitting his propped-up rifle to his shoulder.

Reid gripped the sack they had filled with coins and rocks to give the illusion of it holding the ransom that they did not possess the time to collect. He strode out into the packed red dirt patch which led to the massive boulder that balanced perfectly on a mound of rock. It looked as if a single push could topple it, but the bottom of the boulder was somehow fused with the mound, holding it into place. He dropped the sack at the edge of the clearing. "Grant. I have your money!" Reid shouted, lifting his hands above his head.

"Grant's not making this exchange. I am." Jill strode out from behind the boulder, gripping Lorna's collar, a gun at the ready.

Lorna's hands were still bound, and from here, he could spy the blood dripping from her palms to her fingertips to the earth.

"Lorna." Everything in him urged him forward, no matter the danger to himself.

"Gaston, don't! Rifles everywhere!" Lorna cried out.

"Quiet." Jill shoved Lorna to her knees.

She collapsed, rolling to the edge of the mound. The drop wouldn't kill her, but it could break a bone if she fell incorrectly. Reid stiffened, wanting to race to her aid, but he kept his hands high.

"Where is the money, Reid?" Jill shouted.

"I have it twenty yards back. I didn't want to take the chance you'd shoot me and take the money. Give me Lorna, let us ride away, and then you can have the money."

"I don't think so." Grant appeared from the shadow of the scraggly trees, his revolver pointed at Reid's chest. "The ransom has changed. I require the money *and* you. The girl goes free, and you take her place."

"I knew you only had to see his face again." Jill cackled. "Welcome back, husband. I've missed your bloodthirsty side."

Grant grinned down at his wife. "I always knew you were worth the trouble of marrying."

"So, marriage is trouble again? I'm guessing that means we are cancelling that wedding?" She rose on her tip toes and kissed his cheek.

Grant's crooked grin appeared. "Don't need to tie myself down a second time, not when I found myself again and can have the best of both without that extra baggage that comes with another wedding."

"As loving as this conversation between a husband and wife may be," Reid interrupted, "let's get on with the exchange. Release Lorna. Your argument is with me, Grant."

Lorna pushed herself up to sit on the back of her heels, her focus tearing from Grant to Reid. "Please. Don't. I'm not worth it, Gaston."

Reid scowled. Didn't she know how much she was loved? He only had a family in the East who wanted him to continue the family line. Sure, the Elliot family loved him, but she was their daughter. He could be killed without many to mourn his loss. Lorna on the other hand . . . he could not bear to live without her. "Honey, you are everything." *To me. And your family.*

Tears filled her eyes. "No, please . . . You don't understand. I-it's my fault."

"It is the Death Riders' fault. You remember that when this is all over." He took one step closer to her. "Let her walk to me, Grant."

"No." Grant sneered. "Take off your gun belt."

He gritted his teeth, but he had known this was coming. He unbuckled it and tossed it to the side. He didn't usually wear any guns under his coat, but he had begun to wear a shoulder harness since he sent Grant to prison, but Grant did not know that. "The least you can do is let me hug her goodbye."

"You have mistaken me for a man with a

heart." He clicked back the hammer. "That peace loving man died the moment he laid eyes on you. Grant Lawson, Death Rider leader, is back."

Jill giggled. "Who's the desperate one now, Reid? Grant, we got him dead to rights. Let the man have his goodbye." She grinned at Lorna. "I did promise the girl she could say goodbye to her husband."

Husband? Reid twisted about to look for another man hiding in the shadows. Lorna hadn't gone and married someone like Belle Parish had, did she? *It's all happening again!* He looked to Lorna, her face contorting at the word 'husband.' *What's happened?*

"Fine." Grant rolled his eyes. "But, if they try anything, it is on you and your infernal weakness for romance, wife. And if you try anything funny, Reid, I'll shoot your bride where she stands."

My bride? He thinks that . . . Lorna is my wife? He shifted toward Lorna again, but now was not the time to question, or correct, Grant's thinking. If it got him close to his Lorna, that's all that mattered. "Thank you."

"Ranger Reid is thanking me now?" Grant snorted. "This keeps getting better and better. Thank you, wife, for allowing me to have such a wonderful reunion with my enemy."

Lorna paled, but kept her eyes fixed on Reid. The terror in her usually warm and bubbly spirit sent a surge of fresh anger through his veins at those responsible for causing her such harm.

Jill jerked Lorna to her feet and pushed her to him. Lorna scrambled down the side of the rock, but without the full use of her hands, she was likely going to have scratched and bloodied limbs. She shoved off the mound of rock and gripped her ill-fitting calico skirts in her tied hands, bolting for him. She slammed into his chest, wincing from the heavy plates, no doubt. Her hands pressed against his chest. He could feel her tremors through the plates. "Oh, Gaston. You shouldn't have come. They are going to kill you. Why did you leave yourself so exposed?"

"I am prepared for what they are going to try, but do you really think I wouldn't come for you?" His arms wrapped about her quaking body. He ached to turn his back to the danger, to shield her from bullets. "I wasn't lying when I said you are everything to me."

She jerked back to stare up at him. "We have to run for it," she whispered, eyes frantic. "They will kill us both, or I'll be as good as dead once they shoot you."

"Grant is a crack shot. There is no way we can outrun them at this close of range."

"I'm a crack shot too. You've got your gun under your coat."

She must have felt it when she ran into him. "Yes, but—"

"Hands where I can *see* them!" Grant protested.

He lifted his hands once more.

"I can pull the gun and end this. You know I can."

"Time's a wasting!" Jill shouted. "Kiss her and move on."

"How can you get it?" He bent his forehead to hers, as if they were having a tender farewell. Perhaps from the outlaws' angle, it might even look like they were kissing.

"Kiss me," she whispered.

He stilled, his gaze flicking to her lips and back to her dark eyes. "What?"

"Kiss me like your life depends on it." She seized his vest and tugged him toward her.

He faltered. He wanted to kiss her. He had been dreaming of kissing her, but—

"Tarnation! Gaston Reid, kiss me before he shoots us both."

His heart hammered in his ears as he cupped her chin, eyes flicking to Grant before he bent low to her, his lips nearly brushing hers as he whispered, "Don't miss."

"You either."

His lips crashed into hers, his chest exploding at the contact and his head feeling light as she slid her hands up his vest and into his coat, tugging the pistol free from the harness in a single motion as she broke the kiss, whirled, and shot Grant in the upper chest below the collar bone and winged Jill, making her drop the gun as she screamed for her husband.

Bullets pinged against the rocks at their feet, Lorna screaming. Reid swept her into his arms and raced back for Tanner, who was covering for him. Something struck his back and he stumbled, nearly dropping Lorna. He sank behind the rock beside Tanner with Lorna cradled in his arms. He groaned but knew that if the bullet had found its mark, there would have been a searing, blinding pain.

He ripped the knife from his boot and sliced her bonds, cursing under his breath at the raw skin of her wrists and the cuts on her palms, but he didn't have time to tend to her with bullets raining down on them. She flipped on her belly beside Tanner, her revolver at the ready. It would do little good at long range, but his woman was a fighter.

He grabbed his own rifle from beside Tanner and waited for the chance to wing a shooter. Bullets died out and the dust of the battle settled. Jill groaned at the bottom of the balancing rock as she crawled to her gun and husband.

Reid got to his knees and lifted his hand as Lorna did the same. "Stay put."

"You risked your life to save me. I will do

the same for you," she countered, sitting back on her heels. "I'll cover you."

"Lorna Elliot. For once in your life, please listen to me. I beg of you. I cannot go out there if I have to worry about your safety."

She sighed, the fight visibly leaving her. She gripped his vest, pulling him back to the ground as she wrapped her arms about his neck. "Thank you. Please, don't get killed," she whispered into his neck.

He wrapped his arm around her petite waist, wishing he could stay like this forever. "I don't plan to." He kissed the top of her head and darted away, taking care to stay in the shadows and behind any cover he could manage. He knew the general directions the shots fired from, and he kept his gaze ever roving across possible hiding spots of their enemies, as he knew Tanner was doing as well. Reid kept low and raced to reach Grant before any more bullets filled the air.

Jill stumbled to her knees in a faint, her weapon falling to the ground beside Grant. It was the opening he needed. Reid bolted to them. He kicked her weapon away, cuffed Jill, and moved to Grant, snatching up the rifle. Grant appeared to be unconscious. He rolled over the giant of a man and removed all his weapons. The outlaw was bleeding pretty bad, his skin far too pale for a man who spent most of his time out of doors.

No further gunshots had followed him to the leader's side, so he wasn't surprised when Lorna and Tanner appeared.

"Is he alive?" Lorna whispered, the red curls framing her face making her look younger. "I-I didn't want to just wing him. Sometimes that only makes men angrier . . . or so you said from your stories."

Her voice roused Jill, who rolled and slowly focused on the situation at hand. "Y-you shot my husband, you—" Jill screamed a word that burned Lorna's ears as Jill pressed against the earth to raise herself to her knees.

"I know I shot him, but I didn't deliver a death blow on purpose." She bent and tore a length of cotton from Jill's gown and tossed it to Tanner who made quick work of binding Grant's wound and then used the remaining cloth to dress Jill's arm.

"This should hold him until we can get him help before he is locked up again. Jill, you walk ahead of us. You try anything and it's over." Tanner gripped Grant under the arm and proceeded to drag him to his horse, Jill stumbling in front of him at gun point.

Lorna handed the gun back to Reid, her hand trembling. "You better take this. I'm feeling a little weak after all the excitement."

He fitted it into his shoulder harness and wrapped his arm about her, steadying her. "Good work, Lorna. It took a lot of guts doing what you did." His gaze rested on her lips. He would need to find out about why they thought Lorna was his wife, which had led to that kiss. The fresh memory of her lips on his sent his heart to pounding. He had never had a kiss like that in his life. There had been kisses on the cheek from women in the past. He'd been a recipient of stolen kisses too when he was a young man, but this was nothing like those. Her kiss was perfection—it was more than perfection. It was fire. And he wanted more of them. His hand reached for hers. It was small, but strong. Why hadn't he seen this Lorna sooner? His gaze fell to her lips again and it felt as if he were being pulled to her.

"You too."

He blinked from his stupor. *Good work kissing?*

"For finding me."

CHAPTER 11

Gaston tightened his hold on her hand as they followed the man he had brought with him, the action bringing an inadvertent whimper to her lips.

"I'm so sorry, Lorna." He released her at once and cradled her injured hands to turn them in the moonlight. "I forgot about your cuts." He hissed, reached into his pocket, and withdrew a handkerchief.

Her lips parted at the embroidery on the corner. After all these years, he still kept a handkerchief from the set she had made for him.

His gaze met hers and he leaned toward

her as if . . . as if he were going to kiss her? Her heart stuttered. No, not kiss her. He inspected her hands. She sagged. She needed to stop her dreaming of a love with Gaston even more now. After that ghastly fib about him being her husband that led to her first kiss—the most magical kiss she could have ever imagined in all her years—she needed to keep herself and her imagination in check. She withdrew her hands. "Thank you. I'll see to them as soon as we have supplies."

"*I'll* see to them when I have the supplies," Gaston corrected. "You can hardly wrap them tightly enough when your hands are cut so badly. I should have been better prepared and brought medical supplies with me to see to any injuries. Seems my time as sheriff really has dampened my ranger training. Maybe Tanner has something in his pack."

Tanner? As in Tanner Sterling? She well knew his name and of his heroic deeds as Gaston had awed the family at Sunday dinners over the years with stories of the Angel of Justice. Gaston had gone to great lengths to rescue her. "One can't be prepared for everything," she rushed to reassure him. He'd just saved her life, and now he thought she was being neglected by him?

"Out here, one must be."

"Grant and Jill are secure." Tanner called from his mount where Grant was draped over the saddle and Jill's hands tied to the horn. Tanner stood with the reins in hand. Looked like he would be walking. "Even if there aren't any more bullets flying, I'll feel much better when we are out of here. We are too exposed. I want to take them down the foothills to Manitou Springs. You take Lorna through to Colorado Springs. I want to keep them separate, just in case."

"You sure that is wise?" Gaston returned. "I could take Jill with me."

"And take the credit, along with *my* bounty?" He scoffed. "No, thank you."

"After all you've done for me? I'd never—"

"Come on, Reid. I'm trying to help you out." He widened his eyes as if it were some sort of code between the men.

Gaston coughed, his face reddening. "I'll fetch Lorna home then."

"That's a good man." He grinned and looked to Lorna. "Can you give Reid a thorough description of each woman working for the Death Riders for the wanted posters, miss? Likely, they are long gone from these hills by now."

"I can. And you are probably right. They packed up their residence pretty well when we left the cliffside. Someone mentioned their hideout was close to Manitou Springs. I doubt they will be returning to their cliffside home. These women are too smart—smart enough to manipulate Grant to bend to Jill's will."

"So, would you say that Jill is running the ranks now?" Tanner frowned, eyeing Jill.

Jill smirked. "Never thought a woman could run the Death Riders?" She chuckled. "Who do you think helped plan all those holdups over the years?" She nodded at her unconscious husband. "Not him, that's for sure. But, to his face, I'll always let him have the credit because it makes him so happy."

Lorna lowered her voice for only the two men to hear. "For the time being, she was in charge as Grant was too focused on Sylvia." Her heart dipped. *Sylvia.*

Gaston grasped her elbow. "What's wrong? You look awfully pale. You aren't going to keel over, are you?"

"I-I was supposed to help Sylvia."

Gaston frowned. "You mean the Harvey Girl who got you into this mess in the first place?"

She rested her hand on his muscular forearm and drew it back at once, casually putting a pace between them by petting Bunny. "There's much more to the story. She was tricked, and there is an argument to be made that she was momentarily out of her mind."

"People say that all the time to avoid the consequences of their actions," Tanner interjected.

"I'm sure they do, but I believe Sylvia truly was misled by Grant—one might even say brainwashed." She shivered. "If it hadn't been for Sylvia, the riders might not have believed a lie that saw me safe enough until you got to me." She swallowed. There was no way on God's green earth that she was going to expose that lie now, in front of Tanner Sterling, the Angel of Justice. *Soon, but not now.*

Tanner tipped the brim of his hat. "Thank you, miss. I'll see these two in jail and then check out that cliffside house. Can't leave nothing to chance when it comes to this group."

Gaston clasped his hand. "Thank you. I owe you one, brother."

"You are finally right about something. I would have gotten these two with or without you." He winked. "It only may have been a little longer in the capturing. I'll take back my vest."

"I was hoping you'd forget about that. I want one of these." Gaston laughed. He pulled off his long coat, his vest, and Lorna's mouth parted as he shrugged off his shirt, revealing a bulky vest beneath.

He unbuckled it and hauled it off, his thick muscles bulging as he handed the vest back. His back was shockingly tan, as if he made a habit of removing his shirts after every capture. His back bore a wide circular mark that was beginning to bruise beneath his shoulder. Her mouth dried. The vest had saved his life. *How near he came to death for me.* Her gaze moved over him, checking for injuries. Her attention rested on his sculpted stomach and to her horror, Gaston's jaw was dropped in a lopsided grin as he watched her watching him.

Heat sparked to life across her cheeks, and she spun around, but did not miss the chuckling from the men, followed by Tanner's farewell. She waved, calling out her thanks, but kept her gaze to the moon, which raised more laughter. Yes, this was humiliating, but it was going to get even worse after her lie came to the surface. Could she get away without telling him? Or maybe just a half truth?

"It's safe to turn around now, Lorna. All muscles are covered." Gaston teased.

She lifted her chin as if she hadn't been ogling him seconds before. "I saw your bruise. Are you hurt elsewhere?"

He settled his Stetson into place. "I'm more worried about you and those hands.

We need to see to them before infection sets in, but I want us out of these red rocks before I take a moment with Tanner no longer watching my back."

She whistled low, Bunny's ears perking as he trotted over, nudging her with his nose.

Gaston's hands were on her waist, lifting her before she could even climb into the saddle. She settled astride, her skirts bunching around her knees as he mounted up behind her, his arms caging her in, protecting her. "Why don't you lean on me and rest until we reach the station. You look done in."

"You sure know how to make a girl feel pretty." Her eyelids drooped and her limbs ached from the drain of the fight as they rode through the red rocks. "Don't you need me to watch out for the women in the rocks?"

He gently pressed his hand to her cheek, leaning her against him. "I've got you, Lorna. You can sleep. Trust me."

His chest felt so nice—much nicer now that it didn't feel like a metal plate. "I've always trusted you." She closed her eyes and allowed herself a moment of weakness to draw strength from the man she loved with all her being.

REID KEPT his focus on the rocks shooting up on either side of him as they rode out from the formations at long last where the swelling foothills flattened and the road into Colorado Springs straightened before them. The moonlight gave way to dawn, and the glow illuminated the mountains behind him, and slowly the chill in the air ebbed.

Having Lorna in his arms was doing something to his chest, and, if he were better at ignoring these feelings tearing through his body, he would have ridden to the doctor's office to check out the condition of his erratic heart.

She moaned, her head lolling. He clasped her to him with his free arm and heaven help him, she snuggled into him. She felt right in his arms and after the terror of thinking that he might lose his dear friend, his soul ached at the thought of her ever leaving his arms . . . which posed a problem. Long ago, Gil had warned him from ever courting his sister, but at the time, Reid was focused on the rangers and building a career in saving innocents and the promise had been all too easy to make. He hadn't seen her as anything more than a friend, but the moment he saw her in that Harvey Girl uniform, looking all ladylike and graceful, it was as if a door unlocked in his heart and Lorna Elliot held the key.

Lorna stirred, groaning and muttering, as if reliving the nightmare.

He halted Bunny and gathered her in his arms, gently shaking her. "Lorna, love. Wake up. You are with me. You are safe."

"G-Gaston?" Her lashes fluttered open, and with a little cry, she wrapped her arms around his neck, pressing into him as she shivered. "I-I forgot where I was for a moment."

He pressed a kiss atop her hair, and she stilled. He gritted his teeth. He may have been able to get away with the action when they were in the red rocks and the dust was still settling from the spray of bullets, but now, with the light of dawn bursting over the mountain ridge of the Rockies, he could not hide his actions. She slowly pulled back, her wide brown eyes searching his.

"I'm sorry I worried you. I should have listened to you. Sylvia lured me out, but I should have known better. You worked so hard to keep me safe and yet, I still set aside my better judgement by going out alone." She dipped her head. "Is my family terribly worried?"

"I did my best to reassure them that you would be safe. I've chased criminals for over a decade, so that should bring them some measure of comfort until we are able to send a telegram."

She adjusted in his arms to face the approaching town. "We will be home soon enough. At least you won't have to worry about watching my every move anymore with Grant and Jill in custody."

He scowled. "I wasn't put out by watching you. In fact, that was the best I ever ate."

She snorted. "Food would be your bright side to this situation. My bright side is that my bed at the Montezuma will feel infinitely more comfortable than before."

"You deserve the rest."

She sighed. "Which I will have once I cover my shift. I cannot afford to take any time off. The Harvey House can only put up with so many antics before they decide I'm not worth employing, no matter how good I am at my job. I can only hope that my poor choices won't keep Corinna from advancing in the Harvey House chain of command."

Reid weighed his next words as they crossed into town with businesses that were still closed. A few grand townhomes lined the street with smoke drifting from their chimneys. "Corinna was beyond worried . . . as if she knew first-hand what cruelty at a man's hand was like. Has she talked with you about her life before the Harvey House?"

"She has been very tight lipped about her past, but I do know that she is running from something painful."

"You have made many good friends in your short time away."

"I've learned a lot from the other women about relationships."

He had noticed that about her, a confidence filled her that hadn't been there before. Growing up, she had used false bravado . . . cattiness even, to survive in the town of Las Vegas, but when she was away from the town's gossips and disapproval, she blossomed and became the woman she always was underneath the layers of hurt from the town's rejection of the Elliot family. "You like it there?" He grinned. "Gil told me about the dare that saw you signing up."

"I can never resist a dare, as you well know." She laughed and relaxed against him once more. "But yes. I love the work. It's hard but rewarding as I am serving people who are weary from travel . . . it's my version of washing someone's feet like Jesus." She twisted around to look up at him. "What about you, Gaston? Are you happy as sheriff, or do you really think buying a plot of land, like you've always talked about, is your next dream?"

"I never much thought of myself as a rancher before, but over the years, seeing your brother work with the cattle, alongside you and your father, it stays with a body. I always thought I wouldn't purchase a small ranch until I was unable to perform my job as well, but after this last adventure of rescuing you, all I want to do is . . ." *Settle down and marry you.*

"Is?" She prompted.

"Is to put the past behind me and focus on what is ahead, and that is ranching." He guided Bunny through the waking town to the platform.

He dismounted and lifted his hands to her. She rested her hands atop his forearms, sliding her hands up to his shoulders as he slowly lifted her from the saddle. He let his hand fumble and she fell into his chest, her lips grazing his cheek. He turned to face her. All he had to do was lean in and her lips would be his again.

The shrill train whistle jerked him away from her as Bunny pranced to the side. Lorna lifted her hands to calm her horse, running her fingers over the stallion's coat as she gently comforted him, murmuring softly into his ear.

"I'll get the tickets," he mumbled.

Her cheeks paled, and she swayed where she stood.

Reid was by her side in an instant, wrapping her in his arms where she belonged. "Do you need water? Food? Blast it all, I keep forgetting to tend to you."

Her chest heaved, shallow frantic breaths. "N-no. Not that. Please. Please don't leave me." She swallowed and looked up at him. "I'm sorry, but the thought that those women are still out there has me worried. They were as deadly with a weapon as Grant, and I have no doubt they could take me, if they so desired."

He kept his arm about her and grabbed Bunny's reins. "Then I will keep you by my side until we are home. No one will ever take you from me again." *And that's a promise.*

CHAPTER 12

he gentle swaying of the train car nearly lulled her to sleep. Nearly. With Gaston beside her, it was difficult. *"Don't leave me."* Could she have sounded more needy? Her cheeks burned at her weakness, but it was almost worth it when his strong arms stole about her, comforting her. True to his word, Gaston had stayed by her side for the entirety of their journey, even going so far as to escort her to the lavatory, which would have been embarrassing if she stopped and thought about it, but, after her ordeal, she reckoned she could be a damsel for one day and it would not kill her.

She adjusted in her seat so she could take a peek at Gaston through her lashes. Even after a fight in the red dirt, Gaston was wickedly handsome, but the way he protected her, chose her wellbeing over his —it was even more alluring. She had known he was brave, but she had never stopped to consider how it felt to be on the receiving end of his heroism. He was everything a man should be. His strength of character, courage in the face of death, and fierce protectiveness were brought to a whole new light. And she was a goner.

She checked him for signs of exhaustion, but he merely flipped through his newspaper and glanced about the car any time the doors opened for a passenger swaying down the aisle toward the dining car and back. Thoughts of food sent her stomach to rumbling. She closed her eyes fully in case he heard it. *No conversation is good conversation.*

Lorna was relieved at their silent agreement not to talk about a certain kiss that was seared in her memory. Gaston had kissed her soundly. Well, it had been *her* idea, but he had kissed her. *He could have said no.* She shook that hopeful thought from her head. *He was faced with certain death, or kissing me, of course he chose to kiss.* She glanced through her lashes again at him. She just didn't expect it to be so —so magical. She knew he had full lips, but the softness she had not been anticipating. Had it affected him at all though? She felt like her heart was going to burst at the time.

"About that kiss . . ." He folded his newspaper and set it aside.

Of course, he heard her stomach and caught her staring at him again. *So much for our silent agreement. Once again, it's all been in my head.* Her tongue stuck to the roof of her mouth. How did one talk about a staged kiss with the man she was desperately in love with for *years?* She forced confidence into her shoulders as she made a show of stretching her arms above her head. "Yes?"

"It got the job done."

She dropped her arms. Well, that hurt. She had never actually kissed anyone before, so she couldn't be certain of her skills until now. She had no skills apparently. She dipped her head under the guise of wiping off her ill-fitting calico skirt. "Uh, thank you?"

"I mean, that it, um," he raked his fingers through his hair and settled his hat into place. "I meant to say that you must have put them up to the idea of a goodbye kiss, yes?"

Could one die from embarrassment? She had an inkling she was about to find out. "Look, I can explain."

"So, you did set it up." He flicked up the brim of his hat. "It was a brilliant plan. Grant's hubris kept him from realizing what a threat you were, or that I could change my ways with my weapons and not have another gun hidden away."

She nodded, eyes fixed out the sooty window where she could spy a herd of ragged buffalo grazing on the prairie. "Hubris will get you."

"I should know." He grunted.

She dared to turn back to him, but she focused on the single thread of her cuff that was unraveling. Like her lie, if one pulled on it, what would happen? "Why would you say that?"

"I was proud I put away the roughest, toughest gang in the wild West and I was confident I could protect you . . . and I didn't even have the good sense to think a Harvey Girl could turn on one of their own."

This was all about his protecting her and not the kiss? She could work with that, but she didn't like his tormented expression of abject disappointment in himself. "If it weren't for you, Gaston, I wouldn't have made it. You did a great job getting me away from Grant and Jill."

He gritted his teeth. "I doubt your parents would agree on the means."

Her cheeks bloomed and she gripped his hands. "Look at me, Gaston Reid. You *cannot* and I mean absolutely cannot tell them how I put my hands on your gun."

"What? You don't want them to know how you grazed your palms across my chest?"

Her mouth was dust.

"It's not so bad to tell the truth." He

chuckled. "Everyone will want to know how we made the exchange with so many guns trained on us. This will be the first time in history a kiss played a vital role."

She dropped her face in her hands and groaned. "Wonderful. My first kiss, and now it will be told to the rangers, and probably printed in the newspaper, and I will be made a laughingstock even though I am the one that winged Grant and Jill, but will folks focus on that bit of information? No. It will be all about that kiss."

"That was your first kiss?" His jaw dropped, his gaze flitting to her lips and back up to her eyes, staring at her in a way that she was almost certain he could see the depth of her adoration.

And this goes from worse to traumatizing in under twenty seconds. She lifted her head. "I don't make it a habit to go around kissing men unless they are to be my husband, or at least, that's what I promised myself as a girl."

He ran his thumb over her hand. "I'm sorry for playing a part in breaking your promise. No woman should have her first kiss under such circumstances."

It wasn't all that bad. She wanted to change his look of misery right now. It didn't suit Gaston. She bumped her shoulder into his. "Well, for a half a day, you were my husband, and I have to admit that I was impressed at how good a listener you were."

"Pardon?" His wide blue eyes found hers again.

Good gravy. Trying to get him to laugh was a terrible idea. *Who cares if he looks a little disappointed in himself! He's a grown man and will get over it.* She on the other hand, would never get through this conversation. "Um, Jill was going to stab me for my not thinking Grant a worthy enough man to marry when there was talk of adding me to his collection."

His hand tightened over hers. "He threatened you, Lorna?"

"It was terrible, Gaston. You have to know that I never would have made up such a story if it wasn't absolutely necessary." She swallowed, pushing out the awful truth that would surely come to light if she did not say anything now. It would be just her luck for Jill, or Sylvia, to testify in court of Lorna's secret love for Gaston. "I-I might have insinuated that we were madly in love and that we married in secret as you didn't want to wait until my contract was up and I didn't want to pay the forfeit. Sylvia backed my story, and Jill promised me a kiss before you went to your grave."

"As I said, you are brilliant." He grinned, his eyes sparkling. "Making a kiss become the ticket to saving us all."

"So forward." She groaned. "I am so sorry. I know I made a mistake, and it could have turned out much worse—"

He lifted her hand and lightly kissed her knuckles. "If it kept you unharmed and safe from Grant's latest scheme, I do not care if you told them that we were already married *and* had a child on the way."

"Gaston! You shouldn't talk of babies with us being unwed and unpromised." She fanned her cheeks as her blush was creeping down her neck now. She rushed to add, "Not that we are talking of promising anything! I would *never* say such a thing . . . even if I did have to lie about being married."

He gave her hand a little shake, as if to shake her mind free from her guilt. "Lorna. It is okay. I do not hold it against you. In fact, I am proud you had the presence of mind to make up such a convincing lie that ultimately led to you getting the chance to put your hand on a weapon and our arresting Grant and Jill."

"T-thank you," she whispered, unsure where this kissing topic was leading to. *Please, God, let it be over.*

"I do have one question, though."

"Anything as long as you promise not to share that part of the story."

"I promise not a soul outside of the sheriff's office will know." His eyes began twinkling again.

Oh, no. It was never a good sign for her. She squinted at him. "What is it?"

His wolfish grin appeared. "Tell me how you convinced them of our love."

"No. Absolutely not." She jerked her hand out of his grasp.

"You do realize that I need to file a report on this as the sheriff." His eyes were fairly swimming now in suppressed mirth.

"And I feel like you are abusing your power asking me how I described my love—our love." She crossed her arms, flopping back on the bench seat and wincing at the wood striking her shoulder blade.

He reclined and crossed his arms as well, leaning toward her. "Come on, Lorna. It's a long train ride. I need a good story to keep me entertained."

"As I said, Sylvia backed up my story once she had a change of heart regarding Grant."

"And what was the story?"

She licked her lips. She needed water, but there was no way she was going to drink from the communal bucket of musty water. But one glance at him confirmed that he would not let the matter lie. *Best just rip that bandage right off.* "I simply told them that I had been in love with you since my childhood and how unrequited it was until of late when you saw me for more than a friend."

The teasing grin slipped. "Oh."

She hoped he did not know that part of the lie was actually the truth, and *that* was how she convinced everyone. "See? Not as glamourous as you thought." She offered him a wobblily smile, dying for this conversation to be over.

"And then, to save me, you asked me to kiss you." He murmured, his gaze moving to the window as if he too were as uncomfortable with this conversation as she.

Serves him right. She lifted her chin. "It was an emergency. I haven't waited my whole life for a love marriage for Grant to steal the chance at it from me. Now, are we done with your little inquisition? I'm exhausted."

He shot to his feet and extended his hand. "Your stomach has not stopped growling. Let's feed the beast, or neither of us will get much rest."

REID HELD the door of the dining car, motioning Lorna inside. All this talk of kissing was making it harder and harder for him not to give in to another kiss with her. However, Lorna was keeping him at arm's length now that the danger had passed, as if she wished to put the matter behind her. Did she have any idea how she affected him? And every time he closed his eyes, he was back in the red rocks with her in his arms, her kissing him as if their lives depended on it. It sure would be nice to have that experience again without the threat of being gunned down.

Lorna took a window seat at the first vacant linen covered table, perusing up the menu that was lying in wait beside the setting. "I hope a table is okay? I figured we have a long journey ahead, and a boxed lunch didn't sound as good as an actual meal when I haven't eaten properly in days."

He sat in the seat opposite hers, setting his hat on the empty seat nearest the aisle. "Love, you can order whatever you want." *Love?* How did that slip? He cleared his throat. "It's my treat."

"Money." She sucked in a breath through gritted teeth. "I-I'm sorry. I forgot I didn't have any funds with me, but you can bet your hat that I'll pay you back for all the train fare and food."

He rested his elbows on the table and leaned toward her. "I'm not worried about the funds."

"In that case—" She waggled her eyebrows at him over her menu as the waiter approached and Reid straightened. "I'll take the steak, potatoes, and greens with your favorite dessert, please, with water and a cup of strong coffee."

"Very good, Mrs. And that would be the Chantilly cake."

She winced at the man's guess of them being married and handed over her menu. "I've never tried it, but anything with *cake* in the title sounds just right."

The waiter jotted down her order. "And you, sir?"

He grinned at Lorna's squirming and handed over his menu as well. "I'll have the same as the *Mrs.*"

"I should have figured people would think we are married on a train ride unescorted. And you do realize that this is not a Harvey House meal, yes? If the steaks are terrible, we have to eat them, yes?" She whispered over behind her napkin.

"That didn't stop you."

"Anything is better than what I ate at the Lawson's place." She glanced out the window, her brows furrowing.

"Do you need to talk about it? Most people would be traumatized after such an ordeal." He slid his hand over the tablecloth, his calloused fingers tracing circles on her wrist.

She drew back as the waiter delivered their water and she gulped it down. He gritted his teeth. He should have been seeing to her needs instead of teasing that frown away from her face. Another waiter refilled her glass and moved to the next table.

She leaned back in her chair, studying the passing scenery. "I'm surprisingly fine. I've been listening to your stories for years. Perhaps that helped."

"It's not the same as experiencing it first-hand. You don't have to be brave with me. You certain you don't need to talk about it?"

"Not now." She picked at the table linen. "If I do, I'll seek out someone."

"You can seek out me." He reached across the table again, clasping her hand. "I've been through a gunfight many times, but the first is always the hardest."

"Thank you." She pulled back her hand and grasped her knife and fork as the waiter approached with the plates. "Food and a nap will make most any problem better, but when I do need to talk, I think it might be better to speak with Preacher Martin."

"Only as long as you speak to someone. Violence, hurt, fear, and abduction are serious matters, and, even if you feel fine now, you need to see the preacher and at least tell him the story of what happened. He may have a scripture to offer you comfort. Promise?"

"You don't have to persuade me. I can take care of myself, Reid." She took a massive bite of steak and focused on the window as snow dusted the hills, the snow growing thicker by the moment.

"I know you can." *I wish you would allow me to take care of you without you arguing for once.* "But there is a strength in allowing others to help you, and I wish you would let me."

"I wish I could too," she whispered. She turned to him. "You know better than others that growing up in a town where my pa wasn't liked was hard on me. I had no friends and those that tolerated my presence only did so because I lavished them with gifts as a young woman and bought their attention with sweets as a child. I knew that I was buying my friends, but I was so desperate for someone, anyone, to like me. My pa saw that. He showered me with gifts, making people think me spoiled."

He nodded. He well knew of her past, but this was the first time she ever voiced the hurt she experienced at the hands of the town's grudges that ran deep after Pa Elliot accidentally exposed Uncle Lane to the illness that took his life.

"You are well aware of Pa's large ranch, but you might not know that to build it, he bought out ranchers who were here for years before us. Some had gambling debts, others fell on hard times and had to move to small townhouses, and one even wished to move back East. My pa is a businessman. He offered them a price that they could have turned down, but word got out about the amount he paid each rancher, and the townsfolk were furious that he would build his fortune on the backs of other's misfortune. He even bought steer at a good price in the name of helping neighbors, but the number of head he amassed made the townsfolk leery of him. But what was the final straw was the death of your uncle."

He grasped her hand. "And the memory stays alive in the relatives of the previous owners?"

She nodded. "And in their children. Pa's attention and love helped distract me from my lack of true friends. After each shiny new object faded in their eyes, I was once again alone for birthday parties, for holiday parties, and at school. And when I saw that no one liked me on my own merit, I decided I didn't really need anyone . . . until the one person who should never even glance our way, rode down the creek to where I was playing with Gil and wanted to join—you."

He reached across the table and took her hand again, and, this time, she did not pull away. He well recalled her bright braids and skirt plastered to her legs as she and Gil sailed wooden boats down the creek he was exploring on horseback. Aunt Gertrude had managed to keep him away from the Elliots until he was thirteen, but once he met his best friends, his world broadened and life under his aunt's thumb became more bearable.

"You were the first person in town who was kind to me for my own sake. At first, I thought it was only because of Gil, but you always went out of your way to make me feel like I was special—an individual and not just a member of the Elliot clan."

"That's funny because you always made *me* feel special. I was never special to anyone who didn't want something from me before either. As you know, my aunt refused to allow Harriet and I to attend school or socialize much outside of each other and the few town children that she deemed suitable. It was stifling." He dared to rub his thumb across her wrist. "But the moment I met you in that creek, I was drawn to you because of your joy, and vivacity, and genuine spirit. It was because of *you,* and not Gil, that I came over all the time to play as a boy."

"Me?" Her eyes widened.

"If it wasn't for your kindness and spirit, Gil and I wouldn't have become so close."

"And as a man, what makes you wish to continue this friendship when I've been so much trouble?" She offered him a small smile. "You've got plenty of friends besides me now."

The picture of her in her Harvey uniform, her lips on his, and the feel of her in his arms, whispering his name as if he were an angel come to rescue her, flashed to mind, when she in fact, had rescued him all those years ago. But he wasn't certain how another kiss would be received. First, he had to begin the enchanting of Miss Elliot before he laid his heart on the railroad track to be rescued or flattened. "What's always made me want our friendship—you."

CHAPTER 13

The snow had thickened to a blizzard by the time they approached the Raton Pass that burrowed deep through the Rocky Mountains. Her fingernails tinted blue, and no matter how much she blew into her hands, or stuffed them under her arms, she couldn't keep her body from shaking at the rapidly dropping temperature in the train car. She eyed Gaston asleep on the bench across from her, using his great coat as a blanket. She rubbed her arms up and down the horrible, thin calico gown, wishing she had a coat, or at least a shawl. Her teeth chattered despite her clenching her jaw, and her fingers were growing stiff. If she didn't get warm soon, she might never get warm.

She huffed into her hands once more. Even her breath was cold. She groaned and darted to the other bench, slowly lifting his coat, and scooting under it with him and snuggled into his side, hoping he would sleep through her intrusion. She gritted against the coming mortification of him waking to find her under his coat with him, but sheer necessity compelled her. She closed her eyes against her extreme impropriety and slid her arms around him, hugging herself to him, basking in his warmth. He was far better than any baked potato that she usually used to warm her hands during a sleigh ride to and from church in the winter. She burrowed a little closer, her cold cheek pressed to his chest beneath the coat.

He stiffened. "Lorna. What are you doing?"

She winced and slowly lifted her chin to meet his gaze. "I'm cold."

"I can feel that." He chuckled. "Do you want my coat?"

Her teeth chattered. "T-then y-you would be c-cold and it's only going to get colder with this snow."

"You know, we could pretend to be married for a little while longer." He grinned down at her.

"Gaston Reid," she scolded, but without much conviction. She was entirely too cozy after her ordeal to remove her arms from his waist, and even if she wanted to, his arms had already encircled her as well. "This is for survival purposes only."

"If you wanted to cuddle, all you had to do was ask." He teased.

"Gaston!" She hissed. "You are impossible, but only because I am dangerously cold will I stay put. Otherwise, I would shun you for the rest of the journey for saying that."

The train chugged to the pass, whistle blowing as it was engulfed in darkness. Against her will, a whimper escaped. She closed her eyes against the all-consuming black of the tunnel through the mountain. They would be through soon enough. If she focused on the car's swaying lantern light, she would be fine. Her hand was taken, and her gaze flashed to meet his in the flickering light.

"Are you well, Lorna? I'm sorry I teased you. I was only so worried about you during this whole ordeal that I'm afraid my worrying turned into teasing as an outlet."

She shook her head, which was difficult as she was pressed against his chest. "I don't like the dark. I was fine with it . . . before. But having been taken at night and then having to stay awake to keep myself safe—"

"I won't let anything happen to you, Lorna. You are with me now. You can sleep and know that you are safe." At her tremble, his arms tightened about her.

She felt a brush against her hair. *Did he kiss my hair?* The swaying lantern no longer stayed her nerves, but listening to the steady thump of his heart, calm engulfed her. She kept her head pressed against his chest, allowing herself a moment to enjoy his warmth and strength.

The train wheels clattered, and the car swayed, but with him and his arms about her, she drew one breath and then another, quieting her racing heart until they burst through the other side of the Raton pass. He shifted as if to move his arms, but at her muffled protest, he chuckled and kept one arm about her shoulders, the other skimming down to hold her hands.

An elderly woman hobbled past to use the necessary at the back of the train, pursing her lips at them and no doubt, their improper embrace.

She knew they were breaking many rules, but she could not bring herself to care enough to leave the comfort and safety of his arms after everything and slowly, she drifted off to sleep.

HAVING this lovely woman in his arms was a dream. Reid blinked his eyes rapidly, desperately attempting to stay awake. He focused on Lorna's soft snoring for a while, but soon even that was not enough to keep him alert. But he supposed that with Lorna in his arms, and being armed enough to take down any outlaw, they were safe enough should he wish to close his eyes. They would be home in a matter of hours, and once they were back in Las Vegas, he would have precious little time to rest until he saw to the matters of town and then her continued safety.

He rested his head on her vibrant hair that was as soft as it was lovely. She smelled of honey and vanilla—of home. If he could only convince her that he could be more than a friend, perhaps he would not have to say goodbye to moments such as these. Maybe he could convince her to marry him the moment her contract was up. He ached to make her his. *Lord, I don't know how to make a woman fall in love with me. You know I've tried and failed in the past, but now, the stakes have never been higher. I am in love with Lorna Elliot, and, if You are willing, have her love me in return.*

The lack of swaying was the first clue that the train had stopped. The second clue was a sharp clearing of a throat.

Reid stirred, slowly blinking to find Lorna still in his arms with her back cradled into him and his head resting on hers. It had been the best sleep he had in weeks. He moved to stroke back a lock of her hair that was tickling his nose.

"Reid. What do you think you are doing holding my sister like that?" Gilbert Elliot's booming voice filled the train car.

Reid jolted fully awake, Lorna gasping as she scrambled to her feet and fell between the bench seats. Reid hauled her to her feet, steadying her. They were a sight. Lorna's hair had completely spilled from her coiffure, and he was rumpled from her sleeping on him. He snatched his great coat from the floor.

"Gil!" She threw her arms about his neck.

He hugged his sister, glaring at Reid before clasping her face between his hands. "Did they hurt you, Lorna?"

"They almost did." She shook her head. "They wanted to marry me off to Grant."

"What?" He growled.

"But I told them how I married Gaston two weeks ago."

"What!" Gil whipped toward Reid. "You married my sister?"

She held up her hand to stay his arguments. "Grant considered himself a po-lygamist at the time, claiming to be a part of a religion of some type that I've never read about, given he dropped the peace-loving act the moment he saw Reid and wanted to blow a hole through his chest."

"So, you married Reid?" Gil's sharp tone made his sister roll her eyes, even as Reid cringed. "Thought you'd pull a Colt Lawson on an innocent girl, did you, Reid?"

Reid lifted his hands at the accusation. "It's not like that, and if you would pipe down for one second, we can explain everything."

"You explain why I came on the train to find you and my sister sleeping in each oth-er's arms as cozy as two squirrels in a sock."

"Gil!" Lorna gaped at her older brother. "I was *cold*. We rode through a snowstorm."

"You know me better than that," Reid exclaimed at the same time. "And do not insult your sister."

"Stop jumping to conclusions and let me finish." Lorna clenched her fists, scowling up at Gil. "I did *not* really marry him. It was a ruse to keep them from marrying me off to Grant."

"And does Reid know the ruse is over because the way he was holding you does not make me think he does, and y'all might need to go see Preacher Martin to make this right."

Lorna gasped. "Gilber—"

"I'm mighty beholden of your service in recovering my sister, Reid, but this is highly inappropriate behavior," Gilbert continued, ignoring her. "I'd expect it of Lorna—"

"Excuse me?" Lorna gritted her teeth. "I'm a lady, Gilbert Elliot."

"One who has carried a torch for him for years." Gil jerked a thumb at Reid.

She has what? Reid gaped down at her, hope blooming in his chest. "So, you liked me for years, huh?"

She crossed her arms, glaring at Gil. "What a thing to say after I've returned from almost certain death. I would think that berating me for seeking a bit of comfort after all I've been through would be the last thing on your mind. You should be thankful that I am not falling into a fit of hysteria."

Gil slowly unclenched his fists and sighed. "I'm sorry, Lorna. You are right. I am overreacting from my worry. Ma and Pa were beside themselves."

"Well, you and Reid certainly have a funny way of showing your concern," she grumbled.

"How did he show his concern?" Gil whipped back to Reid. "What did you do?"

"The moment he saw me, he kissed me good." She tilted her head, grinning triumphantly at Gaston, purposefully leaving out that it was she who did the asking for the kiss.

The little minx is getting back at me for teasing her. He smirked at her. "Very funny, Lorna."

"He what?" Gil exclaimed drawing the eyes of the now boarding passengers. He poked his finger into Reid's chest. "You kissed my sister?"

"What your sister is trying to say is that it is a *long* story that is best discussed off the train in private rather than with all the gossips of New Mexico within earshot. With the way you are carrying on, I'd suspect you'll read the story in the papers across the United States tomorrow because everyone could hear you *yelling* about a kiss that was so spectacular, people will be writing ballads about it for years."

Gil grumbled under his breath about Reid not denying the claim as Lorna gaped at him.

Reid ignored him, and drew his coat over Lorna's shoulders, and took her arm, no matter that her brother was there. Reid was not letting her go after that debacle. If he had to lock her in the jail cell to keep her safe, he would do it. He directed her off the train and onto the platform of Las Vegas that was now coated in a thick blanket of snow. He instructed the porter to fetch his horse and tie him to the hitching post, pressing payment into the man's palm.

She shrugged off the coat and handed it back to him. He returned it firmly to her shoulders, whispering, "It took a long while to get you warm, and I don't think that your brother would approve of me warming you up again like last time."

As he hoped, her cheeks burst into crimson. "You are incorrigible."

"After what you said about me kissing you to your *brother*, you better believe I'm going to tease you mercilessly to get back at you."

Gil took Lorna's free arm and she protested and wiggled away from them both. "I know you were both concerned, but I am safe now and must get back to the Montezuma before they fire me from the resort."

"About that," Gil tugged his hat into place. "Harriet spoke to her old house mother at the Castañeda Harvey House here in town and convinced them to allow you to move from the Montezuma to here."

"Gil," she began to protest, but halted at his gentle touch on her arm.

"That way, Reid can get back to his sheriff duties while still keeping an eye on you, along with the rest of the Elliot family. The extra five miles up the mountain really is too much for the family, but we would do anything to keep you safe."

"So, you meddled with my *job*, Gil? Honestly, I don't feel like I am being unreasonable for being upset. I made friends at the Montezuma, and I intend on keeping those friendships." Lorna's lip trembled.

"It's not necessary for her to transfer. I can figure something out. I'd hate for her to leave her close friend," Reid interjected.

"Oh, you mean your roommate, Miss Corinna? She is coming along with you."

She blinked. "She is? How?"

"When she caught wind of your pending transfer, she begged to go, and as she is one of the best Harvey Girl waitresses seen out of Topeka, besides yourself, they wanted to keep her happy and agreed. Your things have been moved into the Rawlins dormitory across from the Castañeda."

"That . . . was thoughtful of you." Lorna pushed out, but Reid knew it cost her to give up the place she was making her home away from the town of Las Vegas with its gossiping, grudge-holding townsfolk.

"Look, I know we overstepped our

boundaries, but Pa was about to force you back to the ranch. Reid wrote to us while you were working in Topeka and told us how happy you were and good at your job. Harriet thought it would be better for you if she acted on your behalf. She asked me to apologize upfront for overstepping by the way."

"I supposed I should tell her thank you, but I may have to wait a few days until I calm down," she muttered.

"A less passionate response than I was expecting from my now fiercely independent little sister." Gil pressed a kiss on her forehead and led them down the boardwalk toward the dormitory. "Thank you for making this easier on the family. Harriet really did try to make it a better transition for you." He patted her arm outside of the Rawlins building. "I will tell the folks and Harriet that you made it safely to your new position. They would have come, but the snowfall was nearing a blizzard, and I wouldn't have it, what with them getting over a cold." He pulled her into a hug. "You are sure you are well in body and soul, Sis?"

"Never better." She gave him a little push. "Go back to your bride and tell all that I am hale and hearty after the adventure of a lifetime."

Reid studied her smile that didn't reach her eyes, but Gil seemed to accept her words.

"Let's pray that you never have another such adventure." Gil hugged her again and trotted off with a wave.

She slowly turned to look up at the dormitory and sighed. "I had hoped I would never be this close to Las Vegas again, and now I have to start over making friends."

"It won't be forever, Lorna. We need only to find the rest of the Death Riders women and with the description you gave me on the train, the sketch artist will have the posters at the press already. I think that in a matter of months, your future will be your own again."

"I know it is only a matter of time with you and Tanner Sterling on the alert." She smiled up at him.

Her confidence in him made his chest swell.

"At least you won't have to watch me every hour of every day now."

"Maybe, but old habits die hard." He longed to pull her into his arms, to never let her go—to drop to his knee and propose right now. But he knew this position was important to her. He would have baulked at someone asking him to give up the rangers before he was ready. He needed to honor her request to work.

"And now that I am in town, I expect to take my stallion for a ride when you aren't riding him."

"Of course, Bunny is yours after all."

"Lorna!" Corinna sprinted across the street, her skirts hiked to her knees. She threw her arms about her. "Thank the good Lord. I prayed and prayed for your safety."

Lorna laughed, tears spilling down her cheeks. "You have no idea how much I have missed you. Your prayers made all the difference."

Corinna swiped under her eyes. "I know what it's like to be under the power of cruel people. Prayer is the only thing that got me through my ordeal." She shook her head.

"But, enough about me. Let's get you cleaned up. You smell." Corinna wrinkled her nose and shooed her toward the door with a wink.

Lorna paused at the threshold and looked over her shoulder to Reid before turning and throwing her arms about his neck. "Thank you, Gaston, for everything."

She pulled away and disappeared inside, leaving his heart aching, but he had a job to do, and with the rest of the Death Riders women still on the loose, maybe his sleepy little town wouldn't be quite so boring. He sighed. He kind of missed boring.

CHAPTER 14

*D*espite the ruckus spilling out of the saloon until three in the morning, Lorna awoke feeling like a new woman, especially after bathing, plaiting her hair into a coronet, and dressing in a fresh high collar black gown with a crisp white apron. Corinna had bandaged her hands and as it wasn't quite a good look for a Harvey Girl to be sporting such dressings, the house mother, Violet Trent, allowed Lorna to wear a pair of white gloves of Corinna's over her injuries.

Lorna was stunned by the friendship Corinna offered in coming with her to the Castañeda even though it wasn't as opulent as the resort. But Corinna never once mentioned the sacrifice and eyed the hotel eagerly as the pair of them followed Miss Violet Trent about the small hotel, listening to the house mother's explanations of how things were done in this Harvey House. At last, they reached the bustling dining room with its white and burgundy checkered floors. The potted palm in a blue pot stood near the corner of the room that seemed to mark where guests should not enter as it blocked the area of the Harvey Girls heading to and from the kitchen with rows of shelving for the clean place settings. She frowned at the lack of tablecloths that did wonders to dress up the wooden tables and lend an air of sophistication to the restaurant.

"We are not as elegant as the Montezuma Resort in the Gallinas Canyon, but we have many new visitors throughout the day and there will not be as many chances to right things in the lulls. Here, we must clear and set the moment a guest departs the dining room. . . which takes less time as usual, given the lack of tablecloths." She pinched the bridge of her nose. "I'm afraid we look even less dignified than the resort at the moment as there was a problem with our linen shipment this morning and all of our clean linens went missing."

"Why would someone steal tablecloths?" Corinna whispered to Lorna.

Miss Trent pressed her lips into a firm line. "I have my suspicions that it is the saloon. They've never liked us here, and with the new owner trying his hand at serving meals, I have little doubt that he is attempting to undermine us and has his employees doing his dirty work."

Lorna frowned. "It will take a lot more than missing tablecloths for his restaurant to be considered a threat. Did you report it?"

Miss Trent ran her finger along the chair rail, inspecting it for grime. "I made a statement at the law office to the acting sheriff, but tablecloths are hardly a matter of importance to anyone else in this town." She dusted off her hands. "But I digress. Please apologize to each guest for the lack of tablecloth and offer a free dessert as compensation. We should have linens by tonight, and if we don't, I'm going to have to send for some from the Montezuma." She sighed. "I would hate for Mr. Harvey to catch wind of such a ghastly drop in standards before I can write an explanation, along with news that the situation has been remedied."

While the restaurant did not boast of views of the Gallinas Canyon, the long windows gave a splendid view of the foothills that, she knew from her own dining experience, would be covered in flowers come springtime.

Corinna smiled. "It's lovely, Miss Trent, and I'm honored to work here. It will be nice to be so busy. The Montezuma had bursts of guests, but never a steady flow."

"It certainly makes the day go by faster." Miss Trent gave her a smile and patted her on the arm as she signaled another Harvey Girl to join them, a thin strawberry blonde.

Lorna's stomach sank at the sight of Dolly Matthews. The girl had never been kind to her, or her family. Dolly had never shied away from using her sharp words. Would she never escape an angry head waitress? First Sylvia, who had turned out to be Grant's lover and was now on the run. At the thought of her experience, her stomach flopped again. She probably should eat something. She pressed a hand to her corseted waist. *I am safe here. I'm safe. Gaston is near enough that, should I scream, he could come a running.*

Corinna rested a hand on her arm. "What's wrong," she whispered.

"You'll see in about two seconds," she murmured out the side of her mouth as Dolly stopped in front of them, hands clasped in front of her skirts.

Dolly eyed them, a smile of . . . approval gracing her expression?

Is this a trap? She offered Dolly a tight smile, pushing aside thoughts of all the times Dolly had slighted her. "Hello, Dolly."

"*Miss* Dolly. We are in the dining room. When in private, you may be less formal, of course." Her left brow arched. "I thought you would know better coming from the *resort.*" She drew out the word as if it was distasteful.

So much for the sisterhood of aprons. She

forced friendliness into her smile. "Miss Dolly, I am honored to be working at the Castañeda, and I guarantee you that Corinna and I will prove ourselves to be hard workers."

"And does Corinna actually speak for herself?"

Corinna's eyes widened and she swallowed, bobbing her head.

Anger flared in Lorna's belly. She resisted the urge to take Corinna's hand. "She's shy."

"She works for the Harvey House. We do not pay her to be shy. We pay her to be friendly."

Lorna fought to keep the fake smile in place. "Corinna can out waitress any of us Harvey Girls . . ." She let her words dangle, the insinuation of "even you" hanging in the air.

Dolly scowled but waved them inside to the dining room. "Get to proving your worth as Harvey Girls. You two will have the tables along the windows."

Lorna did not wait to be told twice. She swept into the room that she had dined in as a guest a dozen times with Corinna behind her. They smiled at the nearest Harvey Girl, Fannie Traverse . . . Dolly's close friend.

Fannie gave them a friendly bob of the head. "Glad to have you ladies here. We've been cycling through Harvey Girls with all the marriages and proposals of recent months. First there was Sophia Bird Fairfield, then Belle Parish, and I'm next up." She wiggled her finger, displaying the tiny gemstone in a gold ring.

Corinna admired the piece. "Lovely."

"Thank you. We are to marry as soon as my contract is over in a few weeks." She smiled to Corinna. "We haven't met yet. I'm Fannie."

Corinna reached to take the dishes from Fannie. "Corinna Victoria."

Fannie rolled back her shoulders. "I'm thankful to be released from my shift. I've worked two shifts in a row, and I might keel over if I don't nap soon, but my man is waiting to take me for a drive in his buggy."

"I know the feeling," Lorna procured the rag from Fannie, scrubbing down the table.

Fannie stretched her back. "Topeka was hard on us all, but the training was thorough and will help you feel confident in your movements, but then again, I forgot that Dolly said this isn't your first position."

She shrugged. "Our positions at the Montezuma hardly lasted long enough to call it our first position . . . thanks to circumstances beyond my control."

"That's what I heard." Her green eyes widened. "I don't know what I would have done if Grant Lawson had marked me for his victim." She shivered. "You are fortunate to be back here in one piece."

"He hardly *marked* me. It was more on the account that a wayward, brainwashed Harvey Girl wanted to be inducted into the Death Riders, in a most unique way, and decided to take me as her rite of passage."

"You make it sound like the outlaw gang was a cult." Fannie pressed a hand to her heart.

"If it wasn't, it certainly is now." Lorna pressed her lips together, suppressing the terror of almost being taken for his bride if not for that lie . . . and kiss to end all kisses.

She moved to the next table and stacked the dishes and set to scrubbing away the food and memories.

Corinna set down her armload of glassware and rested a hand on her shoulder, her eyes brimming with concern. "You have good friends surrounding you, a family, and man who loves you. You will be safe."

"Thank you, Corinna." She dipped her head at the man part of her reassurance and set the glasses, only to notice a fingerprint at each rim. "Would you mind fetching new glasses? These all have fingerprints on the glass. And maybe tell the dish boy to dry his hands before he sets the clean glasses in the shelves."

Corinna's eyes widened. "I couldn't do that. It would be rude."

"It will be easier than our making him rewash the entire cabinet of dishes." Lorna countered.

"I suppose you are right." Corinna sighed and turned on her heel to the kitchen.

Lorna bit the inside of her mouth. She could have done it for Corinna. She had noticed over their time together that the poor woman did not like speaking with men apart from the safety of the tables. But it was best she start now with Dolly Matthews waiting for either of them to make a mistake. It was part of the job to speak with the male staff.

The next few hours were filled with blissful busy work and left her no time to dwell on what had happened in the red rocks, nor that ground shaking kiss . . . or the way she had snuggled him on the train. Her cheeks heated at the thought of her brazenness. Being cold could push a body to do something she wouldn't normally. In all fairness, she had never been so cold in her life, nor so comfortable in the next moment. A girl could get used to having such a giant of a man as a real husband to huddle next to for a lifetime. *No. No more imagining more out of the situation, Lorna Elliot. Gaston Reid only came for you because he cares for you as a friend, and he allowed you to stay beside him to keep you from losing your fingers to frostbite. Nothing else.*

"Lorna." His rumbling voice pulled her from the depths of her concentration.

She slowly turned, the stack of dishes balanced in one arm. "Sheriff Reid. Would you like to be seated at the table or lunch counter?" At the question flickering in his eyes, she hoped he caught on that she needed to be formal in the dining room.

He leaned in to whisper, "Which will see me getting more attention from you?"

His breath on her ear sent a shiver down her spine.

"Are you cold again?" His brows lifted and she caught his wicked grin.

She rolled her eyes at his blatant reminder. What game was he playing? "Neither. I'm busy cleaning the tables since Miss Dolly decided Corinna needed to exercise her voice with the guests." She moved to stack the dishes in the dirty bin.

"Uh, Lorna, has there been any trouble since I left?" Gaston swiped off his hat as he followed her to the Harvey Girl's station.

She dumped the dishes and reached for four clean sets. "You've been out of my sight for a half a day. Take a break, Reid." She hated being snippy with him, but she had to cease this flirtation that would only end with her heart being broken again.

He frowned. "Why are you calling me Reid again? I thought we were well beyond that? Seems to me, after all we have been through, we've earned the right to use first names when no one is within earshot."

Her cheeks flamed. "Please tell me you are not bringing up that kiss again?"

"No one said anything about kissing." The corner of his mouth lifted.

"Good." She threw down a napkin that did not pass muster and turned her attention to the shelves of glasses to inspect the drinkware herself. Two rows would need correcting. She tsked and picked up the dirty bin and loaded them straight into it.

"But since you have brought up one of your favorite topics of late—"

"Please do not start on me, Reid." She hefted her bin of dishes into the kitchen, and retrieved an empty bin to take its place. He remained next to the potted palm. "Look, I apologized over and over on that train ride. I did what I had to." She dropped the bin in its shelf.

He caught her wrist. "I was thinking we should try it again?"

Again? Her gaze fell to his lips, her heart pounding. No, it was cruel of him to tease her like this. Not after all her work to see her heart whole again after years of unrequited love and wondering why he never noticed her beyond friendship. Or, why he had never realized that they were perfect for one another in so many ways. She pulled away. "I think you need to leave."

His brows furrowed. "Why?"

"Because you need a break from watching me, and I don't want to be around you right now."

Hurt flashed in his eyes. "Lorna."

She swiveled her back to him under the guise of organizing the linens. "You've teased me for the last time today, and I've got work to do, Reid, and so do you. You are a sheriff, not a ranger anymore."

REID GRUMBLED over the mound of paperwork on his desk, which mostly con-

sisted of complaints against the town's saloon. He despised the establishment as
much as the next citizen, but it was a free
country, and he couldn't rightly go about
closing businesses that he disagreed with if
they followed the law. He was exhausted
with the trivial parts of this office and his
heart was no longer in it. At all. He never
quit anything before becoming a ranger, so
he figured he could allow himself to place
an advertisement for another to take his
place. As soon as it was filled, he could find
some land and make it his own—and maybe
even propose once he got Lorna to fall in
love with him.

Focus, Reid! He squinted over Colt's
scrawled penmanship in the lamplight, a
line about missing linens and another describing a Mrs. Higgins's complaint of the
new batch of saloon girls that just arrived
on the train and how they were already
convincing her husband to stay out playing
cards until the early hours, gambling away
their family's funds. He frowned. He knew
the man well as he had been a regular in his
cell for the last three Friday evenings that

he was in Las Vegas. Perhaps he could help Mrs. Higgins by keeping an eye out for Mr. Higgins—anything to keep his mind off Lorna and her odd behavior toward him.

She had treated him like a forward cowboy that she had to put in his place and not the man she had snuggled next to while traveling to safety. He had thought perhaps the idea of courtship wasn't too far off after their time on the train. And yet, she was almost cold to him today. He grabbed his Stetson and plopped it on his head. He had a job to do first and then he'd worry about how to woo Lorna into becoming his bride and moving out to a ranch with him where he could snuggle her all she wanted.

He crossed the street, the bawdy laughter greeting him. He never had the taste for such places himself but was familiar with them given his former line of work. He pushed open the swinging shutter doors, the heavy cigar smoke filling his nostrils along with pungent whiskey. Laughter trilled and he flicked up his brim, resting a hand on his gun belt at the sight of Higgins sitting at a corner round table with a mound of coins and cash in front of him and a fan of cards in hand. A woman in a brilliant emerald gown and a black feather boa was draped over his shoulder, pointing to his cards, and whispering in his ear, giggling.

Higgins stole a kiss from her, sending the table into ruckus laughter from the men. The woman in emerald slapped Higgins' chest and held out her hand. He dropped a silver dollar in her palm that she tucked in her bodice with a wink.

"Worth every penny!" He shouted and downed his whiskey glass, sucking in a sharp breath over the burn, no doubt.

Reid narrowed his gaze at the woman. She must have been one of the new arrivals. He would have remembered seeing a lady with a porcelain complexion that looked like it had never seen the harsh sun. She seemed vaguely familiar, but where would he know her? He approached the table, crossing his arms. "How's it going, Higgins?"

The man jerked his head up, mirth fading at the sight of Reid. He tilted his wire rimmed spectacles on the edge of his nose as he returned his attention to his cards. He lifted his empty glass to a passing saloon girl, who set a fresh drink before him. "Sheriff. Pretty good night for me."

"Your wife will be relieved."

Higgins snorted, flipping another coin onto the pile of cash in the center of the table. "She don't need to worry about nothing. I've got this under control. I always do."

"Why don't you head home while you still got some money lining your pockets?" It wasn't his place, but sympathy for Mrs. Higgins pushed him to step in on her behalf. "Don't you have a little one on the way?"

The woman caressed Higgins's shoulder. "It's early yet. How about one more drink while you finish this game, darlin'?"

Reid frowned at her. "How about you keep out of this conversation, Ma'am."

"Ma'am?" She drew out the word like it offended her, releasing a shrill laugh that had the few other saloon girls joining in. She preened her black feather boa as she sauntered around the table, hips swaying. "No one's called me that in a while."

He ignored the vixen and kept his gaze fixed on Higgins. "Well? You going home to your expecting wife?"

"Thanks a lot, Sheriff." Higgins tossed down his cards. "You made me lose my concentration." He growled as the man opposite him collected the pile of winnings in the center of the table. "Broke my luck. Might as well go home." He snatched up his ratty bowler hat and shoved back his chair as the woman in emerald arranged her arms about his neck, cajoling him for one more drink.

Satisfied he had done all he could, Reid shot out of that den of iniquity before one of the new saloon girls attempted to lure him to a table—not that he would ever allow them to do so, but he didn't like the idea of being seen near one of the women and word getting back to Lorna, making their already unsteady relationship even more so.

Reid waited outside the swinging doors for Higgins to come out. The man stumbled, his boot catching on the threshold. Reid seized his arm, steadying him. "Have a good evening, Mr. Higgins."

The man waved him off and staggered down the boardwalk, mumbling.

The woman in green appeared in the saloon window, her eyes narrowing on Reid, but when he turned to face her, she swung around to see to her table of clients. She seemed so familiar, but he couldn't place her. Maybe he would remember who she was with some sleep. He scrubbed a hand over the back of his neck and glanced down the street where the Castañeda stood and the adjacent Rawlins building. He found his feet moving before he had even decided to take one last check.

He paused in the courtyard of the hotel under the single massive live oak. The front windows of the dining room were ablaze with light, but only one or two tables were occupied at this hour and Lorna was sweeping while Corinna was replacing the used tapers on each of the tables that were still lacking linens. He recalled the note Colt had scrawled down. It was odd, but not exactly life threatening.

Lorna paused to arch her back and their gazes met through the glass. He could have sworn he felt her pulse quicken in his chest. She glanced over her shoulder and then lifted a finger to him. She disappeared from view for a moment. The front door swung wide.

"I thought I told you to get some rest," she chided and joined him under the branches, crossing her arms against the chill.

He shrugged out of his coat and draped it over her shoulders. To his pleasure, she didn't protest. "And you and I know each other well enough to acknowledge you are not the only stubborn member of this friendship. Maybe I wanted to see you."

Her lips quirked and a smile blossomed. "Well, maybe I wanted to see you too. I'm glad you came by."

The knot in his chest eased at her smile. He reached out his hand. She chewed her lip for a second before her fingers wrapped about his and he could have sworn he heard an infinitesimal exhale of content that echoed his own. After being together, seeking comfort in one another following the terrors of the trail, her absence had left him reeling.

"I'm sorry I was short earlier. It was uncalled for and I regretted my words the moment you left."

"Think nothing of it. But, why were you?"

"The short answer? Fear."

His grip tightened on her hand. . . if only he could help ease her fears. "Do you have time for a walk under the stars? I feel as if we haven't talked in weeks."

She dipped her head, a small smile playing at her lips again. "Corinna is finishing our shift in the dining room now, and, as I didn't take my break during the shift, I am off for the night. Corinna knows and will cover for me to give me fifteen minutes unchaperoned."

He had forgotten the Harvey House rules of courting. The idea of sitting in the Rawlins building's parlor with Miss Violet Trent in the corner reading a book had him tightening his grip on her hand and pulling her away from the Castañeda at a trot. Lorna giggled and followed suit, only slowing when they reached the blue chapel at the edge of town where the cedar trees grew tall and strong from the nearby creek where they used to play after particularly hot Sunday sermons. Brilliant stars filled the dark dome above with a few clouds drifting in front of the crescent moon, made all the more beautiful with this woman's hand in his. He looked down to their joined hands, wishing he didn't have to let her go. "How was your day?"

"Exhausting, but it is so good to be back at work." She lifted her skirt to step over a fallen branch. "And you? Are you bored to tears yet?"

He chuckled. She knew him well. "I've cried twice today, actually."

"I'll sew you some more handkerchiefs to get you through the year." She laughed, pulling away from him to sit beside the creek. She tugged the laces of her half boots, yanking them off, and rolled down her stockings.

He sank beside her and jerked off his boots and socks, tossed them a yard downwind, and immersed his feet into the creek along with Lorna. "Feels like the old days."

She leaned back on the palm of her hand, flicking a flat stone across the surface with the other. "Yes, but not quite the same."

With the moonlight on her lovely hair and full lips, caressing her every curve, he'd agree. He wanted to try that kiss again, but he had a feeling that now was not the time. She needed to recover from the ordeal . . . time to know that he saw her as more than a friend. He dropped his gaze to the babbling creek. "Tell me about your day."

Lorna flopped onto her side, propped up on one elbow, and turned to him, her toes dangling above the water. "What would you like to hear first? How I scrubbed spit from the floors after an uncouth cowpoke dined at the lunch counter? Or when I cleaned up after a sick child with remarkable projectile skills?"

"Both sound fascinating." He grinned as he reached into his coat pocket for the treat he had purchased this morning but hadn't had a chance to give her, and removed a sack of licorice, tossing it to her.

She squealed as she caught it, already knowing what was inside from the sweet smell wafting from it. She handed him a piece and grabbed a strip for herself. She regaled the day, and he was pleased to find out how much fun she was having with Corinna, though he did worry about Dolly Matthews giving her a hard time.

"But I suppose when one has been abducted by outlaws, Dolly has dropped in one's tier of terror." Lorna laughed, finishing off the last piece of candy. At the hoot in the trees, she groaned as she pulled herself up. "We better get back, lest people begin a rumor about the two of us spending so much time alone. Townsfolk might start treating you differently if they think you are more than a friend to me."

"Would it be a rumor if it is true?" His hand found hers.

Lorna's eyes widened, a soft smile playing at her lips before she snatched up her stockings and shoes. She motioned for him to turn.

"We've spent the past hour with your ankles in plain view, Lorna."

"Yes, but stockings take some wrangling when pulling over wet limbs."

He chuckled but put his back to her anyway and fetched his socks and boots. Both properly attired, they wove through the trees back to the edge of town. If he didn't speak now, he wasn't sure when he would have the chance again and with Lorna around so many eligible bachelors day in and day out, he didn't dare wait a moment more. He grasped her hand, tugging her into the shadows of the cedar branches. "Lorna, I want to make one thing very clear."

She scowled. "Gaston Reid, I am not going to let you set in my dining room all day. At some point, we have to put aside our fears of the Death Riders and move on with our lives. I can't have you putting your duties on hold for me."

He smirked. "If I'm a paying customer, you won't have a choice, but that wasn't what I was talking about." He lifted her chin and leaning forward, whispered, "I was serious when I said that I want a do-over on that kiss. And when it happens, you'll know that it wasn't done because we were under gun point."

She gasped and stepped back, stumbling over a fallen branch. Reid wrapped his arm about her waist, not that she was in any danger from sprawling in the dirt, but he'd take the excuse to hold her close—to convince her that he belonged to her and she to him. "Lorna Elliot," he whispered. "Do you have any idea what you do to me?"

She drew her lips in, wetting them and it took everything in him not to kiss her senseless.

"I-I don't."

He rested his forehead to hers. "Shall I show you?

A rustling in the bushes sounded to the left. He threw himself in front of her, weapon drawn when a spray hit him in the chest, sending him sprawling into Lorna.

CHAPTER 15

*H*er eyes watered as she clamped her hand over her nose and mouth. "Fool skunk was climbing the cedar tree. Are your eyes okay, Gaston?" Lorna had seen many a dog temporarily blinded from skunk spray, and she didn't doubt that could happen to a man.

He swiped his arm over his eyes, squinting and blinking rapidly. "They are burning something fierce. Everything is fuzzy."

"Come on. We need to get you back to the creek." She gripped him by the back of his arm and guided him. To his credit, he stumbled along without protest, or complaining about the sting. She removed his gun harness and belt and pulled him into the creek, not caring that the water soaked through her skirt and shoes, even though they would not dry before her next shift. She cupped the water and held it to his face, pushing his head to the water.

"What the—"

"You have to flush your eyes right away, or the symptoms get much worse. You would think you would know this being a ranger."

"Being a ranger doesn't mean I am good at everything, or that I've ever managed to get sprayed by a skunk."

"Well, that's news to me. You showed up at our ranchero mighty malodorous a time or two." She giggled, cupping handfuls of water to his eyes until he groaned and dunked his face into the river a few times.

He flipped his hair out of his eyes, exhaling. "My vision is clearing now."

"Good, because you still stink to high heaven." Lorna smirked and pushed him backwards into the creek, giggling.

He whipped out of the water, sputtering.

He wiped the water from his eyes, a dangerous smirk overtaking his expression. "Lorna Elliot. You are asking for it, missy!"

She squealed as he lunged for her, tackling her into the water and cushioning her landing with his arms. She gasped as she broke through the water, her hair plastered to her face. She couldn't contain the giggle at the sight of Gaston dripping wet beside her on his hands and knees. "We are going to have a time explaining this."

He slathered his hair out of his face once more. "Might see a scandal that forces you to the altar."

She rolled her eyes at his dimpled grin. "Maybe for some of those fancy socialites, but things are different out here in the West thankfully."

"What? You wouldn't want to marry me?" He sat back on his heels.

Her heart stuttered. Gaston had been flirting with her for these past few weeks, but it was going to take more than a few weeks of her catching his eye to make her set aside the walls she had so painstakingly built around her heart in regard to him.

"That's something we shouldn't joke about —ever." She held her hand out to him. "And I only meant that if I had to live such a sheltered life as some of those fine ladies, it would be hard to have much fun."

He hefted her to her feet and together, they scrambled out of the creek bed, which took some doing being weighed down by their clothes.

"I fear I still have the skunk on me." Gaston wrung out his vest. "Does the Harvey House have a barrel of tomato sauce I can buy?"

She wrung out her hem and grinned up at him. "Oh, only baking soda will take that stink out."

He shook his head. "I thought tomato sauce was the answer to getting the stink out."

"Only if you want a huge mess and have to bathe in it for hours. Baking soda is far more effective, and it will save your clothes from the burn pile."

He quirked a brow. "Then why did you push me in the creek?"

She shrugged, giggling. "I felt like it."

He lunged for her again, pulling her back into the water.

"Gaston!"

"I feel like you need a good dunking."

"No!" She squealed, wrapping her arms about his neck. "If I go down, you go down with me."

He halted, his chest heaving as if acutely aware of her plastered against his chest. "Always."

She slowly released her hold on him, sliding down to her feet. "We better head back."

With his guns slung over his shoulder, the pair wove through the trees and into town. Their shoes squished with every step, but thankfully, due to the late hour, only the saloon was busy and as that was not near the Harvey House, Gaston and Lorna were able to sneak to the dormitory door without being spotted by anyone.

"Thank you for the highly relaxing walk," Lorna teased as she stood before her door. "But you better go hide in the shadows across the street while I get the house mother to let me inside."

"And if I want us to be caught?"

"Really, Gaston. The way you are talking would make any girl think you wanted to marry her." At the glint in his eye, she whipped to the door and knocked thrice. "Go now!"

His chuckle sounded further away from her, and she did not dare to look back to see his grin. Whatever game Gaston was playing at was dangerous. If he did not mean to marry her, then she had best not play.

The door creaked open, and Miss Violet Trent appeared, clutching her robe at her throat. "You are late returning from your shift." The door widened as she gestured to Lorna's soaked clothes. "What on earth happened?"

"I went for a walk and had a run-in with a skunk. Thankfully, it missed me, but I still soaked in the creek to clean my clothes just in case." She left out any mention of Gaston Reid. It *was* the West, but some constraints of propriety still remained, especially as a Harvey Girl.

Miss Trent pressed her lips into a thin

line, clearly not fooled, and waved her inside. "They may have allowed you moonlit walks at the Montezuma, but you should know better than to do so in Las Vegas. Consider this your one and only warning."

"Yes, ma'am."

"Good." Her nose wrinkled. "Even if you don't smell, you had an encounter with a skunk. Bathe, toss your clothes in the laundry bag, and set it out on the back porch."

So MUCH FOR his romantic gesture of an amble under the stars and having another crack at that magical kiss. *Pretty sure an attempt at kissing has never gone worse in the history of courtship.* He kicked at a tumbleweed along the boardwalk to his office where his cot awaited . . . that would have to continue to wait until he filled his metal tub with hot water and some baking soda, if the former sheriff had left any in the cabinet, that is. Reid was not a baker.

Slurred singing grated his ear. Higgins

had propped himself against the wood pillar of the saloon's porch with an empty bottle in hand, his tongue licking the rim to get the very last drop. *Not even a Friday night and I've got to lock up Higgins until he sobers up.* "I thought I told you to go home."

"And that pretty lady came and got me." He grinned, his eyes unfocused. "Can't say no to such a pretty lady."

"You most certainly can when you have a *wife* awaiting you at home." Reid snatched his collar and hauled him to his feet, the man yowling in protest.

"You smell worse than a wet dog that's been rolling in nature's perfume parlor."

"Better get used to it. You going to be smelling it all night, locked up in your favorite cell until you sleep off the alcohol." Reid chuckled under his breath and crossed the street. "Putting up with skunk stink all night might teach you to stop drinking so much." He kicked open the door and released Higgins who stumbled to his cell, shut the cell door behind himself, and collapsed on his cot, snoring within seconds.

Reid removed the galvanized tub from

the hook on the outside back wall of the building and lugged it into his room when he caught sight of something in the front window. He quietly set down the other end of the tub and reached for his gun. Who would be poking around the prison? He pressed his back to the wall and peeked out. Emerald skirts vanished around the corner. Why would the saloon girl follow Higgins? He gripped his gun and threw open the door, darting after where she had disappeared. She was nowhere in sight. He would question Higgins thoroughly about the woman in the morning, but right now, his own stink was making his eyes water. Bath first, sleep second, and then figure out who this woman was and why she was so interested in Higgins.

CHAPTER 16

"*D*on't tell me that you cannot come to dinner tonight when I know for a fact that you will be free in exactly one hour." Gil crossed his arms, scowling at Lorna as she poured him a second cup of coffee at the lunch counter.

"I don't think it's a good idea. I'm new to this Harvey House and I probably should spend time in the Harvey Girl parlor to bond more with the women."

Gil gulped down his coffee in a manner that had her wincing and wondering how his throat had not been burned. "You are avoiding coming home. Why, Lorna? Ma and Pa are aching to come see you, but you know how they are whenever one of them is recovering from a cold."

"They never set foot in town."

"Right. Now, am I going to have to drag you home? What's the problem?"

I'm avoiding a certain good kisser. Her cheeks flamed at the memory of his lips on hers that would be seared onto her heart for a lifetime and then again, last night, he had acted like he wanted to kiss her again before the skunk interrupted them. "Gil, you were the one who dared me to do something different with my life. That dare had some serious consequences." *And not only in regard to controlling my schedule . . . but by bringing Gaston Reid into my daily routines.*

"I dared you to become a waitress because you were teasing Harriet about her lack of skills on the ranch, and I thought you should get a taste of your own teasing by becoming a Harvey Girl and see how hard Harriet has worked her whole adult life and the skills it took for her to become a head waitress."

"And I apologized to her for teasing. I honestly didn't know I was bothering either of you. I was trying to banter with her over how she couldn't even milk a cow." She shook her head. "I'm learning more and more what it means to be a good friend. I understand now that not everyone enjoys teasing. And before you ask, I'm no longer upset that Harriet interfered with changing my post."

He pushed his coffee cup to her again. "If you aren't mad at Harriet, then what is stopping you?"

Gaston. He is confusing me with his hints to attempt our kiss again. And I know that he doesn't mean to tease me, but most of my child-hood involved Gaston's teasing me about one thing or another, which led to me calling him by his first name in the first place and now it's hard to tell the difference between his teasing and flirt-ing. But she couldn't say what she was think-ing. If Gilbert knew she still cared for Gaston in that manner . . . well, she could not endure his pity again and with Gaston being a cousin to her sister-in-law, things could get sticky between Gaston, Gil, and Harriet. It was all too complicated. She set aside her preference, along with her brother's empty coffee cup. "Does it really mean that much to you and the family that I attend the dinner?"

"Yes! Have you forgotten what day it is?"

She tilted her head. "Wednesday? It's not our usual Sunday dinner night."

"Which you haven't attended in weeks. We are meeting in the middle of the week because it's Reid's birthday and you know that Harriet is his cousin, so we will, of course, be hosting him."

Her mouth dropped. She had never in her life forgotten his birthday. Maybe the walls around the Gaston section of her heart were actually working? "I suppose I did forget. I'm assuming his aunt will be in attendance?"

"Unfortunately," Gil sighed.

Lorna pinched the bridge of her nose. Gaston's aunt did not particularly care for her, being an Elliot and all. Before her time at the Harvey House, she never really understood how lonely her life was on the ranch. It was a beautiful life, but lonely. Now, these women, Harvey Girls from all walks of life and from around the United

States, accepted her as she was and did not care about her family's reputation in the dusty town of Las Vegas. She was stronger for her time as a Harvey Girl and she would not allow Harriet's Aunt Gertrude to make her feel dirty, or less than worthy. She would smile and be kind, but not allow it to seep into her thoughts and soul.

"Fine. I'll go to keep the peace."

He grinned. "Good, because Reid is riding to the ranch in his aunt's surrey and left Bunny at the stable for your use. I told him that you'd be safe enough riding home in broad daylight. However, Reid will want to escort you home, so you won't have to worry about the late hour after the party."

Which meant he would be riding behind her on Bunny. *Wonderful.* She could be strong. She had to be strong to withstand his hardened muscles. She gave a dramatic sigh that she was certain her brother expected. "Thanks, but am I never to have Bunny to myself?"

"Once you are done working, I'm sure Reid will be happy to stop exercising your horse for you." He slapped on his hat. "Thanks for the coffee."

"It's not on the house."

"Sure, it's not." He winked at her.

"Gil, you are going to get me into trouble."

"What's the point of having a sister as a Harvey Girl if I can't even get a free cup of coffee out of it?" He slid a coin to her. "Since you forgot his birthday, I'm assuming you'll want me to write your name on the card for the gift Harriet and I got him."

She shifted from foot to foot, warring over the merits of confessing that she had already gotten him a gift six months ago when she was still violently in love with the man. Who was she trying to fool? She was *still* a goner when it came to him, but she had pride on her side now. "I, uh, I picked something up for him a little while ago before life got busy." She shrugged as if she hadn't searched up and down for the perfect gift in a catalog and had it special ordered to ensure it would arrive on time. It really was painful when she stopped and thought of how much she had obsessed over him.

His gift rested at the top of her closet at the ranchero, hidden in an overlarge box, already wrapped, and ready to be given to him.

At the end of her shift, Lorna didn't have much time to change into her lovely periwinkle silk gown. She loved the brilliant color after wearing black and white for so many weeks. She arranged her hair into a coronet braid, knowing it would be the surest way to keep her hair neat after the ride home. She drew on her cycling bloomers that she never used as she had crashed her old velocipede on a dare from her brother two months ago. She wasn't about to wear a split skirt to a birthday party with Harriet's aunt present, but neither was she about to give the town a show worthy of the saloon's stage, not that she had ever seen the soiled doves dance, but she had heard enough over the years of their performances to make her skin crawl.

She hurried to the stables, eager to ride her stallion. The stable boy had the horse ready for her and using the mounting block, she settled into the saddle, arranging her billowing skirts as best she could to cover as much of the cycling bloomers as possible. She rode out of the town at a walk, sending Bunny into trot at the last building, then a canter, and a gallop. The wind whipped through her hair and the sheer freedom made her heart light after too much time spent wrapped in her own troubles. She dropped the reins and lifted her arms above her head, laughing in delight with Bunny lengthening his stride and setting a pace that would have had her ma shouting at her to slow down.

Bunny followed the curve of the road around a foothill, and she nearly lost her grip with her legs at the row of horses barricading the road. The riders were slim with hats pulled low and bandanas pulled over their noses. *The Death Riders.* She fumbled for the reins as the leader of the women released a shrill shout as they charged at her. She did not hesitate to direct Bunny off the road and up the steep hill, trusting Bunny's wild stallion's strength and sure footing to keep her safe as the gang charged after her.

She didn't bother to scream for help. No one would hear her. She pressed low on Bunny's neck as they reached the crest, racing down the other side of the foothill. The pounding of hooves filled her ears, but she knew better than to look back yet. Anything that could throw off her speed even by a second should be avoided. The other riders must not have been that talented as they soon fell behind, judging from the hoofbeats.

She risked a glance. The riders halted at the crest behind her. *Are they giving up?* Her throat tightened as her terror caught up with her racing heart now that the danger seemed to abate, but she did not dare stop until she reached the sanctuary of her family's ranch in case it was a trap. A surrey was parked at the front door.

"Pa!" She screamed, even as she longed to shout for the one man who could out-shoot even her. "Gaston!"

The pounding of Bunny's hooves brought the front door slamming open. Gaston ran out to her, reaching up for her as Bunny skidded to a halt, his coat mottled with sweat. She slid into Gaston's arms, shaking now.

He held her, running his hands over her shoulders and back as if searching for a bullet wound. "What happened? Lorna, tell me this instant."

Pa, Ma, Gil, Harriet and Gaston's aunt and uncle appeared in the doorway, but she was trembling so hard she didn't care that they saw her taking comfort in Gaston's arms until Pa drew near and she rammed into his chest.

"What happened, daughter?" Pa's voice trembled. "Are you hurt?"

She shook her head. "No, but th-they were waiting for me."

"Who?" Gaston interjected, planting his hands in his hair as he seemed to attempt to lasso his worry.

"Outlaws . . . the Death Riders."

Gaston released a word that brought a scowl from Ma and a correction from his aunt. He trotted inside.

She pushed away from Pa as the group discussed this turn of events, and Lorna followed Gaston inside to the back kitchen where he gathered his gun belt from the hooks beside the door. "Gaston, you can't go out there alone. There are too many."

"I need to find them." He spun the cylinder of his Colt revolver, checking his bullets and clicked it shut, repeating the process with each weapon and securing them in holsters at his hips and chest. "If I don't catch them, they will keep coming after you—again and again." He grasped her hand. "You have to trust me to know what I am doing."

"It's not that I don't trust you. I do. More than anyone."

"Then what is it?" He settled his Stetson into place and held the back door open for her just as the family moved to the front parlor.

She followed him to the stables. She couldn't be around anyone but him right now. "I thought the danger was over."

"I didn't, and I should have been more diligent with following up on the threat and not relying on the rangers and Tanner to apprehend the gang when I knew I could." He clenched his jaw and grabbed a bridle off the rack and moved to the stall holding a gelding. "I should have never signed on to be sheriff. Not when—"

"Stop blaming yourself right now. How were you to know the outlaw gang would rise again after Grant *escaped* jail and broke out his wife? How could you have prepared for the Death Rider women to attack again even after Grant's second arrest?" She crossed her arms, shivering as thunder rumbled. She glanced out the open stable door to the billowing gray clouds sweeping across the prairie. "Don't head out without backup. They are long gone by now."

"I never needed backup as a ranger, and there will be tracks that I need to study before they get rained out."

"Which will be any second." Lorna rested her hand on his arm, desperate to keep him from riding out to face the outlaws alone. "Please don't leave me. I don't feel safe when you are not near," she whispered. "Please stay." Rain pelted the roof and his shoulders sagged. They both knew the trail would be lost in a matter of seconds.

He pulled her into his arms, resting his

chin atop her hair. "No use now, so there's no need to worry you anymore."

She exhaled, relief flooding her lungs as she sagged into him. The fright had weakened her more than she had realized. "Thank you. Do you think it possible that Jill escaped and is giving orders to the women again?"

"Tanner hasn't sent a telegram about an escape." He tightened his hold on her. "Lorna, it will be well. We will find these women and put them behind bars."

"Will we?" She peered up at him. "I don't know what to do. Wherever I go, they find me. I don't know why they are so determined. I'm no one to them."

"You made Jill look the fool. She will never forgive you for tricking her into letting you kiss me." He sighed. "There really is only one way to keep you safe. You need to disappear for a time."

"Where to?" She lifted her gaze to him. "Should I change my name and move to another Harvey House?"

"Something like that. Let's join the group in the parlor and discuss a plan with your parents." He pressed a kiss to her hair.

She stiffened and nearly vaulted out of his arms as she put some distance between them. "You need to stop doing that."

"Doing what?"

"Kissing my hair." She crossed her arms. "It's not proper."

"No kissing?" He tilted his head, a mischievous glint in his eyes, and slid his hand into hers. "This acceptable?"

It was more than acceptable—it was marvelous. "I suppose so."

***

AUNT GERTRUDE'S hawk eyes pierced him as he darted inside the Elliot's home with his hand in Lorna's, both dripping from the downpour.

Despite his aunt's pursed lips, he kept his hand wrapped about Lorna's. He had never seen her so frightened, even when he saved her from Grant Lawson. Her confession of not feeling safe without him sent a surge of protectiveness through him that was all consuming—as if God Himself had set a fire in his belly and said this was his new calling.

He motioned to his aunt and uncle to join them. "Did you happen to see anyone else on the road here?"

"You were with us. You know as well as we that we did not see a soul that we haven't known for years." His aunt kept her disapproving gaze on him.

He could fairly hear her protests that she would not have a second relation tying them to the Elliots. *When is she going to release this grudge?*

"What is going on? I thought we were coming to celebrate a birthday today." Aunt Gertrude snipped at Harriet.

"We are, but there have been some problems for the Elliots lately," Harriet replied, resting a hand on her belly.

Is she with child? Harriet had been paler of late, but he knew better than to ask after an encounter in church when he well-meaningly asked a woman when she was expecting—she was, in fact, *not* expecting a baby. Thankfully, as a ranger at the time, he could avoid that church for a while, but every time he saw her, he remembered that moment and he was certain she did too. He shook the memory from his mind and focused on the matter at hand.

"Aren't there always issues at the Elliot Ranch? Only months ago, Harriet's husband was shot by the Death Riders."

"It is the same gang." Harriet exhaled, as if her patience was wearing thin. "But this is a new development. An old enemy of Reid's is threatening Lorna."

Aunt Gertrude frowned at Lorna as if she were inconvenienced by this threat. "I see."

Ma Elliot wrapped Lorna in a blanket and offered a second to Reid, whispering, "Reid, change into something of Gil's. Lorna, your spare party gown is hanging in your closet, of course."

"No disrespect, Ma Elliot, but I think your daughter's safety is of paramount importance at the moment, and I don't think that having a party right now would be—"

She smiled softly and patted Reid's cheek. "We know that present fear and sorrow should not allow happy moments to go by unnoticed. One could say that it makes the sweet moments all the more dear, for we do not know when they will come again."

Lorna pulled the blanket tight about her shoulders. "We will be out in a moment. We have a birthday to celebrate after all."

Ma nodded. "We shall start with cake and presents. At the meal, I know you all would like to discuss a plan for my daughter's safety."

While the prospect of a party seemed trite in light of Lorna's ordeal, he would never hurt Ma Elliot. "As you wish, ma'am. Did you say cake before the meal?"

Ma Elliot smiled up at Reid. "I know you prefer your sweets, and, as it is your day, we shall eat dessert first."

"You know me well." He kissed Ma Elliot's cheek and strode down the hall to Gil's old room that was now the guest room with a closet of his Spring clothes, since he and Harriet moved out to a smaller cabin on the Elliot land. Lorna disappeared through the door opposite.

He drew on a red checkered shirt of Gil's

that was significantly tighter and pulled against his muscles in a fashion that restricted his movements. He'd bust the thin shirt if he had to move fast enough to draw his guns. He shut the door behind him and leaned against the wall, intent on waiting for her, even if there was a party in his honor in the parlor. With the threat so near, he couldn't bear the thought of being any further apart than necessary.

Lorna soon appeared in a hunter green gown that complimented her tanned cheeks and dark eyes. She carried an overlarge rectangle package that was stamped with a design and tied with ribbon. He leaned forward, examining the pattern. "Are those Ranger stars?"

Her cheeks bloomed. He liked her blush much more than her panic. She twisted her lips to the side, sheepish.

"I carved a stamp out of a potato and used some of the paint we had left over from painting Ma's kitchen cabinets. The plain brown paper from the general store is hardly festive."

He reached for the gift, examining the

blue stamps. "You had time to do all that for me?"

She dipped her head. "I did it before."

"When you were in Topeka?"

She clasped her hands behind her back and became very interested in a pine knot in the floorboards. "Before that. You'll probably think the gift is silly."

His heart skipped. She had thought of his birthday *months* in advance? He lifted her chin with his fingers. "Coming from you, I know I'll love it."

She twisted her hands. "D-do you want to open it now? Away from everyone else?"

"Why? Did you give me something scandalous?" He chuckled and pulled the string.

MAYBE IT WOULD HAVE BEEN BETTER SIMPLY letting the gift gather dust than reveal to him how much I wanted him to love his gift? It was too late now as he began unwrapping the stamped package, revealing the leather beneath.

His jaw worked as he took in the cattle

trail boots she had special ordered. He lifted one out, running his hand over the scalloped top of tan calf skin above the darker calf skin, giving the pair a fancy design while still being serviceable.

"I-I noticed that you have resoled your boots at least three times. I know you must love those boots, but I figured it might be time for a new pair."

He ran his fingers over the leather, his silence making her ears ring.

"I'm sure I can get my money back for them if you hate them." She had ordered them too long ago to return, but she could sell them for a loss to one of the cowpokes on the ranch.

"This is the most thoughtful gift anyone has ever given me." He lifted his gaze to her, a soft look in his eyes that she had never seen before. He held the boots in one arm and pulled her to him with the other, pressing a kiss to her cheek. "I love the gift."

Her heart stuttered at the contact. "You won't miss your old ones? I know they are special to you."

He chuckled. "I only had them resoled so

many times because I didn't have time to special order any boots for myself before I needed to leave town and then, I kept forgetting the need until the next time I had the boots resoled." He stroked her cheek with his thumb. "These took a lot of thought and must've cost you a week's salary."

"You are worth it," she whispered. "And I wanted to get you something you'd love."

"You guessed right." He tugged off his boots and pulled on the new square-toed ones. He grinned. "Well, I'll be. They fit perfectly. How did you get my shoe size?"

She swallowed thinking of how she had traced his shoe from the imprint in the dirt outside the barn the last time they were both on the ranch, brought it to the cobbler's, determined the size to order, and sent for them. It was too embarrassing to admit. She shrugged. "I have my ways."

"It's a stunning gift to a man who is not your beau."

Her cheeks surged with fresh warmth. What was he trying to do? Make her admit that she had carried a massive torch—*bon-*

fire—for him? "Well, I owed you for coming to my rescue."

"You don't owe me for anything, Lorna. I'll always be there when you need me."

He was trying to make her melt into the hardwood floors, and it was working. At Harriet's laughter coming from the front of the ranchero, they both sighed. She stole a glance up at him. Did he want to stay in this hallway with her instead of visiting with her entire family? She would never admit it, not even to Corinna, how much she missed it being just the two of them on the trail. Certainly, it had been dangerous, but with him, she had never felt safer.

He offered her his arm. "Shall we?"

The family all gathered around the table where a large chocolate cake stood in the center, the Elliots all cheering when they entered. His aunt and uncle had firm smiles in place as if the hullabaloo hurt their ears.

Lorna's grip tightened on Gaston's arm, and she noticed Gil's raised brow at the new boots and her hand placement. She should release Gaston. But she was feeling more and more at home being by him, touching him. And yet, he had made her no promises, and she would not allow herself to return to being besotted with him without any hope of being loved in return. She stepped back and focused on her slice of cake, smiling as expected at each present, and enjoying the following meal.

"Good thing the rain stopped as the present from Ma Elliot and myself is outside." Pa Elliot grinned, rising from the table.

"Outside?" Gaston's grin grew. "What did you do, Pa Elliot?"

Pa waved him out and Lorna followed closely behind. If she had been home, she would have likely been in on the secret, but she was just as curious as Gaston. One of the ranch hands stood just outside the front door holding a lead line. She gasped at the beautiful mare that perfectly matched Bunny, besides its white tail.

"We caught this mustang last month. Finally broke her and thought you'd like to have a horse of your own."

Gaston's jaw dropped. "I couldn't accept such a gift."

"Only cost us the time it took to train her." Pa shoved his hands into his pockets and rocked back on his heels. "You've done a lot for our family, especially in recent weeks, and you need a good mount now that yours is out to pasture, and Lorna will be wanting Bunny again. Please, allow us to bless you."

He stroked the horse's mane, the horse sniffing his hand. He rubbed her nose, unable to hold back his grin. "I can't thank you both enough."

Ma patted his arm. "You thank us simply by being a part of this family, dear boy."

Thunder rumbled overhead, and the men moved to take the horse to the stable, Lorna following. If they were going to begin the discussion of what to do, it would happen in the stables, away from his relatives, and she had no intention of being left out of the planning of her life.

"Lorna, shouldn't you help your ma?" Pa rested a hand on her shoulder, staying her.

"What you are discussing involves me."

"She should be part of the conversation, sir," Gaston agreed.

Pa slowly nodded and motioned her into the stables. Gaston drew the mare into a stall and reached for a brush, running it over the mare's already shining coat, but Lorna knew that the practice would help him stay grounded while bonding with the horse.

Pa crossed his arms, leaning against the stall threshold. "Reid, you and I both know that if the Death Riders have marked her, they will not stop until they find her and finish what they started."

Lorna fought against the urge to tremble. She reached for a bucket of oats and offered it to the mare, who accepted with a single sniff.

Gil reached for another brush, joining Reid in the grooming, and betraying how anxious he was on her behalf. "Then she needs to disappear."

She straightened at that, but kept her mouth closed lest her father send her back inside with the women and Gaston's relatives.

"Where would you suggest?" Pa

frowned. "You are the expert. What will keep my daughter safe?"

Gaston met Pa's gaze. "She needs to go somewhere they will never expect—somewhere they will not dare to chase her."

Before he could elaborate, figures appeared in the stable doors. Of all the times for his aunt and uncle to appear, now was not one of them. Lorna already felt too exposed, but to feel vulnerable in front of them? She met Gaston's gaze, and he offered her a sympathetic smile as if sensing her discomfort.

Ma joined them as well, gripping her coffee cup with both hands, concern leaking from her eyes. "What are we to do, Reid?"

"There is only one thing to be done. Lorna must disappear for a time while Tanner Sterling and the rangers find out the Death Riders' next move."

"Is it in the rangers' jurisdiction?" Ma countered.

Gaston abandoned the brush and motioned Gil out of the stall. "Grant and his crew have committed many crimes in the state of Texas. They will consider this their problem."

"What do you plan to do?" Gil asked. "I know you have a plan. You would never sit by while one of us was in danger. You never did."

"I think she needs to hide somewhere far enough from New Mexico that even the Death Riders will hesitate to follow."

"Where?" Lorna whispered, exhausted from the strain of feeling safe and then having that security ripped away in an instant.

"I want to take you to my family's home in Newport, Rhode Island."

Aunt Gertrude gasped. "You cannot be serious."

"This situation calls for nothing but that," Gaston replied.

Lorna shot to her feet. "Gaston Reid. I've never been out of the West, and you think the best way to keep me safe is to throw me to a different sort of wolf all together?" She released a short, scoffing laugh. "I'd be an embarrassment to you around all those fine ladies and their manners."

"You could never be an embarrassment." Gaston shifted to stand beside her.

"Actually," Ma traced the rim of her coffee cup. "I think it might be a good idea. We will miss you dreadfully, but this way, we can be certain you are safe until the Death Riders are put away once and for all. I do not believe they will go so far as to follow you into the gilded halls of society's elite." She chuckled. "They would be caught in a heartbeat in their western garb and wild ways."

"Gilded halls? Ma, you cannot be serious. Please, please tell me you aren't going to force me to give up my position as a Harvey Girl." To her shame, her voice wavered. She knew it was foolish to be so upset when she had only been a Harvey Girl for two months, but she loved her work. She loved her friendships. She loved the woman she was becoming. Did she really have to surrender all now she was finally at the point that she was maturing?

Gaston scrubbed a hand over the back of his neck. She knew he hated the position she was facing due to evil that he had inadvertently brought near the family. He was the reason the gang had marked Lorna. However, she knew it began because of the funds she could bring them, but the lie Lorna had told them about being married to Gaston had made it personal. She was no longer a way to line their pockets. She was Grant's ticket to the ultimate revenge— tearing out Gaston's heart.

"Do you have a better idea, Lorna?" Gaston grasped her fingers.

Her lip trembled, the truth spilling out of her. "I-I barely fit in Las Vegas. I am finally making friends. Can you imagine how the women in Newport will treat me? A country girl without an ounce of the training those ladies have?" She shook her head. "I'll be destroyed in minutes."

"I will be with you every step of the way. I will take care of you and protect you—no matter what we face."

"And Lorna, never forget, you have one thing that those rich people want." Pa drew his arm over her shoulders as he pressed a kiss to her forehead.

"What's that?"

"Besides a sweet spirit and a heart of gold, you and Gil will one day own Elliot Ranch. You both will own thousands of acres."

She smiled up at him, her soul warmed by his love. "Pa, our ranch is beautiful, and I could never ask for more, but these women are boasting of . . ." She knew she looked shamefaced as she pushed out the whisper, "millions in wealth."

Pa nodded. "We may not be worth millions in cash, but the life we have built out here is priceless, and I have a feeling that one day, this land will be worth far more."

She grasped her pa's hand and gave him a trembling smile. She hated the idea of leaving her job, but as she liked being free and *alive,* she had little choice but to break her contract with Fred Harvey. "Our family is priceless to me as well, which is why I'm even considering this horrible plan."

"Lorna, you scared?" Gil asked, crossing his arms.

Of course I am scared. Lorna scowled at him, seeing at once that he was goading her, preparing to do the one thing that would make her go without hesitation. "Don't even think about it, Gilbert Elliot."

"I *dare* you to spend at least one week in Newport. If you do, I'll be your servant for one week. If you lose, you have to serve Harriet for one week."

She shook her head, even as the childish temptation to boss around her brother took root. "Gil . . . that is playing in an ungentle-manly behavior."

"I never claimed I was a gentleman." Gil chuckled. "Well, Sis? You going to take this dare?"

She sighed. She never could resist his dares. She should know better by now, but this infernal blaze in her belly to rise to the challenge never failed to flame when Gil tossed down the leather glove. "Fine, but it is the *last* dare I'll ever take from you, or anyone else. You hear? I'm not that girl I once was."

"Sure, it is." He winked.

Aunt Gertrude harumphed, turning up her nose in elegant indignation. "You do not think the Death Riders will simply redirect their aim on the Elliot family, or even your own, Reid?"

"You will be safe enough, I believe." Pa interjected, resting a hand on Gertrude's shoulder, sending her skittering to her husband's side. "But, if you feel threatened, you and your husband are welcome to the guest room. The hands are good with guns, and you will be protected."

"If you are so well armed, why send Lorna away?" Aunt Gertrude challenged.

"We do not wish to invite trouble. It will be far easier for all parties if they know Lorna has simply vanished."

"Oh? And I am supposed to take your word on this? That everyone left in New Mexico will be safe from their wrath?"

"They know that Lorna is . . ." Pa glanced between Lorna and Gaston and finished, "special to Reid."

Gaston released his hold on Lorna and crossed his arms. "Of course, she is. All of you are. I would do the same for any one of my citizens who were in danger."

Gil rolled his eyes and slapped Gaston on the back. "You keep telling yourself that. You can pretend it's all in the name of your work, but I've seen the way you defend her and it's more like a man defending his woman than a sheriff defending his town."

Lorna drew in a sharp breath and nearly choked. She looked to Gaston, waiting for him to protest, but he simply planted his hands in his pockets and glared out the stable doors, searching for trouble.

Was it true? Had Gaston defended her like he thought of her as more than a friend . . . as a woman he cared for? Despite her trying to squelch the idea, hope glowed in her heart that maybe Gaston Reid might be hers after all. It was a wonderful and entirely embarrassing revelation to have in front of their families. "I-I suppose I should pack."

Gaston caught her hand. "Thank you for understanding."

"I'll help you." Ma followed Lorna to her bedroom, opening the closet door, sorting through the small array of gowns, and laying out the fanciest on the bed, planting her hands on her hips. "I didn't realize how much of your wardrobe was comprised of split skirts before now." She laughed, shaking her head. "But I suppose that having three fine gowns will be enough as you are going to Newport to be safe and not to socialize."

Lorna lifted the lid of her jewelry box on her vanity, withdrawing three pieces, a ruby ring that had been her grandmother's, a thin gold necklace given to her by Pa on her thirteenth birthday, and the glass bead Gaston had sent her years ago that she had put on a leather string and tied to her wrist as a bracelet. She had only removed it when she had begun working at the Harvey House. She rolled the bead between her fingers.

"Lorna, I hope you know how proud we are of you and how much you will be missed."

She slipped the ring on her finger and fixed the leather bracelet to her wrist. It would be hidden beneath her cuff, and she had the feeling that she needed as much familiarity as she could manage with the journey ahead. "I'll be back soon, Ma."

She cupped Lorna's cheek, a knowing smile at her lips. "But much can happen in a month. Outlaws captured . . . along with hearts."

CHAPTER 17

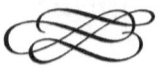

N ewport, Rhode Island

SHE WAS GOING to get back at Gil if it was the last thing she did before the Death Riders came for her. Even though her pretty gowns were made of fine cloth and silk, she knew she looked like a dowdy cowgirl in this first-class carriage to Newport. It had become blatantly obvious that her gown, though made by the town's seamstress, was inferior in every way. The cuts of the Newport women's gowns, along with the details and craftsmanship of each piece was unlike anything she had ever seen, and she suspected they were sent over from that Paris dress shop she read about once. But she kept her head up and pride in her shoulders. *This is the worst idea anyone has ever had. I have got to stop taking dares. It's immature and not fitting a woman of my age.* She jolted at his touch, whipping to face Gaston. "What?"

Gaston chuckled. "We are here. You didn't hear me the first two times I called your name. Where were you?"

"My head is too crowded these days to leave me much time for peace. It takes everything in me, and a whole lot of prayer, to keep myself from focusing on the negative."

"If anyone can overcome this situation, it's you, Lorna Elliot." He extended his hand to her.

"Thank you. I always appreciated how you took note of things in me that I didn't see myself." She rose, legs stiff after the long hours of riding trains. Gaston didn't even allow them enough time to take a night at a hotel, choosing instead to wait on the platform for the soonest train, which was why she felt so wrinkled and filthy. It shouldn't matter. She knew the threat she was under was all too real, but part of her wished to face this giant head on instead of hiding. She could not spend her whole life running from someone who wished her harm.

"It would be impossible not to notice a woman like you." His hand tightened about hers before sliding up to her elbow, escorting her from the train.

Don't fall in love first. Don't fall in love first. She chanted, but it didn't have the same effect as when she repeated it every time they pulled out of a station and the wheels of the train synchronized with her chant. Now, it felt weak in the face of spending so much time alone with him. *Not to mention the fact that I am following him to his home where he is the only one I know.* She groaned at the impossibility of her task.

"It's not going to be so bad." He misinterpreted her groan. "Most families are in New York by now for the Winter season as only a few stay in Newport all year, mine included."

She glanced down at her dress once

more. She should have begged him to stop to go shopping in New York City before coming here, but again, her pride would not allow her to admit that she felt anything less than as beautiful as she did in Las Vegas. Despite years of trying to fit in, she never did, and it irked her. She missed her Harvey Girl uniform that took away the need to impress others by the state of her gown.

Her efficiency was what made her stand out among the waitresses and her friendship with dear Corinna had taken the focus off herself. At the thought of her friend and all that she had hinted at suffering in her short life, Lorna shed her cloak of discontentment and pasted on a smile that she willed to be genuine. She would not allow Gaston to see into her discontented, ungrateful heart. She had a family who loved her enough to send her away. And apparently, Gaston cared enough for her to resign as sheriff in order to see her safe. That alone made her swallow any discomfort.

He released her long enough to disembark and held his hand out to her, assisting her down from the train. She lightly touched his palm and released him the moment her feet hit the platform. These days with him had worn down her resolve to see him only as a friend and touching needed to be kept to a minimum.

She took in the overcast skies and admired the remaining colorful fall leaves clinging to the branches of the trees surrounding the station as a few passengers bustled about, seeking their trunks and transportation.

He gathered their carpetbags in one hand, took her elbow, and guided her away from the train as steam poured out from the wheels.

"What are you going to do after this is all over since you've given up being sheriff? You still thinking about ranching?"

"It pained me to quit." He laughed softly. "The Elliot way has really affected me in that manner, but there is a family in New Mexico who wants to sell their ranch—the Higgins. I found out right before I left town for my birthday party. Apparently, Mrs. Higgins wants to return East and isn't giving Mr. Higgins a choice as it was her money in the first place."

"You would buy their land? Why, we'd be neighbors." She swallowed at the idea of the years she might spend beside his land where one day, he would bring home a wife and then children. She would be happy for whatever woman stood beside him, even if it felt as if a knife twisted in her belly at the thought. Maybe she would have a year before that occurred and she would find her happily ever after before then, or perhaps climb in the ranks of the Harvey House— after she actually fulfilled her first contract that Miss Trent graciously allowed her to take a leave from instead of firing her.

"That's my hope, but I wanted to ask your opinion on the matter before I made an offer."

Was he asking because he wanted her approval? *For a future home?* "Why?"

"Well, I'd be next to Elliot land."

She stiffened. *Of course, you foolish girl. He doesn't want you to be upset that he would be settling down and raising a family next door to the girl who has loved him since she first beheld him, as made so obvious from the boots you got him for his birthday.* "It's a free country, Reid. You don't need my permission for anything."

He frowned and reached into his pocket, withdrawing a folded note. "Shall we stop by the telegraph office while they unload our trunks? I need to send a note to my lawyer to have him purchase the land on my behalf."

REID HAILED a hackney carriage and handed the driver their carpetbags, motioning the porter to gather her two trunks. What had he said to make her go all stiff? Wooing Lorna was proving a lot harder. In the past, she had always treated him like he was special—not many people treated him that way. Sure, Harriet loved him as a brother, Gil was his best friend, and Lorna was . . . well, she was Lorna—his burst of sunshine that was always there with a smile and a healthy dose of encouragement and entertainment should he be feeling down. She was always so in touch with his moods, almost before he was, but something had changed these past few months.

He *had* been somewhat obsessed with Belle Parish and the first bloom of love had been intoxicating. Perhaps he should clear the air. He could claim madness and hope that Lorna forgave him, but then, that would mean bringing up Belle and he didn't think that was a good idea at the moment, but was that what he needed to do in order for them to move forward in their relationship?

He assisted her in the carriage, and she offered him a small smile of thanks. She hadn't been unfriendly, only more reserved. But after the weeks apart when she first left, and that kiss, that world blurring kiss, had enchanted him and he saw Lorna for the first time as someone more than a friend—a beautiful, eligible woman. And every day spent in her company confirmed the matter. He wanted Lorna Elliot for his wife. He just had to convince her, which was partly why he decided to bring her to Newport. He needed to begin wooing her in a way that was so obvious, she couldn't misinterpret his actions any more, and he couldn't do that in New Mexico where she was in danger, and he was always tense. They needed time away from it all.

He settled beside her, watching her observe her surroundings. "Don't be nervous."

She laughed under her breath. "That is easy for you to say. This is your second home."

"Home is bit of a stretch. More like my prison sentence for the allotted time I am forced to return." He kept his gaze out of the window, viewing the pedestrians on the sidewalk as they shopped on Bellevue Avenue. His stomach clenched. He had never told her exactly how big his mansion was in Newport.

Lorna rolled her eyes. "A gilded cage is not to your liking, Reid?"

"It's more about the company." He adjusted his coat that he had changed into in the train's lavatory before they pulled into Newport's station. He learned many years ago that staying in his usual attire only brought strife and more questions than he cared, so despite his metaphorical gnashing of teeth at the idea of wearing such a restrictive suit, he manned up and dressed in the manner that would please his mother. He knew better than to show up in his dusty Western garb, as his mother so lovingly described it. But he did have the jacket altered to hide his shoulder harness with his loaded weapons tucked in their holsters. His mother would complain about the cut, but it was absolutely necessary. "You know the saying about family and fish."

Her brow crinkled. "No?"

"Perhaps it is because you were raised far from the ocean. They say that fish and family begin to stink after three days."

Lorna wrinkled her nose. "Gaston Reid. What a terrible thing to say."

He chuckled. "Day one, my grandfather is happy to see me. Day two, we do all that my family has been wanting to do with me for months, and day three, that's when the claws come out and it is time for me to go."

She rested her hand on his arm. "You come all this way and only spend three days?"

He gritted his teeth. "Most times. But the rangers kept me busy, and I really couldn't afford to be away for longer."

"Do you miss being a ranger?"

"Every day, but I know it is time I settle down." He glanced at her. Dare he hint what he desired? "And find myself a wife for the ranch."

Her jaw clenched. "That seems to be the natural progression of life."

She wasn't making this conversation easy. He grasped her hand, pressing it to his lips. "Lorna, what I mean to convey is—"

The hackney crossed through the gate. Lorna gasped and broke away, sticking her head through the window. "*This.* This is your home?"

"It's the residence where I spent my summers," Reid answered, not bothering to look. He knew the French chateau style home well with its imposing façade and vast gardens that stretched across the acreage that were too precious for a young boy to run through, much like the house. It was a monument to wealth, power, and prestige, and not much else.

His home was in New Mexico in his aunt's modest two-story Victorian home with wooden trellises at the side that allowed him to climb down and ride out to the Elliot's ranch.

"It's an impressive place to spend your summers," she whispered, slumping back in her seat, eyes wide. "You always acted as if it were a trial to return—and here you are, a prince running away from his castle. Are you related to royalty? It would explain a lot."

"Meaning?"

"You've always been chivalrous, even as a boy. And when you became a ranger, your true nature was only amplified."

"As much as my family would wish it, no. We are not related to royalty, but in my experience, chivalry is born from a noble spirit, not by birth." He held back a grin that she thought so highly of him. It was promising for his mission in getting her to fall for him. "I'm hoping this *castle* will aid in protecting you while we are away from New Mexico." The hackney stopped before the imposing building and he grasped Lorna's tiny hand in his. "Don't be nervous. I'll take care of you."

She smiled up at him, eyes twinkling. "You always do, Gaston. Here will be no different, except the scary people are, in actuality, well-dressed socialites and rich gentlemen."

He lifted her hand to his lips and kissed it, her eyes widening as a throat cleared pointedly behind him. He gave her a bright smile and turned to find his grandfather under the portico, scowling at him through the carriage window. Reid hopped out of the carriage, gave the man a nod, paid the driver handsomely, and assisted Lorna out.

"You could have sent for one of our carriages, Gaston." Grandfather crossed his arms, eyeing Lorna. "There was no need to hire one."

A surge of protectiveness sent Reid's hand stretching out and grasping her fingers, intertwining them—his message clear. *She is mine. Do not insult her.* "Sir, this is Lorna Elliot. Lorna, this is my grandfather, Gaston Lane."

She dipped into a curtsey. "Pleasure to meet you, sir."

He gave her a stiff nod and turned on his heel. "Come along."

"I'm sorry for his behavior," Reid muttered from the corner of his mouth.

"Well, I can't say I'm surprised, given his daughter Gertrude." She gave a soft laugh.

Gaston pulled her hand through the crook of his arm, following his grandfather into the vast marble foyer, the rich mahogany lining the walls casting the home in darkness.

"Gaston?" The faint whisper came from the stairs.

He followed the trail of steps to an elegant hem of gold, trimmed lace, and light blue skirt and delicate sleeves worn by the lovely woman that gave him his dark brown hair and blue eyes. "Hello, Mother."

Lorna gave him a hard nudge forward, keeping her smile in place. "Go to her, you nincompoop," she whispered through a gritted smile.

CHAPTER 18

$\mathcal{H}$e crossed the marble floors as Mother descended, hands outstretched to him, a tenderness in her eyes that he knew from experience would fade in a few days—replaced with the crushing disappointment of unmet expectations. Nonetheless, he was happy to see her. It had been three years since his last visit and he hoped that this time, they could make it without descending into arguments over him returning to live with them and taking up the mantle of his grandfather's life's work. He had no wish to take up the trade of shipping and neither did Harriet. He understood their disappointment, but not enough to give up his home in the West and the life he had made for himself there.

Lord, let this be a peaceful visit. Let my family see that I am happy and well. Let me not judge them too harshly either. I know I haven't been a glowing beacon of patience in the past. Let them love Lorna because she is the woman I am going to marry—if You help me convince her to love me.

He escorted Mother to Lorna's side, whose widened eyes betrayed that she felt out of place in these gilded halls, but to him, she was the picture of the perfect lady. "Mother, may I introduce you to Lorna Elliot? She will be staying with us for a few weeks, as I mentioned in my telegram."

"You did not mention a name when you said you were bringing a guest home. Elliot, you say?" Her brow rose in recognition.

Grandfather lowered his voice, "Thank goodness you haven't married the girl before we can talk you out of it. Or have you? Is this what this trip is about?"

Lorna's cheeks flamed and it took everything in him not to correct Grandfather that he was in fact going to marry her as soon as he could convince her to join him at the altar. "Yes, Mother. Lorna Elliot is a very dear friend whose family has been close to me for years."

She smiled down at Lorna and extended her hand. "What an honor it is to meet you. I'm so pleased that Gaston brought you here before any formal attachments have been made." She glanced at Grandfather with a reproving smile. "Isn't it an honor, Father?"

He harrumphed and motioned them into the front parlor with its ornate, burgundy and gold Louis XIV furniture that matched the silk wallcoverings and gold sconces that dripped with crystals. A large crystal chandelier hung in the center under a fresco of a shepherdess and her beau.

Lorna cast Reid a glance over her shoulder as Mother drew her inside. He couldn't help but smile at Lorna's visible swallow and obvious attempt to cover her awed gasp with a cough.

"So, Gaston tells us that you need sanctuary from a gang of outlaws?" Grandfather stared at her, assessing her.

"Yes, sir." Lorna nodded and with Mother's releasing her arm, she strolled about the room, unable to keep from touching a few items on the ornate stone mantel as flames flickered in the hearth. "They've taken me once before. I escaped thanks to Gaston."

"Oh, my." Mother sank atop the settee in a cloud of skirts, her hand flapping at her throat. "Don't tell me it was the Death Riders gang? They were involved with a terrible crime at the Montezuma many years ago while we were there on holiday. In fact, there was a fire that saw the building burnt down a second time, which was the final straw for me, and I simply had to leave New Mexico. I had only been staying for my sister's sake, as my dear husband passed away when Gaston was quite young. I can hardly believe that Gaston loved it there so much that he begged for me to leave him with his aunt for part of the year instead of being sent off to boarding school, but it did have its beautiful mountains and foothills. Have you seen the new Montezuma, my dear?"

"Oh, yes," she beamed. "It is lovely and quite elegant."

"You stay on holiday there?" Mother's eyes sparked.

"Many times throughout the years, yes, but recently, I worked there as a Harvey Girl before all this began."

"A-a *Harvey Girl?*" His mother fairly choked.

Lorna nodded. "Have you heard of us?"

"What in heaven's name is a *Harvey Girl?*" Grandfather sputtered. "They sound like saloon girls."

"They are waitresses." Mother pursed her lips and looked pointedly at Grandfather, but Reid couldn't tell if she was begging him not to say anything or was silently judging Lorna.

Lorna moved to the window, peering out onto the manicured lawn that melted into the stone wall of the cliff walk and the ocean beyond it. "I originally accepted the position as a dare from my brother."

"A dare?" Mother fairly squeaked. "Whatever do you mean?"

"I know, it is terribly immature on both accounts," Lorna sighed with a little smile on her lips. "I can never seem to say no to a dare, but it actually turned out for the best. It has helped to mature me in ways that I didn't really know I needed maturing in. It saw me relying on God more as I faced each day with new challenges and filled my heart with thanks for all the unexpected blessings that came out from serving every day. I made new friends, dear friends, I served my community, and I learned the joy of making my own wage instead of having my pa pay for everything."

"Your pa has money?" Mother picked at her cuff.

Of course, she would fixate on that one fact. But Reid couldn't fault her too much. What society mother wouldn't want to know if her son made a good financial match?

"He owns a ranch, and I am used to helping out on the ranch, roping and herding cattle and sometimes baking in the kitchen with Ma, but I am not nearly as good at baking as I am roping and serving." She grinned up at Gaston. "Isn't that right?"

"I will second that. She has tried making me biscuits, muffins, breads, and pies over the years." He chuckled. "A few were edible, but most even the pigs wouldn't eat."

"I see." Grandfather's scowl deepened.

"Pigs," Mother whispered, snatching a fan from the side table, and flicking it open.

Reid gritted his teeth to contain the laughter burning in his belly. He could have helped coach Lorna on what not to say to avoid any arguments, but he didn't want her to change who she was for his family . . . even if it would've been easier for them not to know about her position as a Harvey Girl, or that she worked on her family ranch. He loved how hardworking Lorna was and he was not ashamed of it, so why should she have to hide herself in shined up stories of her home life?

Reid cleared his throat. "How about some tea? We are pretty famished from the trip."

Mother shot to her feet, relief flooding her features as she pulled the pale blue and gold embroidered bell cord. "I asked the cook to prepare an early dinner." She smiled to Lorna. "Would you like to change first?"

"That would be lovely." She grimaced. "I

hate to think how much dust Gaston and I have traipsed into your fine home already."

"It is nothing." Mother folded her hands before her skirts, her knuckles whitening. *She must be holding her judgements in by a hairsbreadth.* "Gaston made a habit of bringing in a cloud of dirt with him as a child."

A footman that Reid didn't recognize appeared in the door and bowed. "You rang, ma'am?"

"Please show Miss Elliot to the Violet Suite and have her things sent up at once. Have the maid draw a bath as well."

Lorna followed the man without a second glance to Reid. Hopefully, she was fine following the footman to her rooms, but she was different from every young lady in Newport. She was more independent and braver than anyone he knew.

"You cannot be serious, boy." Grandfather fairly growled as the sound of footsteps faded up the stairs.

The fight has begun early. He turned from where he had been staring after Lorna. "I am very serious about the threat against Lorna."

"When you said you needed to visit for a few weeks, I thought you were ready to return, to claim your place here, but you come back with a *cowgirl?*" He sneered. "A Harvey Girl country wildling? Do you really expect her to fit into Newport?"

"No. But then again," Reid added slowly, reaching for his mother's hand to lessen the blow. "I do not plan on living here. I shall be staying in New Mexico now that I have retired from being a ranger and sheriff. My lawyer is in the process of purchasing a ranch for me in my absence."

"And pay for it with what funds? I will not support you if that's what you think. I can still give away the fortune to your cousin, Harriet, even if her marriage was less than desirable." Grandfather stuffed his hands into his pockets, staring down his hooked nose at him.

"I've been working since I was a young man and have a tidy sum to see this dream through. The ranch is, and will continue to be, a working ranch and, Lord willing, I will marry Lorna Elliot."

Grandfather scowled at the now crying Mother. "Looks like we have much to do to convince him to return home from New Mexico, Penelope. First, you married that cowboy turned sheriff, then Gertrude married a banker in the same town, and then our sweet Louise." He dipped his head. "Our sweet Louise married that politician, Clyde Lane, and died birthing Harriet. I bitterly regret the day I ever visited my old friend in New Mexico. History cannot repeat itself with another one of mine marrying outside of our society and staying in the West."

Reid rolled back his shoulders. "Grandfather. Mother. I respect and love you both, but allow me to make one thing *very* clear. Who I choose to wed is my choice and mine alone." He pressed a kiss atop his mother's hand. "You, of all people, should know the importance of choosing your own path. I appreciate you hosting us during this time, but if Grandfather cannot be pleasant to the woman I love, I will find other accommodations."

Mother rested a hand on Grandfather's shoulder, staying his rebuff. "Father, I know better than anyone what it is to love a cowboy against your wishes—and if Lorna Elliot is anything like Gaston's father, I cannot stand in his way, and neither shall you." She gave Reid a smile. "If she is the one you choose, you have my blessing."

LORNA ROLLED over in the too soft bed, the moonlight streaming through the crack in the heavy curtains as her stomach lowed louder than a cattle's song. She grunted and tossed on her shawl over her nightgown. If she didn't eat something, she would never get sleep. She couldn't find her stockings in the dark and given that she had refrained from requesting a taper from the servants, not wanting to be a bother any more than she already was, she would have to find her way to the kitchen in the dark.

Dinner had been a grand affair, but an affair that saw her appetite wane as she observed the dainty portions his mother ate.

Lorna had always had a healthy appetite. She needed food to work, but here, it seemed expected that she have the appetite of the caged songbird in the conservatory. Tomorrow, she'd go back to eating normally again. Tonight, she had merely wished not to stand out.

She padded out of her room down the carpeted hallway, counting the doors until the grand staircase appeared. She followed it down, her hand on the cool rail, the iciness of the floor waking her senses even more than her stomach. She paused in the foyer, orienting herself. The parlor was to her right and to her left was the dining room with another drawing room. The servants had to have another door from which they used to deliver the food from the kitchens as the soup and entrée had been piping hot. She entered the dining room and peeked behind the folding Japanese screen and smiled at the empty butler's buffet table and beyond that, another door. "Eureka."

She opened the door and discovered another hallway with a dumbwaiter to her left.

It was so large she could easily fit inside of it. Beyond the dumbwaiter was a massive stone sink with a faucet. To her right, all the fine China that was not on display in the dining room was neatly stacked behind the window of the cabinet. The hall opened and she clapped her hands at the massive kitchen with its welcoming brick pavers. An overlarge wood table stood in the middle of the room, and the immense stove and oven lined one whole side of the room. It was much larger than even the Harvey House kitchen. Surely, it could prepare a meal for a hundred guests at once.

On the table was a basket with a linen cloth drawn over it. *Hopefully, it's some kind of baked good.* She lifted the corner of the cloth when a door in the back of the kitchen opened, a candle flickering. *Who is working so late?* "Hello? Is anyone there?"

A familiar mop of dark brown hair appeared at the door. "Lorna?" He chuckled and brought out a plate of chicken, cheese, and a glass bottle of milk. "Were you starving too?"

"Completely! But why didn't you eat

more?" She sank down at the stool at the table and reached for the basket, flipping back the linen to see pastries from their dessert tonight.

He shrugged, setting the plate and glass down between them, motioning for her to have some. "I was nervous, and it was difficult to eat with all the questions being aimed my way."

Lorna sank her teeth into the chicken, swaying in delight at the rosemary, butter, and garlic flavors bursting in her mouth. "I know."

"After you departed, they were insistent that we make calls in the morning, but after a lot of convincing them that the reason why we are here is to keep you in a cocoon of safety, they relented." He tore off some dark meat and tossed it into his mouth.

"I have to say, I am a little disappointed that I will not see much of the island where you spent your summers." She reached for the glass and downed half of it.

"I didn't say that." He grinned at her appetite. "I merely said we were not going to

socialize in their circles. You and I, however, can have a grand old time in disguise."

"I do like the sound of that. What do you
recommend we see first?" Lorna reached for
the cheese. She had missed this ease between them. Ever since she had vowed to
release her great love of him, she felt as if
she had needed barriers, but even she could
not deny the lengths Gaston was going to
keep her safe—and the way he had held her
hand in front of his family. It was almost as
if he were claiming her, not to mention his
seeking her blessing about the neighboring
ranch before wiring someone in New
Mexico to see to the purchasing of the land.
But she wouldn't allow her mind to run
away with her anymore. She would wait to
see what was truth and what was her imagination before allowing herself to build
rancheros in the clouds.

"Well, we will see the town of Newport,
but dressed in the clothes of servants. We
will be invisible to my family's friends. It is
the perfect disguise. You brought one
Harvey uniform, yes?"

She nodded. She had wanted to be ready

in case they were able to return home, and she could get back to work right away.

"Then you wear that, and I'll wear my usual clothes, with an old coat that I keep in the attic. We will head out first thing in the morning." He lifted a chicken leg. "What say you?"

She giggled and tapped her chicken leg against his. "To exploring!"

CHAPTER 19

*R*eid lingered until his mother and grandfather departed for their morning calls before he and Lorna snuck out the side door of the mansion and into the servant's wagon that he had arranged to be waiting for them. While he was able to refuse to attend house calls, he knew Grandfather would object to their being out and about dressed as servants. Even though she didn't need his help, he wrapped his hands about her petite waist and lifted her onto the bench seat, and he climbed up beside her, grasping the reins.

"Where are we going?" She asked,

breathless from their escape with excitement brewing in her eyes.

He waggled his brows. "You'll see." He could not wait to see her face when he showed her Bailey's Beach. Thankfully, the day was unseasonably warm and with it being November, the private beach that was used by society's elite would be vacant, which meant that he could take her to his family's beach cabana without anyone being the wiser. Their cabana was next to Newport's affluential Dupré family—the daughters and grandchildren were known to go swimming outside of the fashionable season, but he knew for a fact the entire family was now in New York for the Winter season. He also knew the man who ran Bailey's row of beachfront cabanas. If he spotted them, he wouldn't inform Grandfather, or question their state of dress. Reid drove down the hill and turned to face her when the shore came into view with two bathing machines parked at the edge of the shore in front of the row of cabanas.

She clutched his arm, her eyes shimmering. "Oh, Gaston. The waves are even more beautiful than I imagined. You had the sea every summer and you still complained?" She laughed. "I would never want to leave."

He shrugged. "I missed my best friends. It was hard for the waves to compete against being with the Elliot family."

She pushed a lock of hair from her eyes that the wind had freed from her coiffure. "I love my brother, but this would be hard to give up."

"And you."

She looked up at him. "You considered me your best friend? Even though I was a few years younger than both you and Gil? I always thought I was a bother to you boys."

"You were *never* a bother to me. Gil might have made it seem that way, but I've always enjoyed the vivacity you brought to our group."

She bumped his shoulder with hers. "Vivacity is a polite way of saying that I was rough and tumble and more than a little loud."

"Mayhap. You were so different from the girls I knew here." At her frown, he added, "In the best of ways." He slapped the reins, directing the wagon down the road and near the shore where the road turned to sand.

The wagon wheels slowed, and he hopped down, secured the horses, and lifted his arms to her. She pressed her hands to his shoulders and allowed him to lift her out. She felt marvelous in his arms. He allowed his grip to falter as before, and she gasped as she tumbled forward, wrapping her arms about his neck, her cheek pressed against his. He clutched her to him, their lips the closest they had been since kissing. And boy did he fancy a kiss right about now. He slowly set her down. "Come along, darling. I want to show you the waves." He bit back a groan that he had called her darling out loud. It was one thing to say it in one's mind, and quite another to say it out loud.

Her eyes sparkled in anticipation, so perhaps she wouldn't notice.

He gripped her hand in his and at the question in her gaze, he added, "The sand can be difficult to walk on if it is your first time."

She smirked at him. "I'm sure I can manage."

"I know you can, but I want to hold your hand."

Her lips parted and she snapped her jaw shut.

"Is that agreeable to you?"

"I suppose it can be, if that's what it takes for you to show me the ocean." She laughed and surged forward before dropping his hand and plopping down short of the water and drawing off her shoes and ripping off her stockings.

He averted his eyes at the sight of her shapely calves in the sun and turning, pulled off his own shoes. A hard nudge at his hip sent him sprawling to the sand.

"Race you!" She squealed and ran toward the waves, gasping at the first touch of cold water, but in her excitement, she was undeterred and determined to wade.

He rolled to his feet, laughing as he chased her into the waves, not minding the brisk water on such a sunny day. Everything had always been a competition to her and usually, he gave her a good run for her money, but today, he let her win. How could he not when it was her first time experiencing the sea? The waves crashed against her skirts, making her shriek as she fell to her backside, the next wave crashing into her shoulders and taking down her coiffure in a waterfall of sodden curls. She sat up, coughing, when another wave came. Gaston reached down and scooped her into his arms as she gasped for breath.

"I had no idea they were so powerful!" She shoved her hair back with one hand as the other wrapped about his neck.

"My arms? I try not to boast too much, but it is difficult to hide them, especially when wearing a wet shirt."

She rolled her eyes. "Yes, you are impressively built, but I was speaking of the waves." She shivered in his arms. "Can we go further out?"

He grinned at her confession. "You still want to wade in the water?"

"I've waited my whole life to set foot in the sea, a few waves shall not stop me." She wiggled out of his arms just as another wave crashed into her, sending her smashing against his chest.

He wrapped his arms about her, steadying her as he had done in the river at home. He wanted to live in this moment forever. Newport had never been so wonderful before, and it was all because of this marvelous woman in his arms—the woman he would ask to be his wife, once he was certain that she loved him as fiercely as he adored her. He ran his finger under her chin, lifting her face. Her lips called to him and if her kissing him in return, that day so long ago, was any indication, she might want to kiss him again. He leaned down to her, his heart racing and closed his eyes when a massive wave knocked him to his back. The pull of the waves broke them apart and he scrambled to his knees to see Lorna crawling up the shore, laughing as another wave took him down, his face grating against the sand and water squirting up his nose.

She picked up her skirts and ran the few steps toward him, hefting him to his feet. He had forgotten she was so strong for such a little thing. What had she thought about him and his move to "protect" her a few moments ago? She grabbed his hand and raced up the shore as another wave came and he had no chance to grab her and try to kiss her again as she tripped and pulled him down with her.

He landed beside her in the sand as she giggled and rolled to her back, sand pasted to her gown, hands, and hair. "We are a mess. It's a good thing you brought me here before anyone else this morning. What would people think?"

He propped himself up on his elbow, admiring her bright smile that made her eyes shine with joy. "It's a very good thing."

"I can't wait to tell Gil that you brought me to the sea. He's mentioned it so many times from his travels, I felt like I've already visited it, but there is nothing quite like sand between your toes and saltwater making your hair sticky." She pinched a lock of hair and frowned. "I'll be needing another bath."

He sat up and cleared his throat at her words. "We probably should be getting back before my mother and grandfather return. But, before we do, there is a rock formation I want to show you."

"Is it the spouting rock you told me about? The one with a fifty-foot spray?" Her eyes sparked once again at his nod.

"You remembered that?" He shook his head. It had been a decade since he brought that up.

"I remember all your stories and as I have been dying to see it for years, I have no intention of rushing back, no matter who might spot us." She picked up her soddened skirts, snagged her shoes and stockings, and placed her hand in his. "So, if we are going to get caught coming back to the house soaked, let's make the most of our questionable choices today."

LORNA BALANCED on the massive rock on the edge of Bailey's Beach that led to a natural bridge, connecting one giant rock to another. The gaping hole below displayed the fury and power of the waves beneath, but with Gaston's arm wrapped about her waist, she peered down for a good thirty seconds before darting a safe distance with him, she felt only exhilaration as the water spouted into the sky and the wind snatched the droplets.

She spread her arms wide as the salty spray coated them, washing away most of the sand. The sea had an effect she hadn't been expecting. The sand caressing her feet had calmed her, the salt water soothed her aching limbs from the exhaustion of travel, and the sun stripped her worries of the Death Riders away as the gulls overhead cawed their findings to one another.

She sprawled on the rock, away from the waves, and allowed the sun to bake her skirts dry. Her underthings would take hours to dry, but at least they would appear less haphazard than they actually were with dry outerwear.

Gaston propped himself up on one elbow, watching her. She let him . . . because she was beginning to think that maybe, just maybe, Gaston Reid was starting to fall in love with her.

"Would you like to go home to change before our next stop?"

She rolled to a sitting position, using her hand to shield her face against the sun. "We are going somewhere else? Are you going to take me on the cliff walk?"

"Not today. I thought it might be fun to do some shopping as we explore the town, and, by shopping, I mean having some ice cream. There is a delightful parlor down-town." He extended his hand to her.

"Ice cream? I haven't had ice cream in ages." She hopped up and whacked at her skirts, freeing them of the remaining sand now that it was dryer.

Within ten minutes, they parked beneath the vine covered servant's portico and darted inside, taking the servant's stair to the second floor. Gaston paused outside of her door. "Hurry, because I think they will be home within the hour, and I do not want us to be caught as we are attempting our escape."

"Too late." His mother pursed her lips, eyeing the state of them. "Whatever have you two been doing?"

Lorna refrained from pushing her hair out of her face. Gaston might like her as she was, but she couldn't keep the heat from her cheeks. "Hello, Mrs. Reid. Gaston took me to Bailey's Beach and a wave took us down."

Her eyes bulged. "I see. Well, let us hope you did not get a burn without a bonnet."

She shrugged. "I'm no stranger to the sun, ma'am. A little burn won't hurt me none."

"Except for your complexion . . . which might be even more vibrant with the dress I have out for you on your bed."

"A dress?" Did she look so out of place that his mother thought she needed a store-bought gown?

Gaston's eyes narrowed as if he knew something Lorna did not. "What is the dress for, Mother?"

Lorna pushed open the door and gasped at the silver gown draped over the violet bed covering. Gaston followed her inside.

"Gaston Reid! You know better than to go into a lady's bedroom." Mrs. Reid hissed as she followed them inside.

Lorna ran her fingers over the bead

work of the sleeve. She had never seen anything so fine in her life, much less worn a dress such as this.

"Do you like it?" Mrs. Reid asked, hands folded before her skirts.

"It's breathtaking," Lorna murmured. Gaston had never seen her in something so fine. What would he think?

Mrs. Reid beamed. "I hoped you would like it. I found it in town and the seamstress will be here within the hour to have it altered as much as possible."

"Why does Lorna need a party gown, Mother?" Gaston crossed his arms.

Mrs. Reid's smile grew strained. "I am hosting a small welcoming home ball for you tonight, son, which is why I was gone longer than anticipated today."

"Lorna is in hiding, Mother. Going about town in disguise is one thing, but you cannot expect I would approve of—"

"There's no reason why she can't enjoy a party. If you have concerns, we should discuss them in private while Lorna sees to her needs." She guided Gaston toward the door, calling over her shoulder to Lorna, "A bath has already been drawn for you, my dear."

A ball would be a sight to see, but she was no Newport socialite, and every dance would highlight that fact, no matter if she looked the part in this gown. And then, there was the matter of the danger being surrounded by so many strangers—where anyone might hide in plain sight.

"Thank you for the gesture, but we must decline." Gaston pulled away from his mother and grasped Lorna's hand. "Lorna's safety is of the utmost importance. Colt Lawson is keeping me up to date on the papers in New Mexico. The Death Rider women have had a successful heist or two since we departed. They are filling their coffers and I will not underestimate them. I do not want to put Lorna at risk. Please give your guests our regrets, but for the duration of the ball, Lorna and I will remain out of sight."

"But—"

"I'm sorry, Mother. But there will be expectations for her to dance with others, and no one is to be near Lorna but me."

CHAPTER 20

The next two weeks spent with Gaston in Newport were full of surprises with learning how to poorly play lawn tennis, paint horrific self-portraits, taking out the rowboat, and, weather permitting, walks on Bailey's Beach. And tonight, they were to stroll along the cliff walks to view the full moon.

After their first morning at the beach, her dreams were beginning to burst forward once more and each passing day spent at his side made her suspect he was courting her. He had never actually *asked* to court her, though. So, tonight, she would allow herself one last time to *try* to catch Gaston

Reid, and that was only because he seemed like he was trying to catch her with all his *almost* kisses. She grinned at the memory of him turning her to face him, his finger tracing her chin as he lifted her lips upward, as if he were thinking of their passionate moment in the canyon. She certainly had been.

She was fairly positive that he had been going to kiss her if that last wave hadn't sent them sprawling to their knees and the ocean squirting up their noses. She had never laughed so hard at the sight of Gaston soaked beside her, even though she did wish the wave had waited a moment longer to allow their lips to meet once more and let her know if Gaston truly did want to marry her. She shook the unknown from her thoughts and focused on the enchanting evening awaiting her, and if she played her cards right, Gaston Reid would be hers.

She descended the stairs, one hand on the railing and the other gripping the silver fabric of the magnificent ball gown that Mrs. Reid had given her but she had not yet worn. She didn't dare release her hold, lest she tumble and mess up her grand entrance. She paused on the final curve of the staircase and blinked at the flickering candles in sconces, candelabras, and the crystal chandeliers to where Gaston stood with his back to the stairs, waiting for her. She ran a hand down the glittering silver gown with its diamond clusters that bunched her skirts into lovely rosettes about her knees before falling into priceless rows of lace to the floor.

Gaston turned and at the sight of her, his jaw unhinged. For a man who was always alert and put together, she quite liked being the one to shock him.

He approached the foot of the stairs, holding his hand out to her as she reached the final step. Even with her standing on the bottom step, he could easily kiss the top of her head if he wanted to—and she most certainly did want him to. *A kiss on the lips would be even better, though.* She placed her hand in his. "Gaston. Are you ready for our stroll in the moonlight?"

"You look beautiful, Lorna." He extended his hand to her and led her out the back veranda and down to the moonlit lawn.

"Well, I thought it a pity not to wear the prettiest gown I've ever beheld."

"And it would be a pity not to dance while wearing it." He bowed to her.

She rested her hand on his outstretched arm as he grasped her waist and took his left hand in her right. They swirled about the lawn, laughing as they tripped over a tree root and a series of distant trumpeted honks caught her attention.

"It's just the swans."

"Swans?" She gaped. "Why didn't you show me them right away? I didn't know you had swans! I've never seen one in person."

"Well, we do, but Mother likes to keep them on the far pond as they are rather loud, and the honking can get annoying after a time. Would you like to see them before we take our cliff walk?"

She reined in her enthusiasm enough for him to guide her out toward the far pond. She tugged on his arm, silently begging him to hurry. He chuckled and led her down to the small pond at the west side of the property with a pretty little manmade island in the center with a quaint, arching bridge that would be a pretty place for a private tête-à-tête. He led her up the stone bridge, pausing at the center to lean over the rail to watch as the majestic birds swam beneath them.

"They are lovely. I can see why they are the subject of so many paintings." She chuckled. "If I weren't so afraid of them being gobbled up by a coyote, I'd say we should dig a pond out at the ranch and bring some home, but then, there are droughts too. I suppose it would be cruel to take them away from such elegance."

His hand rested atop hers on the bridge rail. "Guess we will have to enjoy them while we can."

Exhaustion flooded her and she rested her head on his shoulder. She felt his hand slide across her back and rest at her waist. *Is Gaston Reid embracing me?*

He gently turned her toward him, his gaze roving over her gown in admiration.

"W-we should take our stroll before the weather turns."

"And I think we should stay put." He grabbed her wrist and gently tugged her to him. "I dare you to kiss me."

Her lips parted, even as heat flooded her belly at the most tempting dare of her life. She lifted her chin. "I don't do dares anymore, Gaston. It's what got me into this mess in the first place."

"Pity." He stroked her cheek with the back of his hand. "Then I think you should dare me."

She narrowed her gaze. "I won't ever dare you to kiss me."

He rested his forehead to hers, her intake of breath betraying her.

"One day, you will, Lorna Elliot." He slid his cheek to meet hers. "And I was looking for interest, not an excuse." He lifted her chin and bent. His lips crashed against hers.

A whimper escaped her as her arms stole about his neck, pulling him deeper into the kiss that made the world about them blur and the stars shine even brighter. All she was aware of was Gaston and how she ached with the need and desire to be this man's wife. Was this his kiss of a promised future? His kiss of . . . love?

He rested his forehead against hers once more, smiling. He tugged off the signet ring on his little finger and held it up to her. "Lorna, I love you more than anything, and I want you to be my wife—to stand by my side through the good and the bad on our ranch. Your sweet spirit and vivacity enchant me, body and soul. Will you marry me, love?"

She closed her eyes and imagined her future with him beside her every morning, with a baby girl in her arms, a toddler at her skirts, and another, who looked just like his father, running wild on their lovely ranch with a little dog chasing after him. A heaven blessed future. She lifted her gaze and kissed his rough cheek. "Gaston, I thought you would never ask. I'll marry you whenever, wherever. I only want to be with you and only you."

HE WAS FLOATING. He was certain of it. His lungs burned with the need for air. He pulled back, gasping. Reid blinked rapidly to clear the vision that was his fiancée. She had always been a beauty but dressed in that gown with *his* ring on her finger, looking up at him with those adoring eyes, she was a queen—his queen. He grinned. *Queen Ranch* had a nice ring to it. He would get that wooden plaque at the ranch's entrance changed to bear the name first thing after they returned home.

"Lorna, you have no idea how long I have waited to hear those words." He stole another kiss and another.

"I doubt you've waited as long as me." She laughed, her lashes lifting as she gave him a teasing kiss that had him darting forward to claim her lips again.

"Mercy, your kisses will do a man in," he growled.

"I had no idea I had such a power, but now that I do—" She kissed him until they were both breathless. "Hmm, what shall I command you to do with this new power of mine?" Her eyes twinkled.

"I am your servant, my lady." He grinned down at her, full well knowing how mischievous she was.

"Then kiss me again."

"Gladly." He drew her down the other side of the bridge and once out of sight, he did just that. With whispered dreams while embracing beneath a weeping willow, the pair lost themselves and all sense of time until a servant appeared on the back veranda.

He sighed. He led her up the bridge, the footman catching sight of them at once.

"Mr. Reid? A telegram arrived for you."

Reid nodded his thanks and broke the seal, turning so Lorna could read it.

All Death Riders captured. Need you both as witnesses for trial. Return on first train out. T.S.

"We are going home!" Lorna threw her arms about him. "Can a heart burst from happiness?"

CHAPTER 21

*R*eid was sorely tempted to marry her at the next station, but thinking of Ma Elliot was the only thing that kept him from asking Lorna to make good on her promise of whenever and wherever. She deserved a church wedding with her family about her and her new friends from the Harvey House where she only had a few weeks left to work. *Thank God she only signed a three-month contract.*

He glanced down at the sleeping redhead leaning on his shoulder and his chest swelled at the unexpected blessing from the Lord. When he had been infatuated with Belle, he thought God didn't care about his happiness—he never doubted he was loved by God, but the thought of Him caring about his happiness seemed . . . well, distant. Now, he understood why God had told him no to Belle Parish. Belle had not been his person and Reid was certain now that what he felt for that runaway bride turned Harvey Girl had only been an infatuation. With Lorna, it was a raging river of love that ran deep with memories and strong with time. Nothing could get between them because she loved him in return.

The train slowed as it approached Topeka where he knew Lorna had attended church during her time training. *Surely the pastor would be open to marrying us.* If only Reid had thought to invite the family to meet them for a short ceremony there, they could marry. He shook his head. He was always patient and planned accordingly, but when it came to Lorna agreeing to be his wife, he felt as on edge as when he was on the brink of capturing a dangerous outlaw.

The train screeched to a halt and the familiar gong of the Harvey House manager made Lorna stir. Her eyes widened at the sight. "Why, Mr. Heller is on the platform. We are in Topeka!" She whipped to face him. "I didn't place an order, but we might have time."

He wove her fingers through his. "You slept straight through the conductor taking orders, but I ordered your favorite, love."

She hopped to her feet, pulling him up behind her, running her hands over her emerald traveling gown. "We only have a quarter of an hour and I hope to at least get a hug from Freya." Lorna surged off the train and greeted Mr. Heller with a smile and a small wave. He jolted in surprise at seeing her, but he returned her greeting and led the guests to the small Harvey House dining room. Lorna squealed in delight when she spied Freya, the Harvey House head waitress, weaving through the sea of black and white waitresses and guests to her side for a swift embrace.

"What a lovely surprise! What on earth brings you to Topeka on a train from the East?" She eyed Reid. "With Sheriff Reid?"

"It's a long story, but I promise to write

and tell you all about it, but," she beamed up at him, "this is my fiancé."

"Fiancé? You *do* have a lot to tell me!" Freya extended her hand to Reid. "Sheriff Reid, I hope you know what a gem you have."

"I am a fortunate man." He nodded, wrapping his arm about Lorna's waist.

"See, all you had to do was put him out of your mind and you two are engaged only months later," she whispered to Lorna.

Lorna giggled, leaving him wondering why she had been trying to put him out of her mind. He would be asking about that story later, but for now, he let the two women catch up without his interference as Freya ushered them to their table for two by the window that overlooked the small, dusty town of Topeka that hadn't changed since his last time here. His world, however, would never be the same with his fiery Lorna at his side.

The delivery of the drinks and food were fluid with only one mishap when the girl flipped Lorna's cup over in the saucer.

Lorna smiled at the new Harvey Girl

and whispered, "I ordered coffee, so the cup should remain as it is."

The girl's startled gaze met hers. "Oh, thank you, but how did you know? Are you a frequent guest?"

"I'm a visiting Harvey Girl, returning to my post in Las Vegas now."

The girl's shoulders sagged in relief, her smile becoming brilliant. "How exciting! I'm hoping to be placed at Hot Springs in the Montezuma Resort, but they say only the top girls get sent there. I'll probably go to a smaller house before I work my way up to that." She smiled to Lorna. "Enjoy, and hopefully I'll see you around Las Vegas."

SHE RESTED her head on Gaston's shoulder as the train left the station, her heart a swell of emotions. It had been wonderful seeing Freya, but she was glad to be heading home and would be seeing Corinna soon. She couldn't wait to tell her quiet friend all about her adventures in Newport. She knew Corinna was from the East, but didn't know much about her past, other than she had an unhappy life and was looking forward to life in the West for the foreseeable future.

They had the car to themselves, save for three women seated at the rear of the train car, one woman at the front, and in one corner, a man with a handlebar mustache reading a paper. There was an overlarge rolled rug in the top rack above him that spanned four bench seat rows. She supposed the baggage car must be full with a shipment, which allowed the guest's rug in a main car.

"Well, isn't that sweet?" A woman whispered loudly at the rear of the car, the three other women standing all at once, blocking the exits of the front and back of the train.

The woman in green jogged her memory. "Gaston," she whispered, pointing to the woman, a chill stealing to her core. *No. No!*

He jerked to his feet, weapons drawn, the car swaying as it picked up speed. "It's you. You were in the saloon in Las Vegas."

He towered in front of Lorna, using his body as a shield.

The man in the corner fell to the floor, the coward hiding his head under his newspaper, the sheets shaking.

"Took you long enough. We are the wives of the Death Riders and now Death Riders ourselves as we've proven our loyalty to Jill. It's time for Lorna Elliot to come with us."

"Are you so determined to have my money? You know that while I may be from the wealthiest family in Las Vegas, I am not *that* rich." *Like the women in Newport, who are really, really rich.*

"It's never just been about the money." A fifth woman strode through the back door, bearing a sawed-off shotgun in one arm as her other was in a sling.

Jill. Her recent abduction flashed to mind, and she couldn't keep herself from gripping Gaston's arm. "What is happening? I thought Tanner said it was safe to return."

"They tricked us." Gaston gritted his teeth, his grip tightening on his weapons. "Lay on the ground, Lorna."

Her stomach twisted. She was so close to her happily-ever-after with the man of her dreams. God wouldn't allow these revenge-bent women to come between them, would He? *Lord, send us help.* She slunk to the filthy floor on her belly. She had to figure out how to help her man. "You are not going to win, Jill." Lorna challenged, her voice strong and true even as she was on her belly. "Why are you doing this? Grant is in jail for life." *Unless he escaped too?* She gulped. *And Tanner Sterling! Is Tanner alive?*

"Grant's moaning and groaning over his wound provided the distraction I needed to bust out of custody, so I felt compelled to chase you. This will be the ultimate testament of my love for him and my loyalty to the women and their children." Jill lifted her chin. "But who says I will be unsuccessful? We have you outnumbered."

"One ranger, one riot." Gaston interjected, coolly. "Are you so content to go to prison for him again? You escaped Tanner. You could have made a run for it—started a new life. And yet, here you are again."

"And I will keep coming back until *she* is

on her knees before the Death Riders with a ransom on her head so large that it will breathe new life into our gang and *you* are dead, Reid!" She shrieked.

Her viper's words stilled Lorna's racing heart. She needed to face this threat, or never live in New Mexico again. She pushed herself up onto shaking limbs.

"Lorna, what are you doing?" Gaston's voice wavered.

"Stopping this. Jill, if I go with you quiet like, you promise you won't hurt Gaston?"

Jill tilted her head, pulling back the hammer of her gun. "What do you think ladies? Would this act of mercy ruin our reputation?"

"I say we let him go." One of the women voiced. "If we take his woman, and he never sees her again, imagine the pain he will be in—a fate worse than death."

Jill cackled. "Sometimes it pays to be a romantic." She waved Lorna over with the barrel of her weapon. "Get over here, Lorna. Your bargain has been struck."

"Lorna, I won't let you do this." Gaston

kept his guns trained on the women, his attention never leaving the threats.

"If you are to live, I must." Lorna rose on her tiptoes and pressed a kiss to his lips. "Be happy, my darling."

The overlarge rug in the overhead rack above Jill moved. The women didn't notice, but Lorna and Gaston most certainly did. She did not look up, but from the corner of her eye she spied a Colt revolver emerge first, and a shot rang out as Jill screamed and dropped her weapon. Gaston took advantage of the distraction to push Lorna back to the ground. Sounds of a scuffle followed and when she peeked through her hands, Gaston seized two Death Riders, detaining them in his arms while Tanner dropped from the rack, guns at the ready.

The man with the newspaper rose with a revolver of his own in one hand and cuffs at the ready in the other, grinning. "Finally. It took everything in me to stick to my part."

"Cuff Jill, Lawrence." Tanner kept his weapon trained on the still shrieking Jill, who clutched her shoulder, and the fourth Death Rider woman who had run to her aid.

The man called Lawrence secured Jill, and Lorna dove for the last woman who was racing for the back door. She might be small, but she was strong. She launched herself at the woman, wrestling her to the ground like a newborn calf until Tanner tossed her another pair of cuffs. She struggled to fit them to the woman's wrists. The men made it seem easy.

"Stick to your part, huh? The next time you decide to use me as bait, let me know." Gaston fairly growled at Tanner as he knelt to secure the cuffs for Lorna. He softened his glare to a smile when he took Lorna's hand in his, helping her to standing. He pressed a kiss to her head. "Good work. But don't you ever try to sacrifice yourself for me again."

"Can't make that promise."

"I know," he grunted, turning his ire back to Tanner. "What were you thinking?"

"I brought in my brother Lawrence to make sure she was safe. He's about as good with a gun as I am. And our plan worked, didn't it?" Tanner holstered one gun, keeping one out. "Now we just got to round up Grant Lawson, his buddy, and Sylvia Williams.

"They still aren't in jail? You could've gotten Lorna killed!" Gaston bellowed at Tanner.

"After Jill escaped, Grant's buddy got the upper hand. If I didn't have my secret weapon, I'd be dead."

"My love has surpassed even my expectations. He didn't become the leader of the Death Riders by sitting on his hands." Jill grinned.

"But I didn't get her killed." Tanner continued, ignoring Jill's cackling laughter. "And if I had told you, you would have disagreed and then you would have been stuck hiding for another few months and given how much you *love* spending time in Newport, I thought I'd expedite the process by spreading news about town that you were coming home by telling the one person who can't keep his gob shut."

He sighed. "The saloon owner?"

"Yup. I should've guessed that this one was a mite too pretty to be a saloon girl." Tanner grinned, jerking his thumb to the nearest woman that Gaston had recognized from the saloon. "Her name is Ethel Land. She was the girlfriend of Grant's right-hand man."

Ethel narrowed her gaze. "I would never degrade myself to be a saloon girl."

"And yet, you want to be an outlaw? That makes complete sense." Lorna dusted off her hands.

"Our men died for the Death Riders. How would you expect anything less from us?" Ethel interjected.

Lorna shook her head, trying to clear her mouth of judgements. These women needed Jesus, not some man and his outlaw group pretending to be their savior. It felt like grit in her heart, but she pushed out a prayer. *Lord, they need You to open their eyes. Please open my heart to forgive them. They need You. And I need You to help me show them Your love by keeping my opinions to myself instead of condemning them for their choices and leaving that for the judge and jury to decide.* "You don't owe Grant Lawson anything, ladies."

"It's not Grant we are doing this for. Jill paid off our men's debts. She sent us cattle to fill our children's bellies and gold to line our pockets the moment she was out of jail. She respects us." Ethel continued, eyes glistening.

"Because she wanted something from you—she wanted you to become the most loyal band of outlaws yet." Lorna reasoned.

Gaston rested a hand on her shoulder as Tanner and Lawrence directed the five women to the corner bench seat to wait for the next station. "I know you want to save them from the lure of outlaw life, but, love, it is going to take a doctor *and* preacher to break through to them. I'll see to it that wherever they are held in prison that a preacher will come visit them." He grabbed their carpet bags. "It's the beginning of the end for the Death Riders, but I'd rather not look at the women who would see you harmed. Shall we change cars?"

CHAPTER 22

It was a relief to work so hard that her feet might fall off. It kept her mind too busy to think much on the women Jill had brainwashed. With Gaston no longer acting as the town sheriff, he left with Lawrence and Tanner nearly three weeks ago to see to it personally that all the women were tried and put in prison, along with apprehending Grant Lawson, his mysterious buddy, and Sylvia Williams. Gaston had assured her that he would attempt to get Sylvia a reduced charge but emphasized the importance of Sylvia paying for her crimes despite her change of heart.

She glanced at her lady's watch pin. Her

shift would end in a quarter of an hour and when it did, Ma was going to meet her at *Queen Ranch* to finish cleaning the ranchero while sorting out the last details of the wedding that would take place at the Montezuma as soon as Gaston returned. It made for difficult planning without a date, but she didn't want anything stopping her from marrying him a moment longer than necessary—she had already waited years. She smiled again at the ranch name Gaston revealed to her before he left. Her heart fluttered at the memory and of the gift. She glanced at her signet ring and all that it promised.

Not for the first time did Lorna wish she could've married Gaston before he left, but with so little time remaining in her contract for Fred Harvey, she knew it would be prudent to stay put and leave with her full salary intact. It would be lovely to bring her savings into marriage . . . even though fifty dollars was hardly anything compared to the women in Newport's fortune. *But he chose you, not your money.*

A petite lady in a blue gown appeared on

the dining room threshold, a tentative smile on her lips as her eyes met Lorna's. *Belle Parish—Lawson?* She straightened and approached with a smile. "Good afternoon, Mrs. Lawson. A table for one?"

Belle smiled. "Thank you, but I actually came to speak with you. Are you due for your lunch break soon?"

She checked her watch pin again. Five more minutes until she was off duty. She glanced about. The other Harvey Girls were doing busy work and wouldn't need her. She motioned Belle to the lunch counter. "Would you like a cup of coffee or tea?"

She rested her hand on her abdomen. "Herbal tea would be lovely. I'm having such a hard time keeping anything down these days."

Lorna moved around the counter to fetch the correct tea pot, testing its side with a quick tap. *Piping hot.* "Are you feeling ill?"

Belle smiled and reached for the filled cup as Lorna slid over the sugar pot. "Yes, but I'm told that it will get better in the very near future. I am expecting."

Lorna gasped, nearly dropping the teapot on the counter. "How wonderful! Congratulations, Mrs. Lawson."

"Thank you. I've always wanted a large family of my own and I am ever so grateful that I was able to get pregnant so quickly." Her cheeks tinted at the admission, and she hid her blush by sipping her tea. She winced and promptly scooped two teaspoons into the brew. "I came by to see how you are feeling after your ordeal. I would have checked on you sooner, but I've only just been able to get out of bed from the morning sickness. My Colt has told me all about your nightmare."

"I'm much better now that most of the Death Riders crew is behind bars, but I am still anxious while I wait for Gaston to come back with news that Jill and her merry band of women are locked away for good this time." She poured a second cup of tea and joined Belle on the stool beside her. "Once Sylvia Williams is captured, the Harvey Girl who tricked me, she will pay for her crimes too, but with a much lighter sentence. Gaston told me that with my written statement, she will only be given a year of prison time, versus fifteen years."

"That was most generous of you. I, too, look forward to the final trial." Belle sipped her tea. "Colt has been most anxious, keeping me guarded at all hours. When he is not present, he has three armed ranch hands surrounding the ranchero. Even now, they are waiting outside, mounted beside my buggy until we receive word that the *entire* gang is locked away for good."

All this time Lorna had been thinking of her own fears as she was the latest target, but Belle had gotten the harsher torment as she had Grant when he wasn't of a "peaceable" mind. "I'm so sorry."

"I'm sorry for your trials too. I've always had a hard path with fear. It crippled me really, and nearly kept me trapped in an unhappy home in Charleston, but the Lord has shown me that He is all powerful and He will protect me, even when I feel like my world is spinning in chaos." She rested her hand on her abdomen. "Even now, I worry about losing my baby, or what might happen during the birthing, but it is a daily act, giving God my fears." She looked up at Lorna. "How are you handling the trauma from the recent events?"

Lorna gripped her cup with both hands, searching her heart for a truthful answer and not one born out of a false bravery. "I can honestly say that I am doing surprisingly well. I've grown up hearing stories about the Death Riders, and, when Gaston joined the rangers, he never kept anything out of his stories. I knew that Gaston would find me because he was the best."

She smiled. "Reid found me and Colt just in time as well."

Her heart stabbed at that reminder, but Belle was married now and had a baby on the way. It was obvious her heart belonged to her husband.

"If it hadn't been for him, my Colt would have died, and our little baby wouldn't even be here." She rested her hand on her belly again. "God is good." She finished her tea and hopped off the stool. "If you ever need to talk about what happened with Grant and Jill, please feel free to stop by the ranch at any time. Reid is a good man, and I am thrilled for you both."

"You and your husband should come to the wedding!" Lorna blurted. She waited for regret to steal into her belly, but instead, a peace resonated.

Belle's eyes widened in surprise. "We would love that. Do you have a date?"

She shook her head. "The plan is to announce it after church the Sunday we hear from him. Who knows when that will be, but the plan is to have the wedding the following week sometime."

"Fast weddings are such fun," Belle grinned. "Though, I imagine you will have all the help you need with Harriet as a sister-in-law. The woman is a wonder with planning and directing."

"That she is." Lorna laughed. "My shift is over, so I'll walk you out." She threaded her arm through Belle's and escorted her to the wagon, chatting about their Harriet before waving farewell to the former Harvey Girl.

A few more days and Lorna would be out of her contract. She would miss the work, but to be the wife of Gaston Reid would be worth setting aside her apron for a veil. Besides, she had a feeling that life with him would be an adventure every day.

REID, Tanner, and Lawrence approached the cabin in Topeka with the greatest of care. He knew Grant would have expected his women to return by now and must have met with trouble. More than likely, the outlaws were making plans to run.

Reid didn't have much time to put together a plan, but he supposed a surprise attack was the only way to capture Grant and Sylvia anyway. Smoke wafted from the chimney and the flicker of lantern-light streamed through the window. He held up a finger to Tanner, gesturing him to stay along the bush line. While Grant may have claimed to be a peaceful sort these days, Reid didn't trust him further than he could spit.

Tanner shadowed the bushes at the rear of the cabin. It was dangerous to have him on the opposite end of Reid and Lawrence's firing position, but he needed to check the area before they began. Tanner crossed to the other side and lifted three fingers, signaling the number of people inside.

Who did Grant have with him besides Sylvia? Reid didn't feel right running in there with guns a blazing unless he knew that it was hardened criminals behind the door.

Tanner joined the men, planting himself on the ground. "Grant, a man, and that Sylvia woman are inside."

"Did you recognize the man?" Reid whispered.

"Short, thick with muscle, and looked pretty rough." Tanner reached into his saddle bag and withdrew a small telescope and mounted it to his rifle. "I think it is probably a buddy of his."

"Is it me, or has this dynamic gotten stranger with the Death Riders?" Lawrence interjected.

"Didn't think Grant Lawson could get any more depraved . . . then he goes using his charisma to brainwash a second woman to marry him, apparently. Glad we are going to put him behind bars tonight." Tanner lined up his scope with the window, waiting for his shot.

"You confident you won't hit Sylvia or the unidentified male?" Reid squinted at the window, trying to make out the figures from this distance.

Tanner raised a single brow. "You know my reputation. I'm insulted you'd even ask."

"Sorry." Reid longed to pace but couldn't stretch his legs for fear of drawing Grant's attention. His gaze snagged on the necessary, an idea forming. "They've got to come out sometime to relieve themselves."

Tanner's lips pressed into a thin line. "Because we both know that Grant is *so* gentlemanly as to follow common courtesy to use the reeking outhouse."

"Sylvia would be. We get the girl, and they will come looking." Lawrence spun the cylinder of his revolver and locked it into place.

Tanner pointed the barrel of his rifle upward, sitting back on his knees. "Pretty good idea. Do it. I'll cover you, if needed."

Reid snaked on his belly toward the outhouse. He could smell it two yards out and his stomach churned at the thought of camping inside while he waited, but he had to do what had to be done. He glanced back to the cabin and seeing no one opening the door, or peering out a window, he got to his feet and darted inside, wincing at the squeak of the boards, and shut himself inside.

The crescent moon cut out in the plank door let in precious little air flow. He pressed his face against the door to gulp in air without revealing himself through the hole. He blinked against the stinging in his eyes. *Think about something else.* He hadn't smelled stink that bad since he and Lorna were sprayed with that skunk. Lorna. *What has she been up to?* He grinned, knowing she was likely planning their wedding. What a marvel it was to be marrying the woman of his dreams. He had thought Belle was that woman, but since his eyes had been opened to Lorna, that affection seemed trite in comparison.

The squeak of the back door made him straighten. He shoved himself into the front corner where the door's swinging inward would hide him. The door swung and, in the moonlight, he spied Sylvia. He wrapped his hand about her mouth, quieting her before she even released a muffled scream. "Silence. If you value your life, be quiet." That part was a groundless threat, but she didn't need to know his code. He would never hurt a female, no matter if she was a criminal who took off with his woman.

"I won't yell." She managed to say around his hand. "Have you come to save me?" Tears spilled over his hands as she wept, her body growing limp. He slowly removed his hand. Perhaps it was foolish, but the woman would be making more noise with suppressed sobs as she gasped for air. "I-I have been so foolish. My ma would be ashamed of me for what I have done. I-I didn't know what Grant was really like until it was too late."

His throat tightened. She had broken the law and hurt Lorna in the process, but the idea of Grant hurting this woman that he obviously convinced of his sainthood made Reid's blood boil. "What did he do to you?"

"I thought he loved me, but he only wanted me as a w-wife and as a member of his precious gang. Jill—" She sniffed. "She finally got him to open his eyes to revenge again. I honestly thought that he was seeking peace until that day in the Garden of the Gods. He has been obsessed with revenge since and, when I failed to escape, he took me as his wife—so I could not testify against him in court and has been training me with a gun to join his crew. He has an arsenal set up inside that cabin. If you attack now without help, you won't be long for this earth."

He jerked back at this. Lawrence and Tanner were still out there and if Grant did not actually care enough for Sylvia to save her, Reid knew without a doubt that he would shoot the outhouse until it splintered to bits, no matter if his so-called second wife was inside. She had done wrong, but Reid was beginning to think the charges against her could lead to being institutionalized instead of imprisoned. The real criminals were Grant and Jill and, tonight,

Grant's reign of terror against Lorna and this woman would end.

"I'm going to have to gag you. I would be stupid not to." He whipped out his bandana and wrapped it around her mouth and tied it at the back of her head, her large chignon making it rather difficult. He ducked low and darted out into the blessed fresh air with her in tow. He raced to his men.

Tanner eyed him and the woman. "Why didn't you wait, Reid?"

"They have an arsenal inside. They would blast her to bits, along with me, if they suspected anything." Reid rubbed his neck with his handkerchief, feeling disgusting after the outhouse. "I think we need to make it look like she ran. Send a horse down the road."

Lawrence nodded. "I'll watch her while Tanner keeps his rifle on the men."

Reid raced to the stables and did not care to be too silent in his grabbing the horse's halter and pulling him out of the stable. He slapped its rump and ran as the horse's pounding hooves would bring the outlaws to the door. He raced back to their post, taking cover along the way wherever he could find it.

Grant and the man busted through the door, shouting, and sending Sylvia crashing to the ground, terror making her eyes wild as her body convulsed. Anger stirred Reid's heart. Reid hated to think what it had taken to open her eyes to the length of the man's cruel heart.

"She's making a run for it!" The man cursed, whacking his hat against his thigh. "I knew I should have followed her to the outhouse. So much for your idea of making the most loyal riders yet out of a string of wives. I told you it would backfire."

"Shut your mouth and get her while I get the money." Grant bellowed. "She'll have the law on us."

Tanner pulled back the hammer and a crack split the air. Grant shouted and grabbed his thigh, falling to the ground as the other man dove for cover, only for a second crack to bring forth a howl.

"I can see why they say you are the best bounty hunter in the West." Reid grinned at Tanner.

"Someone has to do it. Might as well be me who collects the bounty—seeing as I keep the criminals alive and well enough to stand trial for their crimes, unlike the other hunters who only care for the payout." He withdrew his Colt revolvers and shouted, "Throw your weapons in front of you and keep your hands where we can see them. We have you surrounded!"

Lawrence shot off another bullet to prove it.

Grant and his man lifted their hands in the air, Sylvia sobbing in relief.

Reid untied her bandana. "It's over now."

CHAPTER 23

*L*orna hopped from foot to foot as she waited for the train to arrive. It had been weeks since she had seen him and after receiving his telegram on Monday, she didn't even wait until Sunday service to inform the whole town. She had sent Gil door to door for the past two days, telling all that her wedding would take place tonight. She had waited a lifetime for this man to love her, and she was not going to wait a moment longer.

The Montezuma ball room was ready for them, all decorated with the late blooming purple asters with lovely yards of pale pink chiffon fabric streamers connecting to the chandeliers, creating a tent above the room. Her guests would dine on the Harvey House resort's finest delicacies followed by the beautiful three-tiered chocolate cake standing in the corner of the room that was decorated in vanilla icing with one large white rose atop the third tier. All she needed now was a groom, and, according to his telegram, he should be on this train if there weren't any more surprises.

Her husband-to-be was thorough. He would not have returned to marry her unless she was completely safe. A distant blare from the train made her heart skip. She held onto the hem of her veil as the train moved into the station, the steam blowing her thin veil behind her. She peeked into the windows and squealed when she spotted a familiar Stetson. She wanted to cry out his name and wave to Gaston, but she wanted to see his face clearly when he caught sight of her.

He climbed down the steps, his feet hitting the platform. She couldn't stand it a moment more. "Gaston!"

He turned, his jaw dropping at the sight of her hair braided in a crown about her head with flowers woven in place. She released her hold on the veil and allowed it to billow over her shoulders. Her gown, sewn by her mother and Harriet, complimented her curves, the sweetheart neckline more daring than she usually wore as she would be as red as a tomato with this much skin exposed.

But seeing his face flush with pleasure was worth every fitting and flurry of planning. He crossed the platform in a trot and paused short of her, gathering her hands in his when she really wanted him to wrap her in his arms and kiss her senseless. She twined her arms about his neck and pulled him close.

"Lorna, you are a vision." He blinked. "B-but I'm not supposed to see you in your wedding gown before the day—"

"Which is happening right now." She laughed, tugging him along. "You said you wanted to marry me the moment you got home. Well, the moment has arrived. Tanner said he would make sure you put on your clean suit before you reached the station. Why do you think he insisted on that?" She giggled, waving to Tanner who was giving them wide berth and fairly running down the platform as if to avoid seeing any more of the public display of affection than necessary. "We are heading straight to the chapel and then to our reception at the Montezuma."

"You got all of that lined up in two days since my telegram?" He chuckled. "I thought Tanner was trying to help me with the enchanting of you."

"You've enchanted me plenty . . . for now." She linked her arm with his and picked up her skirts as they ran for the little blue church at the end of the main street.

He paused with her on the steps, grasping both her hands in his. "You didn't even let me kiss you."

"Well, we can't kiss now with everyone on the other side of that door," she hissed, jerking her thumb to the closed church doors. "What if someone comes out to use the necessary?"

His lips quirked. "Come now. Are you

telling me you don't want one last kiss as an engaged couple before we are married?"

Oh, that is tempting. She looked to the door and bit her lip.

"I dare you to kiss me, Lorna." He grinned down at her.

"You know that I gave up dares, Gaston." She sighed. "But, seeing as it is such a tempting dare, I can't seem to find the words to decline my final dare before I become a married woman."

He wrapped his hands at her waist, leaning down as he softly kissed her forehead, her nose, her cheeks, and chin before his gaze rested on her lips. She rose on her toes and pressed her lips to his, their mouths melding together and stealing her breath.

The doors jerked open, and she jumped away from Gaston.

Gil stood in the doorway, pretending to frown at their kisses. "There will be plenty of time for sparking and kissing after you two are married." He motioned Gaston inside. "You get yourself to the altar, man."

Pa appeared as Gaston left with her

brother. He reached out his arm to her. "I've always thought Gaston and you would be a wonderful couple."

She could hardly keep her jaw from dropping. "You did?"

"He is a man of honor, integrity, and strength. I could want nothing more for my girl than a godly man like him. I've been praying for you two to become a couple for the past few years."

Tears filled her eyes. "I have too."

"Let's get you to your groom, daughter. A whole new life awaits you at the end of the aisle, and your mother and I could not be happier for you both."

HE HAD ALWAYS DREAMED of being part of the Elliot family, but Reid had never thought it was a possibility until the day he saw Lorna dressed in that Harvey Girl uniform and his world shifted. Now, as the fiddlers played and stomped the beat to a lively tune in the Montezuma, he danced with the woman in white, his heart overflowing. God knew what He was doing when He made Reid wait for his bride.

Lorna laughed and threw her head back as Reid twirled her around and around. She halted and touched the flower crown that was woven into her coronet braid. The veil was pinned at the back and floated down behind her like wings as the other couples danced around them.

He drew her arms about his neck. "Wife, you are a sight to behold."

"Then, I dare you to kiss me, husband."

That was a dare he would accept again and again. He bent low and captured her lips, promising a lifetime of kisses to follow.

The merriment lasted until midnight when at last, the people living the farthest from the Montezuma had to depart with well wishes for the happy couple.

He drew his bride out onto the massive tower porch and stood with her at the railing, staring up at the stars as the final guests rode back to town. They would be staying the night in the lovely honeymoon suite. Tomorrow, they would begin their lives on *Queen Ranch*.

"You are my dream come true, Lorna Reid," he whispered into her hair.

She turned in his arms to stare up at him. "I love the sound of my new name. It will take some time to feel married, though, after being single for so long."

"Then we shall remedy that straight away." He kissed her soundly and swept her into his arms, intent on enchanting his sweet Lorna for the rest of their lives.

Author's Note

Dear Reader, thank you so much for reading Book Three in the Aprons & Veils series! If this is your first time reading about the Harvey Girls, know that they did indeed exist. In the 1890s, there were not many respectable jobs for women, so when Englishman Fred Harvey created his chain of fine dining restaurants along the Atchison, Topeka, and Santa Fe railroads, single women without an education, or in need of earning their own way, were given a chance to earn an honest wage without the speculation that they offered anything else but food as a service.

With Mr. Harvey's strict rules about the waitress's code of conduct, the women were given their independence while still maintaining their good name and place in society under the protective, fatherly arm of Fred Harvey. These extraordinary, brave women became known as the Harvey Girls, the ladies who tamed the Wild West with fine china, good pie, and exceptional service with complete propriety.

The first Montezuma resort did indeed burn down. After a year of rebuilding with new architects, the second resort opened for only four short months before the "fireproof" hotel burned to the ground with only a partial stone structure remaining. Fred Harvey lost no time and re-built the Montezuma a third time, dubbing it *The Phoenix.* The resort eventually reverted to its former name, though, so their superstitious guests would not think it likely to burn down again. It did not, and you can still see the third Montezuma building, as well as stay as a guest in the Hotel Castañeda, today.

For the purpose of my story, I did take some small liberties with the Montezuma resort and the Hotel Castañeda, such as the opening date of the hotel. Sources claim different years, so I decided to begin this series the year the Castañeda was built. I also changed the hotel's dining room floor appearance. I did attempt to stay as accurate as possible with the Fred Harvey system and layout of both Harvey buildings based on the historical pictures and references available. The Castañeda Harvey House is one of the few still standing and has been fully restored to operate once more.

If you enjoyed the story, I would love if you could please take a moment and leave a review or rating. Happy reading, friends!

Grace Hitchcock is the award-winning author of multiple historical novels and novellas, including the American Royalty, Best Laid Plans, and Aprons & Veils series. She holds a Master's in Creative Writing and a Bachelor of Arts in English with a minor in History. Grace lives in South Louisiana with her husband, Dakota, sons, and daughter in a farmhouse that is always filled with the sounds of sweet little footsteps running at full speed. When not writing, chasing her toddlers, or tending to her chickens and golden and labrador retrievers, she's baking something delightful and can usually be found with a book clutched in her fist.

APRONS & VEILS
BOOK FOUR

The Vanishing of
Miss Victoria

GRACE HITCHCOCK

VALMONT
HOUSE PUBLISHERS

CHAPTER 1

*L*as Vegas, New Mexico
November 1898

CORINNA IGNORED the fresh blister on her right heel as she served another plate of flank steak and potatoes to a dusty rancher. Her black skirts swished over the crimson and white tiles as she wove about the Harvey House's pristine tables, begging the busyness to keep the haunting memories at bay. But no matter how many extra shifts she took on, the ache in her chest from her mistakes was ever present.

"Miss Corinna!" The rowdy man from

her table shouted, lifting his china cup in the air and sending her jumping and nearly knocking over the pot of hot coffee on the lunch counter. His friends shook their heads at his outburst, one elbowing him.

She smiled apologetically to the Harvey Girl working the counter. Corinna grabbed the heavy pot to refill the man's cup, commanding her racing heart to slow. After months of working as a Harvey Girl, Corinna had hoped that she would cease jumping at every shout of her name, but with her past chasing her very shadows, it was difficult not to fear the reckoning seeking her.

"How about you finally stop teasing me and agree to step out with me, Miss Corinna?" The lanky cowboy grinned up at her as his friends dug into their lunches of beef stroganoff and tenderloin tips of beef picante.

Buck Bridger was a handsome enough man, but Corinna couldn't afford to be distracted—distractions could end with her becoming too comfortable and her wrists in irons. "Mr. Bridger, I sincerely thank you for your daily invitation, but I work every day."

"They give you off every Sunday morning for church and a full day off every ten days, don't they? I've been coming here long enough to know the rules." He lifted his fried chicken leg in a salute and took a bite.

"Some girls get days off, but *I* am always working," she returned with a smile and filled the other men's cups as she dodged Buck's questions. It was becoming harder and harder to avoid telling falsehoods to shield herself. She returned the pot to the counter as one table of guests in her section vacated.

She smiled at the young family leaving and tucked the tip into her apron pocket. A quarter had seemed so paltry a sum not too long ago, but now, every coin was precious, and she was grateful for anything extra. She piled the dessert dishes and cups in such a way to only make one trip to the dirty dish bin. Sweat dripped from the golden curls framing her face, but she did not heed them. She couldn't afford to take a break while

Buck Bridger was near the Harvey House. If Buck caught her on the back porch taking a breath of fresh air, he'd talk her ear off and try to get her to talk too—and that was something she could never allow.

Life on the run was exhausting, especially when one was innocent, but did her thieving in-laws care? No. They only wanted her to pay for her husband's murder with her life and her fortune. . . if one could even call that rat of a man a husband. But the marriage certificate that Corinna Victoria Alistair-Roberts kept hidden in the box under her Harvey House dormitory bed said William Roberts had been *her* rat.

She moved behind the potted palm that marked the staff's area, set the dishes in the dirty bin on the shelf, and reached for the rag and bucket to clean off the table and draped a fresh tablecloth over her arm.

Corinna scrubbed the table and tossed the linen into the air, watching it settle over the wood like a discarded wedding veil. She ran her hands over it, smoothing out the wrinkles. She hadn't even had a veil when she'd married—even though she had kept her mother's wedding gown in a trunk in the attic for such a purpose. She and William had eloped too suddenly to even retrieve it.

She collected the cutlery and set them atop the table, aligning the silverware perfectly. Order out of chaos brought her a sense of control—something she desperately wished for after her world tumbled everything out of place. *Will anything be set to right again?*

After their hasty elopement last Thanksgiving, William had discovered she didn't get a dime of her inheritance until her father's death. He only remained long enough to take all her cash, gold, and any jewels she had brought with her. If that rat had stayed, he would have been overjoyed to know that Corinna had come into her inheritance quickly after all. She may not have killed her late husband, but she had certainly killed her father. Father's death had been at her hand as sure as she was waitressing in this quaint, dusty little town—not from any weapon, but from a broken heart at her deceit and choices.

She hated giving up her father's surname of Alistair, almost as much as she hated that Roberts had legally replaced it. Thankfully, no one here knew about either surname. The lies by omission and forced silence made for a rather lonely existence and it didn't help her loneliness when her only friend in the Harvey House, Lorna Elliot, married yesterday.

The other waitresses were friendly enough. It was her past that was the problem. Any questions about her past from others left her breathless, tongue-tied, and anxious, which resulted in her being very difficult to befriend ... apparently.

"He's back," Freya Lacy sang under her breath.

Corinna turned to the blonde waitress at her elbow, balancing the coffee cups and saucers as she finished setting the table. "Who?"

"That gorgeous friend of Lorna's husband, Tanner Sterling!" Freya fanned her cheeks with her hand. "Now, that's a man that could make a girl give up her position as a Harvey Girl."

"Maybe for you," Corinna muttered. "I'd much rather an apron than a veil."

"And he's staring at you again," Freya whispered.

"A-always stare," Corinna aligned the chairs about the table and nodded. *Perfection.*

Freya wrinkled her brow. "Pardon?"

Corinna forced the full sentence out and grabbed the full pot of coffee in anticipation of the guests' needs. "They always stare. Not unusual."

"Yes, but usually our guests are not quite as handsome as that one. Whew." She flapped her handkerchief and dabbed her cheek. "Gentlemanly with perfect manners, tall and broad as they come, with dangerous, piercing blue eyes under golden hair and sun-kissed skin? How could you *not* notice that he's a dream come to life? Why, he's fairly walked out of the pages of those dime novels I see you reading in our Rawlins dormitory parlor." Freya procured the coffee pot from Corinna. "I'll serve him."

"My section." Corinna ground out. She could not afford for the head waitress to catch her passing off her duties on another waitress after last week's warning. Corinna had attempted to give away Buck Bridger's table to Pernilla and, of course, Dolly Matthews had caught her in the act. Dolly never seemed to catch Corinna doing all the extra tasks for the rest of the girls though.

"Oh, don't worry about that. I know it makes you uncomfortable to serve any good-looking man." Freya swished away, smiling down on the broad-shouldered Mr. Sterling before Corinna could explain that neither his stares, nor his good looks, unsettled her. Serving never unsettled her.

She was used to working in a restaurant from a young age and was used to stares, but it was *conversing* that was the issue. At the clearing throat behind her, she started again. She sucked in a breath as the white linen cloth between her hand and the silver coffee pot slipped. Her fingertips burned against the scalding side. She plunked the pot down on a nearby vacant table and gritted her teeth at the smattering of coffee seeping into the white tablecloth. She adjusted her grip and closed her eyes, bracing herself at the tell-tale *tap tap* of heels approaching her. *Blast.*

"I've held my tongue for weeks now, Corinna Victoria, but I cannot continue to allow you to push all your tables onto others when you encounter an *enthusiastic* guest. It isn't fair, and if you cannot perform your job, there are twenty others who will do so."

Corinna didn't have to turn around to know who chided her, but she forced her chin down and turned, curtsying. "I'm sorry, Miss Dolly, b-but—"

"But nothing." Dolly Matthews held up her hand to stop the flow of excuses and fished around the little basket she had draped on her arm. "I had planned on waiting to announce this at the meeting before the evening shift. However, it seems you need to know now. I've decided more advanced methods are needed to encourage you all to improve your work." She lifted the shining bronze badge from the basket and turned it over in her palm. "I just picked these up at the post office. I heard about this method at another house and decided it was time to adopt it here at the Castañeda. As you can see, the badges have numbers. The waitresses will all be numbered from one to fourteen." She motioned to the tiny circular bronze pin with an engraved "1" in the center that Corinna hadn't noticed on Dolly's bodice. "As head waitress, I'm, of course, number one, and always will be, unless the house manager decides otherwise." She dropped the pin the size of a penny in Corinna's palm.

Corinna gritted her teeth against the gleaming "14." She wanted to protest that she was a wonderful waitress. Corinna knew it. But when she didn't stand up to the others and keep her sections, no matter how handsome the guest sitting in it happened to be, Corinna would of course *appear* the weakest link in the Harvey House chain of fresh-faced waitresses. "Miss Dolly, I didn't give—"

"Go on. Pin it on your bodice. It's a reminder that we waitresses value hard work at the Harvey House. However, if anyone should retain position of fourteen for longer than two weeks, they will be dismissed."

"Yes, Miss Dolly," she murmured. "I'll set this table again—"

"Oh no." Dolly planted a fist on her hip. "I think you are overdue for your break. Take some time and think long and hard about your position here."

She eyed the watch pin on Dolly's bodice. "I still have an hour left of my shift, though."

"I know. I have an errand for you while you think. Take this and move out of the way, please." Dolly Matthews fished an envelope from her pocket and shoved it into Corinna's hands. In following of the Fred Harvey standards, Dolly snatched a clean dish and began stacking the plates and silverware, grabbing the now-spotted tablecloth, and draping it over her arm. It all had to be cleaned and replaced.

"Let me help, and then I can post it for you." Corinna tucked the mysterious envelope into her apron pocket, removed the coffee pot, and reached for the clean stack of dishes. "It's my fault that we have to reset the—"

"No, thank you, Miss Corinna." She dismissed her with a wave. "Your shift is almost over, and we need to take a breath from each other. Bring that letter out to Queen Ranch. It's Lorna Elliot *Reid's* final pay. She forgot to pick it up before her wedding."

"This is highly unorthodox," Corinna whispered as her fingers grasped the sealed envelope even as the idea of visiting the peaceful ranch called to her. Lorna *had* asked her to drop by the ranch to check on her stallion, Bunny, while she was on her honeymoon in Colorado Springs.

"So is handing off every table that makes you uncomfortable," Dolly retorted.

Corinna glanced over to Tanner Sterling's table. He downed his cup as Freya brought him a plate of pasta. Corinna swallowed her protest.

"The carnival for raising money to build the new children's home is in two days," Dolly continued, "which is hosted by the Harvey

House, as you very well know, and you haven't even signed up for a booth yet. I suggest you think on it too while you walk, or else you'll be stuck with a booth that no one wanted." Dolly nodded toward the door. "You better get a move on it if you want to be home by dark. I do not want to be held responsible if you twist your ankle in a gopher hole if you tarry and are stuck finding your way home at night."

Corinna bit back another protest that it was Freya who had *taken* her table without asking, but as that would take some explaining and draw more attention to herself, she nodded and sped for the kitchen's swinging door while Freya giggled at Mr. Sterling's table again as she lingered with her pot of coffee, but, of course, Dolly ignored the breech of etiquette.

Corinna wove about the bustling kitchen staff, tugged off her apron, and tossed it in the dirty laundry basket in the back corner of the kitchen. She slipped out the back door, drawing deep breaths of fresh air, cleansing her anger of Freya's stealing her table and Dolly's unfair treatment. If only she was free to stand up for herself—to unleash her tongue. *No. Do not wish for things to be different. You are lucky you have avoided a jail cell thus far with those Roberts after you, especially with only changing your surname to your middle name. Head down and work hard.*

She unbuttoned the top of her high collared black gown and tucked the envelope inside before buttoning the stifling collar once more. Her feet ached at the thought of the long walk ahead of her with her already throbbing blisters, but she didn't dare remove her shoes and risk getting the cuts filled with dirt and making the situation worse. Avoiding the main street, and therefore avoid any chance of meeting Mr. Bridger, who seemed to be everywhere these days, she strode behind the hotel toward the ranch.

At the cut through to Queen Ranch, she found a raging river in the place of the quiet creek she had encountered merely two weeks ago when she had walked down here with Lorna to visit her friend's future home. Corinna squinted up at the blue sky and the position of the sun as Lorna might do. She sighed. She had no idea how to tell the hour by it, but as the walk likely took up the last bit of her shift, she knew it was getting too late in the afternoon to take the long way around to the wooden bridge leading to Queen Ranch. If she didn't complete this task, Dolly would most certainly come up with another horrid chore to make Corinna regret her choices all the more.

She strode along the bank, watching for any spots where the waters quieted, but it only raged. At last, she found a spot with a trio of staggered boulders that created almost a natural bridge if one leapt. She sank down on the muddy bank and tugged off her black half boots, sighing in relief as the leather and hose came off, allowing her poor aching feet the chance to breathe, if only for a few moments.

She withdrew from the bank and bouncing on the balls of her feet, she charged forward and leapt from the bank. She laughed as she landed atop the first stone easily, despite her feet slipping a tad. She gauged the distance to the second. With the furious water beneath her, this boulder seemed a little further away than it had from the bank, and a hint of doubt curled around her heart. "Lorna could do it. Can't be too hard."

She crouched and sprang forward. Her soles slipped on the smooth surface of the second boulder, and she stumbled, the stone striking her knees through her skirts. "Ow!"

She sat back and rubbed the agonizing spot, blinking back her tears and questioning her abilities again, but she was almost to the other side, and the funds had to be delivered by *her* for some reason and not wait until Lorna returned. Corinna winced as she stood and swung her arms back and forth. "Come on, you frightened rabbit. Remember the stories you read with Father of daring women and brave bounty hunters. This is nothing to daring, dead-shot Drake. Nothing!" She simply needed to try hard enough.

She tossed aside the last of her inhibitions and leapt. Her foot met not the solid rock, but the freezing water as she plunged, the river engulfing her and sweeping her away.

Sign Up for Grace's Newsletter!

Keep up to date with Grace's news on book releases and giveaways by signing up for her email list at GraceHitchcock.com

FREE from Grace Hitchcock

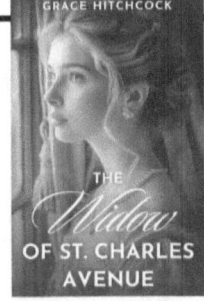

New Orleans, 1895

Colette Olivier, a young widow who married out of obligation, finds herself at the end of her mourning period and besieged with suitors out for her inheritance. With her pick of any man, she is drawn to an unlikely choice.

The Widow of St. Charles Avenue by Grace Hitchcock
a Second Chance Brides Novella
GraceHitchcock.com

Scan to Claim Your FREE Novella

More in your favorite series . . .

Forced into a betrothal with a widower twice her age, Charleston socialite, Sophia Fairfield is desperate for an escape. Much to her dismay, Sophia finds herself falling in love with the wrong gentleman—a man society would never allow her to marry, given Sophia was supposed to be his new stepmother. The only way to save Carver from ruin is to run away, leaving him and all else behind to become a Harvey Girl waitress at the Castañeda Hotel in New Mexico.

The Finding of Miss Fairfield by Grace Hitchcock
Aprons & Veils #1
A Friends-to-Lovers Runaway Bride RomCom

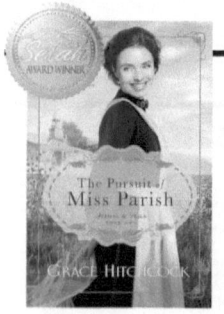

With a hope for belonging, Belle Parish leaves her position as a maid in Charleston to travel to New Mexico to become a mail-order bride. Colt Lawson's letters hold great promise, but something does not add up. Belle flees straight into the Castañeda Hotel Harvey House. Giving up the prospect of marrying, she focuses on her role as a Harvey Girl waitress until a strong Texas Ranger rides into her life.

The Pursuit of Miss Parish by Grace Hitchcock
Aprons & Veils #2
A Mail-Order Bride RomCom

Tanner Sterling has hunted his last bounty. As a new foreman, he wasn't expecting to rescue a sweet Harvey Girl from a raging river his first day. But, when he sees her on a wanted poster, he knows hunters will be coming for her. Despite wanting to hang up his past along with his gun belt, Tanner will do anything to protect her from the coming storm . . . even if he has to claim the bounty himself.

The Vanishing of Miss Victoria by Grace Hitchcock
Aprons & Veils #4
An Enemies-to-Lovers RomCom

You May Also Like . . .

Upon her father's unexpected retirement, his shareholders refuse to allow Willow Dupré to take over the company without a man at her side. Presented with thirty potential suitors from New York society's elite, she has six months to choose which she will marry. But when one captures her heart, she must discover for herself if his motives are truly pure.

My Dear Miss Dupré by Grace Hitchcock
AMERICAN ROYALTY #1
GraceHitchcock.com

A very public jilting has Theodore Day fleeing the ballrooms of New York to focus on building his family's luxury steamboat business in New Orleans and beating out his brother to be next in charge. But he can't escape the Southern belles' notice, nor Flora Wingfield, who is determined to win his attention.

Her Darling Mr. Day by Grace Hitchcock
AMERICAN ROYALTY #2
GraceHitchcock.com

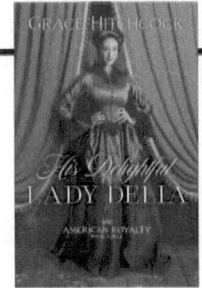

After years of being her diva mother's understudy, it's time for Delia Vittoria to take her place on stage. Attempting to make amends for a grave mistake, Kit Quincy is suddenly pulled into Delia's plot to win the great opera war and act as her patron and an enigmatic phantom. But when a second phantom appears, more than Delia's career is threatened.

His Delightful Lady Delia by Grace Hitchcock
AMERICAN ROYALTY #3
GraceHitchcock.com

www.ingramcontent.com/pod-product-compliance
Lightning Source LLC
Chambersburg PA
CBHW030348030726
47497CB00002B/233